OF GHOSTS AND MAGIC

By Alfred M. Albers

ISBN 0-7414-4121-7

Published by:

INFINITY
PUBLISHING.COM

1094 New DeHaven Street, Suite 100
West Conshohocken, PA 19428-2713
Info@buybooksontheweb.com
www.buybooksontheweb.com
Toll-free (877) BUY BOOK
Local Phone (610) 941-9999
Fax (610) 941-9959

Printed in the United States of America

Printed on Recycled Paper

Published July 2007

Dedication:

Felicita: I found the real magic in my life – you.

Ann, Elizabeth, and Al Jr.: "Those who do a kindness because they expect to be repaid are always disappointed."

– Chinese Proverb

Acknowledgments:

Thank you Al Pepper and Terri Lukach for your candid feedback, suggestions, and editing savoir-faire. To quote the late William Faulkner, “Others have done it before me. I can, too.”

With your help, I have.

CHAPTER ONE

June 15, 2000

The letter had arrived in Thursday's mail. It was unobtrusively stuffed between other correspondence and the newest catalog from the largest magic shop in the world: Nate Howard's Magic, in New York City. Dropping the other mail on the desk in his home office, John Michaels kept hold of the mysterious envelope and stared at the return address: 1218 Saw Mill River Road, Tuckahoe, NY 10710. He sat down in his chair to contemplate whom he knew that lived there. No one readily came to mind, so he reached across his desk to retrieve the letter opener and then carefully sliced open the envelope.

It was an invitation.

> You're cordially invited to the Thirtieth Reunion of Catholic High School's Class of 1970. Festivities will be held on Friday, June 30, 2000 at Crestwood College Linwood Hall Auditorium, 84 East 64th Street, New York, NY 10021.
>
> Reception: 4:00 p.m.
> Opening Commencements: 5:15 p.m.
> Dinner: 5:30 p.m.
> Entertainment: 7:00 p.m.
>
> R.S.V.P. (914) 555-9540
> Drew Wagner

John couldn't help but wonder how Drew managed to get his private mailing address in Virginia Beach, since 99 percent of his mail was delivered to a post office box at the Princess Anne

Station. It's not that John had any reason to hide from the public, but as America's Foremost Magician, his celebrity status had been a mixed blessing throughout the past 23 years. Nevertheless, he was elated to receive the invitation. He spun his chair around and looked at the calendar on the wall. June 30th was slightly less than three-weeks away. He had nothing scheduled for that day, or weekend for that matter.

Looks like I'm going to a reunion, he mumbled to himself. *It'll be interesting to meet up, once again, with my old high school friends to relive the trials and tribulations of our teenage years.*

John wrote a note on his "to do" list to call Drew later that day and then he quickly sorted through the rest of the mail. Except for two utility bills, and the magic catalog, the rest was junk mail that was addressed to the home's "Resident." Many people don't reside at the same location for more than a couple of years, and companies don't have the manpower or time to continually update their mailing list database. It was probably a marketing specialist who came up with the idea to address business-related advertisements to a home's Resident. John set the magic catalog aside and then placed the two bills in the middle of his desk; he'd pay them later. The junk mail was tossed into the trash bin.

First things first, he said to himself. *It's time to peruse the catalog to see what new tricks were available to the myriad magicians around the world.*

He picked it up and then headed for the kitchen. When he got there, he placed the catalog on the table and without missing a step continued on towards the refrigerator. Just as he reached for the door, the phone rang. Turning around, he began to walk across the room towards the wall where the phone was mounted above a collection of pens and notepads, but he suddenly stopped in the middle of the kitchen. His intuition was telling him to let the answering machine take the message.

"Mr. Michaels," the deep voice on the other end began, "this is Bob Waverly from the New York Mirror newspaper. I heard the Class of 1970 is having a 30th Reunion in three weeks. If you plan on attending, I'd like to interview you for a feature article for next Sunday's newspaper supplement. Please call me at your convenience; my toll-free number is 800-350-3186."

News travels fast, John said, as he listened to Mr. Waverly record the voice mail message. *I wonder how he also managed to get my home phone number, since it's unlisted.*

John had met many journalists through the years, but he didn't know Bob Waverly. Besides, if John were going to give someone an exclusive interview it would be his friend Brian Watson who covers the entertainment beat in New York City.

I need to call Drew now, rather than later, to let him know I'll be coming and to ask him if he was the one who tipped off a staff reporter, or Mr. Waverly. Browsing the new magic catalog would have to wait a little longer.

* * * * * * * * * * * * * * * *

Drew was short, five-foot-five, with a flattop haircut and a stocky build that was suggestive of a college wrestler. Although he had the build of an athlete, he had worn glasses all his life and without them all he could see was blurred shadows. It's impossible to wrestle shadows and expect to win. But, what he lacked in vision he made up for by making everyone laugh. It didn't take long for word of mouth to quickly travel amongst the students at Catholic High that one of its freshman, Drew Wagner, was a clever humorist who was always ready with a one-liner, often at the most inopportune times. It was enough, the students had heard, to cause a teacher to lose his train of thought during a classroom lecture.

If there had been "open-mike contests" at local clubs in the mid-1960s for up-and-coming comedians, Drew would have been an instant success story. Perhaps it was better that they didn't; Drew stayed in school. And, in spite of earning the distinct honor of being the only senior ever to have accumulated the most after-school detentions, Drew graduated and stood proudly alongside his other friends and cohorts from the Class of 1970.

* * * * * * * * * * * * * * * *

Thirty years. It seems like only yesterday that the seniors from the Class of 1970 were making plans for, and trying to decide whom to take to, the prom. And let's not forget: would 1970 be the year the punch bowl was spiked?

It wasn't.

CHAPTER TWO

"Good morning, thank you for calling Wagner and Associates, how may I direct your call?"

"Good morning," John replied. "Drew Wagner, please; this is Mr. John Michaels. I'm returning his call."

That wasn't exactly true, but the invitation did say R.S.V.P. That was close enough to the truth, for John.

"Mr. Wagner is talking with a client on the phone. Would you mind holding for a few seconds, Mr. Michaels? I don't think he'll be much longer."

"I don't mind holding," John said.

"Thank you," she said.

John looked out the kitchen window into his back yard while he waited for the receptionist to come back on the line. It was a cloudless day; the mid-morning sky was a light blue and the old oak tree's limbs were swaying slightly. He watched distractedly as a flock of sparrows landed on the grass in search of anything that was edible.

"Thanks for holding, Mr. Michaels. I'm going to put you through right now," the receptionist said, a few minutes later.

"Thank you," John replied.

"My pleasure."

"John; it's been a long time, my friend."

John recognized Drew's voice immediately; it hadn't changed over the years.

"Indeed it has been a long time, too long I might add. How have you been, Drew?"

"I'm well, thanks. You must have received the invitation, eh?"

"As a matter of fact, it came in this morning's mail. I'm very surprised that you were able to get my home address since 99 percent of my mail goes to a post office box. Which search agency did you contact?" John asked.

"Well, John, you know that some professionals never reveal their personal trade secrets."

A moment later he started laughing and so did John. Drew hadn't changed; he could still deliver a one-liner on a moment's notice. They spent half-an-hour talking about old times before changing the conversation to the upcoming reunion.

"How long have you been working on this?" John asked.

"I started a little over a year ago."

"That long, eh?"

"Yeah; I didn't realize how much work was involved in organizing a reunion. I'm glad I started early, though."

"Was there anyone not in favor of having a reunion?"

"Yes and no."

"I take it that many didn't share your enthusiasm for having one."

"Actually, quite a few said that they had been looking forward to a 25th Anniversary Reunion in 1995, but when that didn't happen they had hoped someone would organize a 30th Anniversary Reunion instead."

"Were you able to contact everyone from the Class of 1970?" John asked.

"Just about," Drew replied.

"What's the roll call looking like so far?"

"Of the 220 graduates, fifty-five said they wouldn't attend and eight said that they already had other plans for that weekend."

"That's not bad – roughly 29 percent who aren't coming. Drew, I wouldn't let those numbers dampen your enthusiasm."

"It won't. Say, do you remember Jimmy Taylor?" Drew then asked, changing the topic.

"I sure do; he had a part-time job in the school's book store," John answered.

"That's right. When I spoke with Jimmy, he told me that Bobby Marcellas was killed in Vietnam."

"I'm sorry to hear that; I only saw Bobby once while I was in Vietnam," John said. "I simply assumed he transferred out on time. He was a good guy, and a remarkable handball player."

"Yes, he was. He made All-City every year, and was the High School Athletic Association champion in 1968 and 1969," Drew said.

After pausing a moment, Drew continued.

"I still have five others who haven't responded to the invitation. Of those five, I know that four of the addresses are correct, so I'll be making some follow-up phone calls later today."

"When did you begin mailing out the invitations, Drew?"

"Four months ago; except for yours. I didn't think I'd ever find your home address."

"Who is the fifth person that you're having a problem finding?" John inquired.

"Our former senior-year president, Alex Holloman," Drew answered.

* * * * * * * * * * * * * * * *

Alex Holloman and John Michaels had met at the Catholic High School's freshman track team tryouts during the first week of school, in September 1966. When they arrived at Macombs Dam Park on 161st Street, in the Bronx, they were surprised to see that they were the two tallest freshman contenders. Both were, at a minimum, six inches taller than the others: John was six-foot-two and Alex six-even. John and Alex easily made the track team. John's forte was the 100-yard dash, the 220 and the 440; Alex was the opposite, he excelled as a long distance runner. By the end of the second week they had become best friends. Even though Alex lived in Manhattan and John lived in the Bronx, they often traveled to each other's homes to hang out. By the end of their freshman year, they were like brothers: inseparable.

Unlike baseball and basketball, where some team members sit on the bench until placed into the game, being a track team member meant you were going to participate in every track event, regardless of how short or long the race. Both Alex and John had their fair share of individual wins and losses throughout the 1966/1967 track season, which helped Catholic High's freshman team win second place in the High School Athletic Association Track and Field Division. Their toughest competitor was Parkway High; they won first place by a scant three points. When track season ended in May 1967, John and Alex had decided that they weren't going to rejoin the team, as sophomores. There were other things they wanted to do and having to train four times a week was not high on their priority list.

* * * * * * * * * * * * * * *

"I took a chance and mailed a letter to his address as it appeared in our 1970 yearbook. Unfortunately, my letter was returned by the post office a few weeks later, stamped 'Undeliverable.'"

"Did you call Stella?" John asked.

Stella was Alex's cousin. In December 1966, Alex introduced her to John and after their first date together, they were a couple all through high school.

"Yes, I did. I asked her if she had Alex's address and/or a phone number and, if so, would she give it to me," Drew answered.

"What did she say?"

"She told me that Alex disappeared in January of '74 and she hadn't seen or heard from him since."

There was complete silence on both ends of the phone for a few seconds before John began the conversation, again.

"That's not like Alex," John said.

"Here's what I know, John. Stella said that Alex had called her in May 1973 to say he was home from the Army, for good. After some small talk, they made plans to meet at her parents' house for lunch a few days later; I think it was a Saturday, if I remember correctly. She told me that Alex didn't talk about his two years in the Army, apart from mentioning you by name ... something about you two crossing paths periodically while in Vietnam. She went on to say that he looked somewhat tired, but that he was happy to be alive and back home. As for his plans, Stella said he did nothing during the summer and then started working, I believe, in September."

"Did Stella say whether he stayed at home the whole time or if he went anywhere outside of New York City?" John asked.

"She didn't say and to be honest I didn't even think to ask."

"Did she say if anything specific happened after he started working?"

"Nothing that I remember," Drew replied.

"I can't imagine him packing up and leaving, and not telling anyone why or where he was going," John said.

John waited a few seconds for Drew to reply, but he didn't.

"Drew, count me in for the reunion. Is there anything I can do to help you?"

"Well, I'm glad you asked. I was wondering if you would be willing to perform for us that night. I heard that you have officially retired from live performances, but..."

"Drew, it'll be my pleasure. I'll be happy to revive my show for an encore performance."

"Thanks, John. Rest assured, I won't say a word about this to anyone. It'll be a wonderful surprise and a spectacular way to wrap up the reunion. Thanks so much."

"You're welcome, Drew. Before we hang up, I've a question to ask you."

"Certainly, what's on your mind?"

"Earlier this morning I received a call from a gentleman named Bob Waverly who said he was from the *New York Mirror* newspaper. I didn't speak with him so I don't know how he managed to get my unlisted phone number. As an aside, I doubt he would have told me. He left a voice message asking if I would be interested in doing an interview for the newspaper's Sunday supplement. Do you know this guy and have you spoken to him about the reunion?"

"No, I haven't. Perhaps some other classmate contacted the newspaper and Mr. Waverly presumed you'd be attending."

"Okay, thanks."

"I take it you're not interested in the interview."

"I don't know Mr. Waverly, but I do have a journalist friend who covers the New York City entertainment beat and I'd just as soon give him the exclusive."

"That's certainly understandable," Drew replied.

"Well, Drew, if I'm going to plan a show, I need to make some phone calls to my crew and make preparations to schedule some rehearsal time at my magic warehouse. Let me give you my home phone number; it's 622-9311. The answering machine is on all the time so if you call and I'm not home, leave a message and I'll call you back as soon as possible."

"Okay. I'll be in touch."

"I will too."

As he placed the cordless handset back on the phone unit, John saw the neighbor's black cat, Ace, outside, on the prowl. John stayed by the window, watching. Ace would walk a few steps, stop and then look around. His ears moved in different directions as he turned his head to listen to the various sounds. Then, as suddenly as he stopped, he'd walk a few more steps and start the process all over again.

He could be hungry, John thought to himself, *or perhaps Ace decided that today would be a great day to take a walk around the neighborhood, in the cool breeze.*

Whatever the reason, there wasn't a bird or dog in sight. Who said black cats are unlucky!

As soon as Ace disappeared from sight, John picked up the phone and called his chief assistant and illusion builder, Dave Marsh.

CHAPTER THREE

John Michaels and Dave Marsh struck up a conversation on the bus ride to the Army's Basic Training Facility at Fort Dix, New Jersey. It was mid-February 1971. John learned that Dave lived in the Whitestone section of Queens, a neighborhood in close proximity to the Throggs Neck Bridge. It was about a 40-minute drive from John's house in the Bronx. Six-foot tall and 175 pounds, Dave could have easily played on the White Oaks High School football or basketball teams. He did neither. He chose to work part-time, after school, in his father's cabinetmaking business. From the time Dave was able to hold a hammer, his father taught him the basics of carpentry. There'd be no better person than his own son to, one-day, run the family-owned business.

* * * * * * * * * * * * * * * *

In January 1975, John began a yearlong task of putting together a full-evening magic show that he could easily take on tour, with minimal costs. An integral part of this process was the need for an experienced carpenter to build and maintain the custom magic illusions John required for his show. On a cold Saturday morning, John called Dave at his home in Queens.

After a few minutes small talk, John said, "Dave, can you build some magic illusions for me? I'll pay you in advance for the materials, and your time and labor."

"I'm not sure I'm the right person for the job," Dave began. "I've no prior experience building something as meticulous as a magic illusion."

"As long as you can read carpenter blueprints, you'll do fine," John replied. "Besides, if you have a question, you can always call me collect."

Dave was sure there was more to it than carpenter blueprints, but he agreed to give it a try.

"Okay, John; I'll do my best," Dave said.

"Great; I'll mail them on Monday."

They talked a few more minutes and before they hung up John said that he would send Dave a cashier's check, separately. Later that day, John rolled up five different illusion plans and stuffed them into a mailing tube. Paper-clipped to the plans was a handwritten note to Dave reminding him to call collect, if he had any questions.

Dave didn't call.

Two weeks later, while looking out the window from inside his home office, John watched a delivery driver slowly back-up his truck to the beginning of the driveway. John didn't wait for the driver to knock on the door or ring the doorbell; he stepped outside the front door and waited.

"Mr. Michaels?" the middle-aged man asked as he walked up the driveway with a clipboard in his hand.

"Yes, sir," was John's reply.

"I have a special delivery letter for you as well as some crates. Where shall I put them?"

"I'll take the letter; I'd like the crates placed inside the garage," John replied.

After signing for the letter, he went back inside the house and placed it on his desk. He opened the service door that led to the garage and then pressed the control button that remotely opened the garage door. John ducked under it as it slowly rose up and back on its metal tracks. The driver had already positioned the three shipping crates alongside each other at the very edge of the truck bed. After stepping off the back of the truck, he grabbed the first crate and carefully placed it onto a hand-truck.

"Any place inside the garage is fine," John said, as the driver tipped the hand-truck backwards and began pushing it up the driveway.

"Mr. Michaels, I've been a delivery driver for close to 12 years now. I've never seen a garage with so much empty space. Many people have theirs packed to the brim with – well – stuff. It's a wonder they can get in and out without tripping over something."

"That was the state of my garage the first two years after I bought this house," John replied. "I finally got tired of trying to blindly find things. That's when I decided that I needed to organize the place. It's been this way ever since."

After the last crate was placed inside the garage and the hand-truck was stowed away, the driver picked up his clipboard, made a few notations on the delivery order receipt and then asked John to sign his name at the bottom, accepting delivery.

"Thanks, Mr. Michaels."

"You're welcome," John replied, as he handed the clipboard back to the driver.

I guess I should read the letter first, John said, after pressing the control button again. As the garage door slowly closed, he slit open the envelope with his forefinger, reached inside and pulled out the letter and read it.

* * * * * * * * * * * * * * *

February 8, 1975

John, here's your first illusion.

As I started building, I realized that it would be easier if it were built in three modules. Constructing it this way would also make it easier for you to assemble, disassemble and transport it from place to place.

Call me after you've put it together and let me know what you think. If you like how it turned out, I'll start working on the other ones.

Dave

* * * * * * * * * * * * * * *

It only took 10 minutes for John to assemble the illusion according to the instructions Dave had placed inside the crate labeled Number 1. With the illusion sitting in the middle of the garage floor, John looked at it from all angles. After he had finished inspecting the illusion, he called Dave.

"Hey, Dave."

"Hi, John; you must have received the illusion."

"I did."

"Did you have any problem putting it together?"

"Nope; the parts fit together perfectly."

"Cool," Dave said.

"For someone who has never built a magic illusion before, you've certainly done an outstanding job," John said.

"I'm glad you like it. Based on that vote of confidence, I'll start on the next one, tomorrow," Dave added.

"Okay; I'll send you another cashier's check."

"You don't need to, I used less than half of what you previously sent," Dave answered.

"There are four more to build," John replied. "I'll send you the same amount again; let me know when you're running low."

"Okay, John," Dave replied.

Four months later, in mid-June 1975, the last illusion was delivered.

"Hi, Dave," John said.

"Howdy, John," Dave replied.

"The last illusion is here and, like the others, it looks great. How much more do I owe you?" John asked.

"We're squared away," Dave replied.

After a long pause, John said, "Dave, I'm looking for a person to be chief assistant and illusion builder for the magic business I started two years ago. Are you interested in a job?"

"Thanks for the offer, John, but I don't know if I want to leave Queens. I work for my Dad, you know, and I'm making a decent living."

John persisted.

He eventually convinced Dave to at least give this new opportunity a chance, and if after six months he still felt the same, then they would part company amicably. In January 1976, Dave packed all his belongings into his station wagon and drove to Virginia Beach to begin a new job with John's magic company, John Michaels' Magic, Inc.

* * * * * * * * * * * * * * * *

"Hope I'm not calling too early, Dave," John said.

"Not at all; what's up?" he asked.

"This morning, I received an invitation to the 30th Anniversary Reunion of Catholic High's Class of 1970, from a high school friend of mine, Drew Wagner. I just spoke with him on the phone and told him I would attend. During the course of our conversation he asked if I would consider performing a show for the reunion guests. I agreed. Have you any plans for June 30th?"

"No; my calendar is wide open," Dave replied.

"You interested?"

"Of course I'm interested. I've never missed a gig in the past so there's no reason to start now, even though you've officially 'retired' the show."

"I was hoping you'd say that, even though it is on such short notice."

"Have you called the ladies yet?" Dave asked.

Dave often referred to John's three assistants, Patty Malone, Sally Griffin and Maria Segal, as "the ladies." He usually called them by their given first names, but every so often he'd slip and say, "Where are the ladies?" or "The ladies have this under control." When that happened, they always gave him one of those "if looks could kill" glares.

It was all in good fun.

* * * * * * * * * * * * * * * *

Patty Malone, Sally Griffin and Maria Segal were high school classmates who graduated from the Virginia School for the Performing Arts, in June 1973. Like their respective parents, they were lifelong residents of Virginia Beach (originally called Princess Anne County; the name was changed in 1963). In September 1973, they were offered a 9-month contract with the Stage Right Theatrical Troupe as supporting actresses in a play that would be presented throughout the Mid-Atlantic States of New Jersey, Delaware, Maryland, Virginia and North Carolina, from mid-October 1973 through the end of May 1974. Because the theatrical season is dark during the months of June, July and August, the girls were told that they would be on unpaid vacation until rehearsals for the new season began the week after Labor Day. Patty, Sally and Maria readily accepted the employment offer; they'd figure out something to do over the summer months.

* * * * * * * * * * * * * * * *

Henry Fitch was also a lifelong resident of Virginia Beach. He and his wife, Marybeth, lived on the same street as the girls, and knew them and their parents quite well. Henry had first-hand knowledge of what life on the road as a traveling performer was like. He was a full-time professional magician; Marybeth was his assistant. Together, they had etched out a living touring the United States since the 1950s performing at schools, festivals, State and County fairs, carnivals and trade fairs. Henry would be the first to tell you that life on the road was not all glory. It was damn hard work.

It was during John's first visit to the local magic club, in 1973, that he met Henry. After watching John's performance, Henry knew that John was a diamond in the rough, just waiting to be polished. John had exceptional technical skill and charisma. It was everything he would need to ensure his success as a full-time professional magician. Henry decided to become John's mentor.

Prior to the Memorial Day weekend in 1974, Henry had just finished booking a 45-day tour through Virginia and West Virginia, to present a two-hour, full-evening magic show during the hot and muggy summer months of July and August. In need of three assistants, he asked Patty, Sally and Maria if they were interested in some part-time work. They were up to the challenge of learning something new and readily jumped at the opportunity. After all, it was a paying job and it still allowed them to return to the Stage Right Theatrical Troupe in September. The tour was so successful that Henry decided to repeat the tour in the summer of 1975, with a brand new show.

On a Saturday afternoon, in October 1975, John and Henry met for lunch at Red's Seafood Restaurant on Independence Boulevard in Virginia Beach.

"Henry, I've some good news to tell you. I've put together a four-month tour of the South and I'm adding more shows each week. I think this tour will eventually become a 10 or 11-month tour."

"That's great news, John, congratulations," Henry replied. "When does it start?"

"Thanks. The tour starts on October 2nd of next year with a kickoff show in Elizabeth City, North Carolina," John replied.

"Henry, I'm looking for some assistants who would be interested in working with me on a full-time basis. Do you know anyone?"

Without giving it a second thought, Henry immediately recommended Patty, Sally and Maria.

John politely declined.

"The girls are perfect, John. They are professional actresses, they have stage experience and they've worked with me for the past two years during their summer downtime."

"I don't feel right taking your assistants, Henry. Especially since I know you're planning to do another tour next summer."

"John, my tour ends in mid-August and we'll be back in town a few days later. You'll have plenty of time to rehearse your show with the girls. Besides, this is going to be my last tour. Marybeth wants me to retire ... and I told her I would."

John was still hesitant, but Henry would not take "no" for an answer. He knew that John would have a very successful tour once he got on the road and word of his show was publicized in the local media. After much cajoling, John finally gave in.

"Okay, Henry, it's a deal, but on one condition: you don't cancel your 1976 summer tour."

Henry nodded happily and they shook hands on their gentleman's agreement. Two weeks later, on November 1, 1975, Henry introduced John to the girls, and their parents. Patty, Sally and Maria had just finished a two-week engagement at the Gordon Wells Theatre in Charlotte, North Carolina and had a week off before heading back out on the road. That first meeting was the beginning of a highly successful twenty-plus year career.

* * * * * * * * * * * * * * *

The silence on the phone was deafening.

"Hey, John, are you still with me?" Dave finally asked.

John snapped out of his daydream.

"I'm sorry, Dave. I'm still here; your question brought back memories of my first meeting with Patty, Sally and Maria."

John paused a moment.

"Getting back to your question; not yet. I thought I'd call you first," John replied. "In hindsight, I should have held off agreeing to do the show until I had asked everyone."

"I'm sure the ladies wouldn't mind a working trip to New York City," Dave said.

"They may not, but their husbands may have had other plans for that weekend. What about Melissa? She, too, could have made plans."

* * * * * * * * * * * * * * *

It was almost a year to the day after he moved to Virginia, that Dave met Melissa, an airline flight attendant with Eastern Airlines. They dated for a year and a half before Dave proposed, and in December 1978 they made it official by tying the knot. Melissa was now a senior flight attendant for Midland Eagle Air Express Airlines and though her schedule pretty much had her home every night, there has been a few occasions when she has had to work a flight to the west coast because another attendant was sick or on vacation.

* * * * * * * * * * * * * * *

"You're right, but I'm looking at our calendar and it is wide open, so I'm safe. I'll tell Melissa when she calls me later today, so she can plan accordingly. Do you want me to call the ladies?" Dave asked.

"No, I'll call them."

"Okay. Next question: do you have anything special in mind for this show?"

"Yes, I do, but I need to work out some details first. Is Melissa due back tonight?"

"No; she's due back tomorrow afternoon."

"Have you anything planned for this evening?"

"No, I don't."

"Can you swing by the house about 5:30? I'll fill you in on my idea, then."

"Sure can."

"Okay, Dave, thanks."

* * * * * * * * * * * * * * *

John called Patty, Sally and Maria right after he finished talking with Dave. They were excited about going out on the road, once again, even though it was for just one show. John didn't tell them that during his conversation with Dave that he had referred to them as "the ladies." It wouldn't have taken long for them to converge at Dave's house to read him the riot act and give him the "if looks could kill" glare.

All in good fun, of course.

CHAPTER FOUR

June 15, 2000

After talking with Patty, Sally and Maria, John sat down at the kitchen table, intent on perusing the magic catalog. He only got as far as the first page. Drew's comment that "Alex had disappeared and no one knew why," seemed to reverberate over and over. John's mind was miles away.

The last time I spoke with Alex, heck the last time I saw him, we were in Vietnam, John said to himself. *I was about three weeks shy of being transferred out; Alex still had about four or five more months to go. I remember telling him that I was due to leave, but, unfortunately, I couldn't tell him where I was going because I didn't know, at the time.*

The Army did its best to keep its soldiers informed in a timely manner, but John had heard about a couple of soldiers who only had a few days advance notice. As it turned out, he was one of the lucky ones: he received ten days notice that he was being transferred to Fort Story, in Virginia Beach, Virginia.

* * * * * * * * * * * * * * *

After his discharge from the Army, in February 1973, John remained in Virginia Beach. Intent on beginning a new career as a full-time magician, he started a business using money he had managed to save while on active duty. John aggressively marketed his company and slowly built up a large clientele base, both locally and statewide. After establishing a niche in Virginia, he looked beyond Virginia's border to the neighboring States of West Virginia, North Carolina, Tennessee, Kentucky and Maryland.

It was during the first week of June 1973 when John received a phone call from the Charleston South Carolina Media Arts and Communications Commission, the lead agency for that city's "Fourth of July Festival." A last minute decision had been made to extend the holiday festivities from one day (a Wednesday) to five days (ending on Sunday, July 8th) and they needed additional entertainment. John told them that he was available and then asked how they got his name. He was told that a gentleman named Henry Fitch had strongly recommended him.

John was asked to perform two shows (mid-afternoon and early evening) on July 5th, 6th and 7th and he quoted what he thought was a reasonable fee. They promptly agreed to his asking price and promised to send a contract by the end of the week. John didn't know it at the time, but his performances in South Carolina, that week, would help him get his foot in the door when, a few years later, he would put together a tour of the southern States that stretched along the eastern seaboard and across the Gulf of Mexico.

* * * * * * * * * * * * * * *

I remember calling his house one day during the last week of June 1973, believing that he would have already been discharged and home by then, but no one answered the phone. And, I remember calling his house on July 3rd, but again no one answered. In hindsight, I should have flown up to New York City on the 3rd to see Stella, and Alex. Then early the following morning I could have flown back to Virginia, packed up my car and made the trip to South Carolina.

John got up from the kitchen table and walked towards the refrigerator.

Whatever happened must have really upset Stella. Thinking back, none of her letters to me, over the years, mentioned Alex so I just assumed that he was doing okay. Obviously, I was mistaken; I guess I should have taken the initiative to ask her, but I didn't.

He pulled open the door and grabbed a bottle of spring water.

There were only two times when Stella had written me with bad news; that was when her parents had passed away, within a year of each other.

He uncapped the bottle and took a large gulp.

I can't undo the past, but I can certainly write the future. If I can find Alex before the reunion, I'll include him in the show and reunite him with Stella.

* * * * * * * * * * * * * * * *

Searching for Alex would have been an easy task if John could have simply picked up the phone and dialed Alex's home phone number. But he couldn't and neither could anyone else. No one knew Alex's whereabouts. Well, almost no one: Alex knew, but he wasn't talking. The United States is a big country and for all John or anyone else knew, Alex could be living anywhere. John's gut feeling, though, was that Alex had never left New York City; he was living right under everyone's nose. But, for whatever reason, he simply wanted to be left alone. John picked up the phone to call Stella, but then changed his mind. He wanted to try and find Alex without Stella's help.

If I can't find him through local means, then I'll call Stella and tell her what I'm doing.

John knew that time was of the essence with the reunion slightly less than three weeks away. That's hardly enough time for a couple to find the house of their dreams. Yet John was about to embark on a quest to find a friend who had chosen a life of seclusion for the past 26 years. And somewhere in between these few weeks, he would have to find time to plan and rehearse the reunion show. John took another long sip of water. Staring at the magic catalog on the kitchen table, he dwelled on how and where to begin the search. Suddenly a thought crossed his mind.

The branches of the Armed Forces have a repository where they keep permanent records of everyone who served within its ranks.

John remembered hearing about it from the Drill Sergeant, during Army basic training. He left the kitchen and headed for his office where he kept the white pages telephone directory, the back of which have blue pages with government listings. On page 17, under United States Government, he found a local Army Recruiting Services listing and dialed their number.

* * * * * * * * * * * * * * * *

"Good afternoon, United States Army Recruiting, Master Sergeant Wilkens speaking, how may I help you sir or ma'am?"

"Good afternoon Master Sergeant, my name is John Michaels. I'm trying to locate a former Army friend of mine. I understand the Army has a central repository where the records of all former soldiers are kept."

"Yes, sir, that's correct."

"Could you tell me the repository's name and its location, and possibly a phone number for me to call?"

"The repository is called the Army Worldwide Locator. This command is located in Indianapolis, Indiana, but the Army Worldwide Locator Assistance Command, in Alexandria, Virginia, manages it. If you can hold on for a few seconds, I'll look up their phone number for you."

"Thank you very much," John replied.

A few moments later the Master Sergeant came back on line.

"Mr. Michaels, the phone number for the Army Worldwide Locator Assistance Command is (822) 325-3732. When the switchboard operator answers, tell her you want to speak with the Central Records Division supervisor and she'll transfer your call."

"Thank you very much, Master Sergeant."

"You're welcome, sir."

* * * * * * * * * * * * * * *

Since Alex was an Army veteran, there was a good chance that they might have a mailing address that no one else had. It was a long shot, but John wanted to cover every possibility and this was probably as good a place as any to start.

CHAPTER FIVE

It was 5:15 p.m. when Dave rang the doorbell at John's house. He was dressed casually in blue jeans, sneakers and a pullover black shirt with the words, "Magic is a Vanishing Art!" silk-screened in white letters on the front of the shirt. For Dave, it was always casual. The only thing that changed was a short or long-sleeved shirt, depending upon the season of the year.

"I'm early, as usual," he said, after John opened the front door.

"Hey, Dave, come on in. I was just finishing up some work in the office so let's go there."

As John affixed return address labels and postage stamps to his outgoing mail, he told Dave the rest of the story from his early morning phone call with Drew and the local Army recruiting office.

"Do you think there's a possibility of finding Alex?" Dave asked.

"I don't know, Dave. I really don't."

John paused a moment to gather his thoughts before continuing.

"I'm hoping that I haven't bit off more than I can chew, especially in light of the fact that we haven't done a show in almost a year and have yet to shake the cobwebs off the illusions sitting in the warehouse."

"Once we start rehearsals everything will fall into place. Do you have any idea why Alex disappeared?"

"None whatsoever. It doesn't sound like something Alex would do for no reason."

"It could be post-traumatic stress syndrome from his tour in Vietnam. You know it affected a lot of servicemen."

"Yes, that is definitely a possibility. But we can't diagnose a ghost; Alex needs to be found, first. Trying to find him will be like creating a new illusion. I know what the final outcome should be, but I have to work on the *'modus operandi'*."

"Speaking of magic, John, you mentioned that you wanted to do something special that night. What did you have in mind?"

"If I can find Alex, I thought we could magically make him appear. Since no one would be expecting him that evening it would be the perfect way to end the show. What do you think?"

"I think it's a great idea. Have you given any thought to which illusion you want to use?"

"We have that old packing crate escape illusion. We could modify it to work somewhat like the Tip-Over Trunk illusion. Perhaps mount it on a small base so we can roll it around 360 degrees," John replied.

"I'll look around the warehouse and see if we have anything else we could use first. If not, then I'll work with the crate illusion. We also have a number of different platforms we can choose from so that won't be a problem."

John looked at his wristwatch: it was just past 5:30.

"I was thinking of going to that French restaurant, Le Palais du Jardin, on the boulevard for dinner; I haven't eaten there before. Are you interested in tagging along?"

"Sure. Melissa and I had dinner there once before; the food is excellent. I think you'll like it."

"Okay, let's go. We can discuss the illusion in a little more detail while we eat," John said.

* * * * * * * * * * * * * * *

Le Palais du Jardin is conveniently nestled in a four-store strip mall on Virginia Beach Boulevard, three blocks west of the Wind Crest Mall. The restaurant was situated in between George's Ceramics' Shop, and the Tidewater Sewing and Vacuum Super Center; Bill's Auto Transmission took up residence in the other corner. As they approached the parking lot they were surprised to see at least two-dozen cars already parked there.

"Either the restaurant has a Thursday night crowd or the ceramic shop is teaching a night class," Dave said.

There was only one open spot left, close to the ceramic shop's bay window. As they pulled in, John and Dave saw about a dozen people sitting at a large round table in the front room with paintbrushes in their hands and small jars of paint in front of, and behind, clay vases of various shapes and sizes. They could see the instructor walking around giving advice to her students.

"That explains the parking lot," John said.

John and Dave stopped in front of the bay window to watch. The instructor glanced their way, waved and invited them to come in. John waved back, but shook his head, silently declining the offer. The thought of eating French cuisine was much more appetizing than painting ceramic clay.

As soon as John opened the door and stepped inside the restaurant, the aroma from the open kitchen tempted his senses with a promise of authentic French cuisine, and his mouth began to salivate even before he had a chance to sit down and order a drink.

"*Bonjour*. Welcome to *Le Palais du Jardin*," the hostess said. "My name is Marie."

Marie was wearing a white blouse, a black skirt and black flats. Her auburn hair was short and straight, and fell loosely to her shoulders. She accentuated her youthful look with only a slight hint of makeup.

"*Bonsoir, Marie*," John replied with a smile.

"*Bonsoir; comment allez vous*?" Marie answered.

"*Bien merci, et vous*?" John replied.

"*Bien merci*," Marie said.

"I didn't know you spoke French!" Dave said, unconsciously jumping into the conversation between John and Marie.

"*Oui*," Marie answered.

"No … I didn't mean … uh …"

Dave quickly stopped speaking and turned towards John who was doing his best not to laugh.

"John," Dave said, but was quickly interrupted by John.

"*Oui*," John replied.

Dave opened his mouth to speak, but whatever reply he had planned to say it wasn't to be; he said nothing at all. Unable to maintain a straight face any longer, John began to laugh. A moment later, so did Marie and Dave.

After the laughter stopped, John said, "I took one year of French and one year of Spanish, in high school. Unfortunately, I only remember a few phrases from each language. When Marie said hello, in French, I thought it would be appropriate to reply in French. I then realized that if she were to continue speaking French, it wouldn't be long before I'd have to revert to English and apologize for not being able to continue."

"You had this attractive young lady thinking you spoke fluent French," Dave said.

Marie blushed at Dave's comment.

"That's quite all right; it's nice to hear someone other than my college professor, speaking French," Marie said.

Marie paused a moment and then asked if they had any seating preference.

"The non-smoking section, please," John answered.

"This is a non-smoking restaurant," Marie replied.

"Even better," John said.

"Would you like a table or booth?" she asked.

"A table, please."

"Very well, follow me."

After reciting the special of the day, she handed both of them a menu, took their drink orders and left. John ordered a carafe of the house red wine and Dave asked for a carafe of Chardonnay.

Marie returned a few minutes later with their wine selections.

"Are you ready to order, or will you need a few more minutes?" she politely asked, as she placed the carafes on the table.

"I'm ready," Dave said.

"And so am I," added John.

"What would you like?" Marie asked.

"I'd like the special of the day," quipped Dave, "the oven-roasted lamb with lentils and pearl onions."

"Same for me," John said, before Marie had a chance to ask.

"An excellent choice, gentlemen," replied Marie. "I'll be back momentarily with your salads."

Marie gracefully turned on her heels and headed towards the kitchen.

"Okay, John, let's talk some more about the illusion. On the presumption that you find Alex, what is it exactly that you want to do?"

"I want to present the illusion right at center stage with no scenery or extra backdrop curtains. We'll use the stage's existing back curtain, only. In a nutshell, the curtain opens and the audience sees a tall box sitting at center stage. After it's turned completely around, it's opened to show the audience that it's empty. I then step inside, the box is closed and a moment later it's reopened ... I've disappeared. The box is closed a second time and when it's reopened ... I'm back. Finally, the box is closed one last time and when it's reopened a moment later, Alex steps out."

"Where does this illusion fit in the show?"

"It'll be the only thing we do for the second-half part of the show. The first-half will run about 55 minutes and then we'll break for 15 minutes to prepare for the show's finale."

"Now that I know exactly what you want to do, we can forget about the packing crate illusion," Dave said. "I have an idea that will be perfect, but it'll have to be built from scratch."

"That's fine."

Marie had just returned carrying a small tray with two salad dishes on it. She gently placed the tray on the empty table across from where John and Dave were sitting, and then picked up the two dishes and served them.

"Can I get you anything else?" she asked.

"No, thanks," they both said.

"Very well, enjoy your salad. I'll be back in a few minutes with your dinners."

Dave picked up an extra napkin from the table and in between bites of his salad he made a rough sketch of the illusion. At the bottom of the napkin and on its reverse side, Dave jotted down notes on how he envisioned its presentation and made a few additional, smaller sketches. Periodically, he would look up in a blank stare, and then drop his gaze back to the napkin and write something. When he finished, he turned the napkin towards John and began to explain his plan for this new illusion.

"What do you think?"

"I like it. How long do you think it'll take to build and paint it?"

"It'll take me a day to make a miniature working model, first. As soon as that's done I'll fine-tune it for any needed changes before I build and paint the full-size model."

"When do you think you can start?" John asked.

"First thing tomorrow morning," Dave replied.

From the corner of his eye, John glimpsed Marie walking towards them; her left hand was holding a large tray high in the air.

"How long will it take to build the full-size model?"

"One day to build, and two days to prep and paint."

"All right."

Marie set the tray down on the same empty table she used a few minutes ago.

"Can I get either of you some more wine?" she inquired, as she carefully placed their dinners on the table.

"None for me," John said.

Dave also declined the offer.

"*Bon Appétit*!" Marie said before leaving.

They ate in silence. John was thinking about a plan for finding Alex. Dave, on the other hand, was definitely doing some brainstorming on this illusion because he was constantly shifting his gaze from his dinner plate to the napkin. Marie returned to the table about 15 minutes later to see if they wanted or needed anything else. They didn't. Shortly after they had finished eating, Marie returned again.

"Can I get anyone some dessert or coffee?" she asked.

They both said no.

"Okay, I'll be right back with the check."

When she returned, she placed the bill on the table and thanked them. The bill was $48.

"I got it," John said.

"Well at least let me leave the tip," Dave replied.

"Next time," John answered.

Marie watched in amusement the banter between John and Dave. But she was not prepared for what was to follow. John removed his wallet from his pants pocket and as soon as he opened it, flames burst out from inside the wallet. Marie quickly stepped away from the table, unsure what to do. Dave, on the other hand, calmly sat and watched the entire spectacle as if nothing was wrong.

"Money really can burn a hole in your pocket," John said after he closed his wallet and placed it on the table.

Marie ignored John; her eyes were steadfastly focused on the wallet. Still motionless, she watched a thin, final wisp of smoke billow up into the air. When he re-opened the wallet a few seconds later, it looked exactly like a normal wallet. John pulled out three 20-dollar bills, gave the cash to Marie and told her to keep the change.

"*Merci, Mademoiselle*," John said to Marie.

"*De rien, Monsieur*," Marie replied as she cautiously extended her hand.

Dave was right: the food and the service were excellent.

After they returned to John's house, Dave got in his car and headed home. John went to the kitchen to check the answering machine – no one had called – so he turned around and headed to his office. He sat at his desk and jotted down some notes on a pad of paper and started a list of things he needed to do the following day. Chief among them was to call the Army Worldwide Locater Assistance Command. The outcome of that phone call would determine how he would begin the search for Alex.

CHAPTER SIX

January 9, 1971

Alex remembered that chilly Saturday afternoon when his best friend, John Michaels, called.

"Alex," his mother hollered, "the telephone is for you, it's John."

"Okay, Ma, I'll be right there," he shouted back.

"Hold on John, he's on his way. I'm going to put the telephone down so don't hang up."

"All right, Mrs. Holloman," John replied.

A few moments later Alex picked it up.

"Hey, John, what's up?"

"Alex, man, you won't believe what I received in the mail this morning. Hell, I can't believe it myself."

"So tell me, already. How bad can it be?"

"It's my draft notification. I have to report to the Army Induction Center on Whitehall Street next Friday."

"No shit?"

"As sure as I'm alive."

"Does it give a date when you leave?"

"Thirty days later."

"Fort Dix, New Jersey, for basic training; right?"

"That's the place."

"Your folks know yet?"

"No. They left early this morning to go shopping at Kleins' Department Store."

"When are you going to tell them?"

"I guess after they get back or maybe after dinner."

"You worried?"

"Yeah, somewhat. My father told me stories about his three years in the Army during World War II."

"You could always try and join the Navy or the Air Force, John."

"I think it may be too late for that now, Alex, since I've received official orders to report."

"What a bummer, man."

"The Army will always need more people, Alex. You'll get your 'invitation' in the mail, too. Just wait and see. Why don't you enlist?"

"No way, man. I'm going to take my chances."

* * * * * * * * * * * * * * * *

After completing Army basic training, John was given two weeks leave. His orders had him returning to Fort Dix for 10 additional days of training at the Advanced Infantry School and then, upon completion, he'd board a military transport aircraft heading for Vietnam.

John made the most of his two weeks. He and Alex made the rounds visiting old school friends in the evening, which usually included having a few drinks at The Trolley Car, a local tavern on 116th Street and Lexington Avenue that had become a favorite hangout for Catholic High alumni. The night before John was to return to Fort Dix, Alex and Stella hosted a farewell party for him at The Trolley Car. It didn't take long before a deck of cards was tossed onto the table with a request that John "do a few tricks" before he headed off into the sunset. Everyone at the party knew of John's expertise in sleight-of-hand. Word had quickly spread amongst the students at Catholic High the day he bamboozled the Freshman English teacher, Mr. Bill Landers.

As he looked around at the faces of his friends, his mind wandered back to that day.

* * * * * * * * * * * * * * * *

Bill Landers was one of 12 laymen who taught at Catholic High, an all-boy school located at 124th Street and Lenox Avenue, in Manhattan. Mr. Landers always wore a suit and tie, and by the end of the school day there would be streaks and blotches of chalk dust on his tie, shirt, pants and jacket. Perhaps he felt that if his clothes weren't somewhat smudged then he wasn't doing his job.

It was the last day of the first week of school. Mr. Landers had just finished writing a long sentence on the blackboard that was devoid of punctuation. As soon as he turned around, Drew raised his hand and without waiting to be acknowledged he blatantly asked Mr. Landers why he wiped his dusty hands on his clothes. No one dared laugh. Mr. Landers' response was that high school freshman attended school to learn, not analyze or question the teachers' habits. It wasn't the answer Drew was hoping to get, but he knew that a smart-ass reply would only result in detention. He decided to save the wisecrack for another time.

"Mister Michaels, please step up to the blackboard. Make it quick, we have a lot of material to cover today, young man," Mr. Landers' voice bellowed out.

John got up from his seat and headed towards the front of the classroom, while Mr. Landers walked down the opposite aisle, towards the back.

"Pick up the chalk and insert the correct punctuation, Mister Michaels."

"Pardon me, Mr. Landers, but there's no chalk to write with," John replied.

"It's on the blackboard ledge, Mister Michaels, look for it. Quit trying to waste valuable class time by stalling."

"I've already looked on the ledge, there isn't any chalk there," John replied.

"That's impossible," Mr. Landers said, "I just placed it there."

Mr. Landers walked to the front of the room, in a huff. Sure enough, the chalk was missing.

"Are you sure it's not in your jacket pocket, Mr. Landers?" John innocently asked.

Mr. Landers instinctively placed both his hands inside his jacket pockets and then quickly withdrew them. He turned towards John and gave him a menacing scowl for upstaging him. Mr. Landers walked around the front of the room, scanning the floor; there was no sign of the chalk stick. The students' eyes were transfixed on Mr. Landers' every movement.

When it became obvious that the chalk was, indeed, missing, Mr. Landers walked over to the podium that he kept in the corner of the classroom. He bent over, placed his hand on the inside shelf and retrieved a box of chalk that he kept there, all the while keeping his eyes focused on John and the other students seated at their desks. Something funny was going on and Mr. Landers was not in the least bit amused. If this were some sort of freshman stunt, he was going to have the last laugh by giving someone – Mister Michaels – after-school detention. He'd have none of this claptrap in his classroom. He removed the last chalk stick and then threw the empty box into the waste paper basket that was alongside the podium.

"Here you are, Mister Michaels."

Mr. Landers wiped the chalk dust from his hands on his pants.

"Don't lose this one; it's all I have left, at the moment."

Mr. Landers turned and headed towards the back of the classroom.

"Excuse me, Mr. Landers," John began, "but you just gave me a stick of chewing gum."

"What did you just say to me?" Mr. Landers growled as he spun around. His face began to turn beet-red.

John held the stick of gum up, high in the air. Everyone's eyes opened wide and their mouths dropped opened. They clearly saw Mr. Landers give John a chalk stick, but they had no idea how it suddenly changed into a stick of chewing gum right in front of their eyes.

"It's gum, this is what you just gave me," John said, with as serious a look on his face as he could muster.

"Give it here, Michaels!" Mr. Landers demanded, as he lunged towards the front of the room, his hand outstretched.

As soon as he was within arms distance, John placed the gum onto Mr. Landers' hand. Mr. Landers quickly turned around to face the class and then began to slowly turn his head from side to side, scanning the classroom, looking for anyone who had a smirk on his face. The students sat stone-faced as John held up both pieces of chalk so everyone, except Mr. Landers, could see them. As soon as Mr. Landers turned towards the podium, John quickly and gently placed the two pieces of chalk into Mr. Landers' jacket pocket, and then took three quick steps to the left. Much to Mr. Landers' dismay, when he placed his left hand, with the stick of chewing gum, into his jacket pocket, the look of astonishment on his face was priceless when he withdrew his hand holding both the gum and the two missing pieces of chalk.

"I see you found the chalk, Mr. Landers," John nonchalantly said, as he held out his hand, confident that Mr. Landers would give him one of the sticks.

"Mister Michaels, you can return to your seat. I don't know what you just did, but I'm going to keep my eyes on you for the rest of the school year."

Damn the bad luck, John mumbled under his breath as he walked down the aisle, towards his seat.

"Did you just say something?" Mr. Landers loudly asked.

John stopped, turned around and said, "Yes, I did, Mr. Landers. I said, 'I know I could have correctly punctuated that sentence'."

No one dared laugh as John turned around and continued towards his seat. Mr. Landers never did get that sentence punctuated. He erased it off the board and had the class open up their literature book, instead.

* * * * * * * * * * * * * * *

The hours seemed to fly by and before everyone knew it, they were being asked to wrap things up for the night. The only way John could think of thanking everyone for coming to see him off, was to offer a toast. Since they were the last ones in the bar, John asked Tony, the bartender, if he would bring over a bottle of cognac and some glasses for everyone, including himself. After Tony poured everyone a drink, John raised his glass and offered a toast.

"Thank you all for coming tonight. I wish circumstances were different, but, hey, I'm looking forward to doing this again real soon."

Everyone stood up and gathered around, and as they touched glasses, John said, "Cheers."

"Cheers," everyone replied in unison.

* * * * * * * * * * * * * * *

It would be one month before Alex and Stella would each get their first letter from John. He apologized for not writing sooner. He said he was okay, but that things were extremely hectic. He also said he would try to write more often, time permitting.

Alex was looking out the window of his parents' third floor apartment on a cool Saturday afternoon in late March 1971 when he saw the mailman leaving the building. He had hoped that today's mail would bring him a letter from John. Alex removed the mailbox key from its hook by the hallway telephone and then headed towards the front door. He raced down the stairs two at a time and when he reached the main landing he turned left into the hallway alcove that held a tall bank of metal mailboxes. He placed the key in the mailbox lock, rotated it counter-clockwise a quarter-turn and pulled open the mailbox door. There was a single letter inside. He quickly pulled it out and turned it over. It was addressed to him, but it wasn't from John. It was from the Selective Service System.

A feeling of queasiness overcame Alex. It only lasted a few seconds, but to him it seemed like minutes had passed. An adrenalin rush quickly followed this queasiness and Alex could feel his heart pounding inside his chest. He closed the mailbox door and relocked it. As he placed the key into his pants pocket, his hands began to tremble. Alex walked around to the stairs and sat down. Nervously, he slipped his forefinger under the envelope flap and gently slid it across from one end to the other. Reaching in, he removed the tri-folded letter and flipped it open. At the very top, in bold capital letters, it said, ORDER TO REPORT FOR INDUCTION.

The upper portion of the letter contained detailed instructions on where and when to report, as well as a specific reporting time. Alex was to report to the Army Induction Center on Whitehall Street in Manhattan, for initial processing, at 8:00 a.m. on April 2, 1971. The bottom portion of the letter stated that he had 30 calendar days to get his affairs in order and report back to the induction center at 7:30 a.m. on May 2nd for further transfer to Fort Dix, New Jersey. There were also some additional instructions on what he would need to bring, including enough money for 30 days.

Alex refolded the letter and placed it back inside the envelope. Then he stood up and slowly walked back up the stairs to the apartment. His mind drifted back to the day when his best friend, John, had called to say he had been drafted. He also remembered telling John that he had no intention of enlisting in the service, but would take his chances on being drafted. That day had now come. And, unfortunately, Alex couldn't call John to tell him the news; John was already in Vietnam.

When he reached the apartment he inserted the key into the lock, rotated it clockwise and pushed open the front door. He waited for the door to close, locked it, and then headed towards the living room, the place where he last saw his parents. Sid and Mary were sitting next to each other on the couch; she was busily knitting and he was reading the newspaper. The television was on, but neither one was watching it. They both looked up when Alex walked into the room.

"Son, are you feeling all right?" Sid asked. "You look rather pale."

After seeing the look on her son's face, Mary's motherly instinct told her that Alex was about to give them some bad news. Before he had a chance to say a word, she began to weep. Surprised by his wife's sudden crying, Sid looked first at Mary and then turned to look at Alex.

"Mom, Dad, I don't know how to say this, but … I've been drafted."

Alex gave the letter to his father to read. He then turned around and headed for his bedroom. Alex wanted to call Stella right away, but he first needed to come to grips with this sudden and unexpected turn of events. Alex's parents were devastated that their only son was being drafted into the Army.

"Is there anything we can do or anyone we can call, Sid?" Mary asked, tears streaming down her face.

"I don't know, dear," he replied.

"How about our Congressman; do you think he could help us?"

Sid and Mary weren't against the war, but this was their only son and only child. Should something happen to him, there would be no one to carry on the family name.

"Maybe," Sid replied as he placed his hand on top of his slightly balding head and slowly slid it down towards the back of his neck. "I'll call his office tomorrow."

"Tomorrow is Sunday, Sid. Do you think he'll be there? Why don't you call his office now?" she pleaded.

Sid placed his hand on Mary's shoulder, and in a calm and reassuring voice tried to allay her fears.

"Okay, Mary, I'll call right now, but I need you to try and compose yourself."

Sid got up from the couch and headed for the telephone in the hallway while Mary stayed in the living room. The office manager in Congressman Paul Watkins' office picked up after the first ring.

"Good morning, ma'am, my name is Sid Holloman; I'd like to speak with Congressman Watkins, if he's available."

"I'm sorry, Mr. Holloman, but Congressman Watkins is in Washington, and will not be back in the Bronx until the start of the Memorial Day holiday. Is there anything I can do for you?"

In a calm voice, Sid expressed his dismay over his son, and an only child, being drafted.

"I guess what I'm asking is, can Congressman Watkins arrange to have my son placed in the Army National Guard, rather than the regular Army?"

"Mr. Holloman, the best I can do for you, at the moment, is to forward your concerns to Congressman Watkins' primary office in Washington, DC."

"I understand," Sid replied.

Sid thanked the office manager for her kindness and then hung up the telephone. When he turned around to head back to the living room, he was startled to see Mary standing a few feet behind him; her eyes were red and puffy from crying.

"He's going to Vietnam, isn't he, Sid?" Mary sobbed.

Before he could answer her, Mary turned on her heels and headed for their bedroom. When she got there she gently closed the door behind her.

* * * * * * * * * * * * * * * *

Two days before Alex left for basic training, he borrowed his parent's car and drove up to the Bronx to say goodbye to Stella, and his Aunt and Uncle. He told them he'd be back in a months' time and would come up to see them before he left, again. He was sure that, like John, he would be going to Advanced Infantry Training before going to Vietnam.

* * * * * * * * * * * * * * *

Alex had set his alarm clock for 4:30 a.m. and when it rang he quickly turned it off. As he was getting dressed he could hear his parents talking, their voices effortlessly reverberating through the apartment. Mary had prepared a breakfast of ham, eggs, toast and coffee for everyone. Alex wasn't really hungry, but he ate because he wasn't sure when he'd have an opportunity to get another meal, that day. They ate in silence. Alex didn't know what to say and considering the emotional state his mother was in, he decided that perhaps it would be better to not say anything.

After he had finished, Alex looked at his watch and said, "I'd better get going. I don't want to get there late."

He got up from the table, went back to his bedroom to pick up his carryall bag and then headed towards the front door. Sid and Mary were close behind him. After he stepped out into the hallway, Alex put his bag on the floor, turned to his father and shook hands. He then gave his teary-eyed mother a hug, kissed her and said goodbye.

"I'll be fine, Mom, don't worry. I promise I'll write whenever I can. At any rate, after basic training is over I will have two weeks of leave, so I will be back then."

Mary started sobbing uncontrollably and Sid put his arm around his wife to console her.

"C'mon Mary, let's go inside. Alex needs to get going. Take care, son; don't worry, Mom will be all right and so will I. We'll see you soon."

Alex picked up his bag, turned and slowly walked down the stairs. A moment later he heard the apartment door close and the lock being engaged.

CHAPTER SEVEN

August 19, 1972

Alex had only spent a year in Vietnam, but that one-year seemed like an eternity. The death of some of his Army friends, days, weeks and months after arriving in Vietnam, was unsettling because it made him wonder if he would be the next casualty. These kids were too young to die; hell, they couldn't even vote for the electors who were sending them to fight in this war. Something was definitely wrong with that concept, but that all changed when the Twenty-Sixth Amendment to the United States Constitution was formally certified by then President Richard Nixon on July 1, 1971. The amendment lowered the right to vote to age 18 and prohibited Federal and State governments from denying these citizens their constitutional right.

Mail was extremely slow, although the Army did its best to get the mail to the soldiers in a timely manner. It was not uncommon for Alex to receive a stack of five, six or more letters at once. The letters from home were lengthy and cheerful, and although his Dad was the one who actually wrote them, his Mom also signed each letter. In contrast, Alex's letters back home were short and upbeat. He knew that the daily newspapers and evening news reports on television would be filled with stories about the war. There was no need for him to retell the horrors he saw, in his letters. The least he said; the better. Alex generally talked about the new friends he made, the few times he crossed paths with his best friend John Michaels and his plans after he was discharged.

Eleven months after he arrived in Vietnam, Alex was promoted to the rank of Sergeant. Unbeknownst to him at the time, better news was forthcoming. Exactly one week later, at morning muster, the company's First Sergeant told Alex to begin packing his duffel bag; he was being transferred to Camp Zama in Okinawa, Japan for the 8-month remainder of his two-year Army commitment. Alex was elated by the news and by week's end he was on a military transport plane bound for the land of the rising sun. Alex was extremely grateful that fate would dictate he would be one of the fortunate soldiers' leaving Vietnam alive, and with all his extremities.

Alex had no formal Army schooling other than basic and advanced infantry training, so after he completed the check-in process he was assigned to the base Security Department. It was the most logical place for him to work. The days turned into weeks and the weeks quickly turned into months. Thirty days prior to the two-year anniversary of the date he officially reported for active duty, the Army served written notice to Sergeant Alexander Patrick Holloman that his enlistment was up and he was eligible to be processed for an honorable discharge. The letter also asked if he would be interested in re-enlisting. He wasn't.

On the morning of May 1, 1973, with his duffel bag packed for the last time, Alex picked up his Form DD-214 discharge papers, signed for his plane tickets, was paid up-to-date and given a courtesy ride to the airport. His military obligation completed, he was finally heading home. Alex didn't know the young man who drove him to the airport; he was a local national who worked on the base. The short trip from the barracks to the airport was a time of reflection. Alex had seen more death and destruction in the one year he had spent in Vietnam than all his life in New York City. He had mixed feelings about the war, even though it finally looked like peace was just around the corner. He didn't mind being drafted, but as an only child he had hoped that he would be classified as such, thereby reducing the chance of being called to serve on active duty. It wasn't to be. So when he was drafted, he obligingly went without protesting the unfairness of the system or running off to Canada as many others had chosen to do.

After he checked his bags at the departure counter, Alex looked for the nearest telephone. He was anxious to hear his parents' voices once again and he knew that his mother would immediately begin crying as soon as she heard those magic words "I'm coming home." The telephone rang and rang. When no one answered after the tenth ring, he hung up. He'd try again after the plane landed in Hawaii. There was nothing else to do except walk down to the departure gate and wait for the loudspeaker announcement that the plane was ready to begin boarding.

* * * * * * * * * * * * * * * *

The flight from Okinawa to Hawaii was long and uneventful. After stepping foot onto American soil for the first time since leaving Vietnam, tears began to well up in his eyes. The long journey home was one-third complete. Alex headed for the nearest telephone booth and called home. The telephone rang twice before his mother answered it.

"Hi, Mom, it's me, Alex. I'm in Hawaii; I'm on my way home."

"Alex, oh son, I'm…" that's all she was able to say before starting to cry.

The next voice he heard was that of his father.

"Hi, son!"

"Hi, Dad. I've been discharged from the Army and I'm on my way home."

"That's great news, son. Where are you, now?"

"I'm in Honolulu; the plane landed a few minutes ago. I'll be boarding a plane for San Diego in a few hours."

"When will you arrive back in New York City?"

"My flight from San Diego to Kennedy International is tomorrow. The flight leaves at 7:00 a.m. California time; there's a change of planes in Dallas and then a straight shot to New York City. According to my travel itinerary, the plane should arrive around 4:55 p.m."

"Mom and I will meet you at the airport, Alex. What airline will you be on?"

"Eastern Airlines, Flight 1420."

"Okay, I've written that down. We're looking forward to seeing you, son."

"Me, too, Dad" he answered. "I'm sure Mom is still crying so tell her I said goodbye and that I'll see her soon."

"I will; bye, son."

"Bye, Dad."

CHAPTER EIGHT

June 16, 2000

The switchboard operator at the Army Worldwide Locator Assistance Command transferred John to the Central Records Division supervisor, as he had asked.

"Good morning, Central Records Division, this is Mrs. Rafferty, how may I help you?"

"Good morning, Mrs. Rafferty, my name is John Michaels. A few days ago I spoke with a Master Sergeant Wilkens, at the Army Recruiting Center in Virginia Beach, about contacting the Army Worldwide Locator. Specifically, I'd like to know how I can get a mailing address for a friend of mine who, like me, is a former Army serviceman."

"Hold on a moment, Mr. Michaels, I'll be right with you," Mrs. Rafferty said; she placed him on hold.

The Central Records Division supervisor was sure someone was playing a practical joke. Why would John Michaels, the magician, call here? Surely, he'd have a staffer call on his behalf if he was looking for someone. She quietly stood up inside her cubicle and then slowly strolled around the office looking to see if anyone's phone had a blinking "hold light." Seeing nothing out of the ordinary, she returned to her cubicle. The light was still blinking. She still believed that an office co-worker was putting her on, so Mrs. Rafferty decided to play along hoping to catch the office prankster and then turn the tables on him or her.

"Mr. Michaels," she began, "are you who I think you are?" she asked.

"I know who I am," John cheerfully said, "but my intuition tells me that you're thinking this is a crackpot call. Would that be a fair assumption on my part?"

"I apologize, but to answer your question – yes."

"What if I can offer you some proof, would that help?"

"That would be fine," Mrs. Rafferty replied.

I've got him now, she thought to herself.

"Okay, let me think for a second … all right, I've an idea. Do you have a box of paper clips in your desk drawer?"

"Yes."

"Perfect. Here's what I'd like you to do. Lay out a line of paper clips on your desk; any number between four and ten will suffice. Do it as quietly as you can so I can't hear you, and tell me when you're done."

There was a momentary pause while Mrs. Rafferty opened the box, took out a handful of paper clips and did as she was asked.

"Okay, Mr. Michaels, I'm done," she confidently said.

"Great. Now, I'd like you to lay out another line underneath the first; however, the second line should have one paper clip less than the first line. Let me know when you're done."

Once again, there was a pause.

"I'm done."

"Perfect. Now I'd like you to remove three paper clips from the top line and put them back into the box."

John paused.

"Done; now what?" Mrs. Rafferty asked.

"Silently count the number of paper clips you have left in the top line and let me know when you're ready to continue," John said.

"Okay, I'm ready," Mrs. Rafferty replied.

"Now from the second line, remove the number of paper clips you just counted. Do it as quietly as possible."

"Hold on a moment," Mrs. Rafferty said.

Once again there was a momentary pause.

"Okay, Mr. Michaels, I'm done."

"Excellent. Scoop up all the paper clips in the top line and put them back into the box. Tell me when you're done."

There was a short pause.

"I'm finished," she replied.

"Mrs. Rafferty, I'm going to ask you to stare at the paper clips that remain on your desk and while you do that I'm going to try and see through your eyes."

Right! You're busted buddy, she thought to herself.

After a short pause, John said, "Mrs. Rafferty, there are … two paper clips on the desk."

"Omigod, omigod, omigod, that's right; there are only two left on the desk! You really are John Michaels, the magician," she exclaimed.

"I'm glad I got it right. The paper on the right side of your desk, with the paper clip on the top left corner, threw me off for a second."

The silence was deafening.

"Mrs. Rafferty?" John asked.

"I'm sorry, Mr. Michaels. I'm … umm … how in the world did you know about that other paper with the paper clip? Never mind, I don't want to know. Mr. Michaels, I think it may be better to have you speak directly with the Commanding Officer, Colonel Shaw. I'm going to place you on hold while I transfer your call."

"Thank you, Mrs. Rafferty."

"You're welcome, Mr. Michaels."

* * * * * * * * * * * * * * *

"Good morning, Mr. Michaels, this is Colonel Peter Shaw."

"Good morning, Colonel."

"Mr. Michaels, Mrs. Rafferty tells me that you're trying to locate a former Army serviceman."

"Yes, sir; I am," John answered.

After a short pause, John continued.

"I know your time is valuable Colonel and I appreciate you taking my call, so let me give you the condensed story. In a nutshell, my high school alma mater is having a 30th Anniversary Reunion and I'm trying to find a long-lost classmate friend who, like me, is also a Vietnam veteran. The reunion is less than three weeks away and I'm hoping that I can do something in this short timeframe that no one else has been able to do in over 20 years."

"Mr. Michaels, I'll be happy to try and help you, within the constraints of the law."

"I understand, Colonel. I will graciously accept whatever information you can provide me," John answered.

"Very well; in order to afford you some privacy, I would prefer that we meet on a weekday after normal working hours, or a weekend. I do not want the media congregating around here, if word got out about your visit to this facility. Will this be a problem for you?" Colonel Shaw asked.

"No, sir; it won't," John replied.

"All right, how about this Sunday at noon?"

"Sunday at noon will be fine, sir. Where shall I meet you?"

"Do you know where we are located?"

"Yes, sir; I do."

"I'll meet you in front of the building."

"Thank you, Colonel."

"You're welcome, Mr. Michaels. I look forward to meeting you."

"Likewise," John replied.

* * * * * * * * * * * * * * *

John booked a seat for Saturday's noontime flight on Midland's Eagle Air Express shuttle service from Norfolk's International Airport to Reagan National Airport and then made hotel reservations in the Crystal City section of Arlington. Though there was subway service via the Metro to and from the airport, he planned on renting a car.

CHAPTER NINE

June 17, 2000

It was just past 1:30 p.m. when John pulled into a visitor parking space at the Commodore Virginia Hotel. When he made reservations, he was told that check-in time was 3:00 p.m. He was 90 minutes early.

I wonder if they will allow me to register early and park the car in the hotel's parking lot, John mumbled, as he pulled into an outside visitor parking spot. He shrugged his shoulders muttering, *nothing ventured; nothing gained.*

He got out and headed towards the lobby.

"Good afternoon, sir; welcome to the Commodore Virginia Hotel in Crystal City."

"Good afternoon," John replied. "How are you?"

"I'm well, thank you. My name is Jocelyn, how may I help you?"

"Jocelyn, my name is John Michaels. I called a few days ago and made a room reservation for four days. I know that normal check-in isn't till 3 o'clock, but I was wondering if it would be possible for me to register early and to leave my rental car in the hotel garage so I can get a late lunch."

"Of course, Mr. Michaels, that will not be a problem. Let me pull up your room reservation information."

"Thanks."

A few moments later, Jocelyn said, "Mr. Michaels, I need a major credit card please, and I'll need you to fill out the bottom portion of the registration form and sign your name."

"That's easy enough," John replied as he reached for his wallet.

While Jocelyn finalized the registration in the hotel's computer, John completed the registration form.

"Okay, Mr. Michaels, you're registered; here's your credit card. Your room will be ready after 3 o'clock. There are a few reserved parking spots in the garage and they're plainly marked. All others are first come, first served."

"Thank you very much, Jocelyn."

"My pleasure; enjoy your stay here in Arlington, Mr. Michaels."

John walked back outside, got into the rental car and drove it up the ramp into the hotel garage. He found an open spot on the third floor and pulled in. Since he still had over an hour wait before he could get his room key, John decided to stop in at Bill Eastman's Magic Shop and invite Bill to lunch.

John hadn't seen Bill in well over two years so he knew he'd have an opportunity to catch up on the latest news from the nation's capital. Anyone involved in magic has been to his shop at one time or other and on some days it's not uncommon to find some of the full-time touring professionals in the shop trading magical secrets or asking Bill for advice on a particular trick.

Bill is the best demonstrator in the magic business. He has a knack for taking a new trick and adding the Eastman-touch to it so that it becomes an instant seller in the shop. It's a win-win situation. Bill makes a sale and the magicians get a great trick with some additional handling ideas to work on.

The doorbell chimed when John opened the door and the young man behind the counter looked over in his direction. He didn't recognize John.

"Welcome to Bill Eastman's Magic Shop, how can I help you?" he said.

"Good afternoon," John said in a low voice. "Is Bill in today?"

"Yes, sir," the young man whispered. "Bill is in the back of the shop; he just returned from running an errand."

John put his finger to his lips to indicate that the young man not say anything.

In a loud voice, John shouted, "I'm looking for the proprietor of this business because I'm interested in buying this store."

Within seconds, Bill appeared in the doorway that leads to the backroom.

"What's this about buying … well I'll be … its John Michaels. It's been quite some time since you've been in town," he said as he extended his hand. "How are you?"

"Hi, Bill; I'm well, thanks."

"John, this is my ace demonstrator, Greg Riley," he said, as he turned to the young man who greeted John when he walked in.

Greg and John shook hands.

"Mr. Michaels, it's certainly an honor to meet you."

"The pleasure is all mine," John replied with a smile.

"Greg and I share the duties up front. Well … actually, Greg does 90 percent of the demonstrating for the customers and I take care of everything else. So what brings you to town, John?"

"It's a long story. Listen, I haven't had lunch yet, any chance we could make a run to a decent fast food place and get something? I'll fill you in on my venture over lunch; I'm buying."

"Sure, sure; we can do that. Would you mind if we ate here in the shop?"

"Not at all."

"Okay. Greg, would you like something?" Bill asked.

"No, thanks, Bill."

"We'll be back in about 15 minutes."

"All right."

* * * * * * * * * * * * * * * * *

It was almost 4:30 when John looked at his watch. He and Bill had been talking close to two hours.

"Bill, it's getting late so I guess I'll be going. You've got a shop to get ready for closing and I need to make a few phone calls."

"I think your idea of ending the show by magically producing Alex is great. If there is anything I can do to help, please let me know."

"I will."

"And don't be a stranger, now that you've retired."

"I won't."

As John exited the backroom, Greg looked up from the counter where he was demonstrating a new card trick to some potential customers. Not wanting to interrupt him, John waved goodbye and headed out the door. Greg nodded his head in return and without missing a beat continued his presentation.

* * * * * * * * * * * * * * *

John called Dave shortly after settling into the hotel room.

"Dave, I'm in Arlington."

"Well that explains why you didn't answer the phone earlier this afternoon."

"Sorry about that," John said. "I meant to call you yesterday to give you a heads-up, but forgot all about it in the rush of trying to make plane and hotel reservations."

"Not a problem. So what's happening in Arlington?" he asked.

"I've a meeting with Colonel Peter Shaw, tomorrow at noon. He's the Commanding Officer of the Army Worldwide Assistance Locator Command. I'm hoping the Army has a forwarding address for Alex. If not, I'll be going to New York City tomorrow afternoon."

"Anything I can do at this end?"

"If you could swing by my place and pick up any mail I may have received, I'd appreciate it. Just leave it on the kitchen table for me. The phone answering machine is on, so I'll call in to check for any messages. And the house lights are on an automatic switch so they'll turn on and off."

"Okay, I can do that. You know that a forwarding address doesn't mean much, John."

"Yes, I do. But it's a start. Also, if Alex has moved around since returning from Vietnam, I might be able to track him through the post office, the phone company or the Department of Motor Vehicles."

"That's if he provided them with a change of address, had a phone number or had his driver's license renewed after he returned home."

"You're absolutely correct and with the amount of public transportation available in the city, a driver's license is not really needed unless you wanted to leave the city. Even then, there's bus service from the Port Authority Bus Terminal and train service from the Penn Central Station."

"Exactly."

"I'm also going to call Stella."

"But didn't you say that Drew had already spoken to her?"

"Yes, he did."

"Why do I suspect that you believe Drew didn't ask enough questions?"

"Drew was a close friend, but I suspect that there's something else that Stella isn't comfortable talking about. I think she'll tell me, if I ask."

"Sounds like you've got a handle on this."

"Well, I'm working it as I go. I'll call you tomorrow after my meeting to give you an update."

"Okay."

"Call me at the hotel if something comes up."

"Roger."

* * * * * * * * * * * * * * *

Rather than going down to the hotel's restaurant for Sunday brunch, John opted to order room service. His meeting with Colonel Shaw was scheduled for noon so he wasn't pressed for time. It was 11:30 a.m. when John left the hotel garage, heading south on Jefferson Davis Highway for the 20-minute drive to the business center complex where the Army Worldwide Locator Assistance Command was located. When he reached Duke Street, he turned right and continued straight, heading west.

Approximately four and one-half miles down the road, he took the right-hand exit that lead onto the Eisenhower Avenue overpass, which circled around and crossed over Duke Street. To his left, a quarter of a mile down the road, John saw the business center's two, four-story office buildings. They were on an open parcel of land, devoid of trees, behind Eisenhower Avenue. There was no one behind him so he drove slowly down the street, looking for the access road's entrance. The two welcome signs were strategically placed at 45-degree angles at the intersection of Center Point Drive and Eisenhower Avenue. John turned left into the business center complex and followed the weeping-willow-tree-lined roadway leading towards the two buildings. After rounding a curve in the road, he entered the compound's expansive parking lot.

The two buildings were, by design, built in the center of the property. Both were painted white and all the windows were heavily tinted, which helped keep the building cool during the summer and warm during the winter. The advantage of having the two buildings in the center of the property was that employees would not have to endure an extended walk through a huge parking lot, especially during inclement weather days. Employees and visitors could easily park in front of, behind, or on the sides of the buildings. The front and rear entrance doors of both buildings were unadorned and simply indicated the street address number. From the outside, there was no indication whatsoever that the U.S. Army leased office space. After John parked in one of the four visitor spots in front of the leftmost building, he got out and leaned up against the car so he could look out towards Eisenhower Avenue.

A few minutes before noon, John saw two cars slow down and turn onto Center Point Drive; a minute later they rounded the turn and came into view. As they made their approach, John stepped onto the sidewalk to wait. The two cars parked in the visitor spots to the right of John's car. There was a middle-aged man and woman in one car, and a younger man, probably in his early-30s, in the other one. John watched as the elder man emerged from the driver's side and quickly walked around to the passenger door. He opened it and waited for the woman to exit. As they both walked towards John, the man in the second car got out and followed the couple.

"Mr. Michaels?" the elder gentleman asked.

"Yes, sir," John replied.

"Good afternoon, I'm Colonel Peter Shaw; how are you?" he said, as he extended his hand.

"Good afternoon, Colonel; I'm well, thank you. How are you?"

"Fine thanks. Mr. Michaels, this is my wife, Mildred, and this is Master Sergeant Gibbs, my Administrative Non-Commissioned Officer."

"Good afternoon, ma'am; Master Sergeant Gibbs," John said to each of them as he shook their hands.

"Peter, what time shall I pick up you?" Mildred asked.

"In an hour, Mildred," he replied.

"Mr. Michaels, it was a pleasure meeting you."

"Nice meeting you, too, Mildred," John cheerfully said.

The Master Sergeant and John stood in silence as they watched Colonel Shaw escort his wife back to the car and waited for her to drive off.

"Gentlemen," he said after he returned, "let's go inside and get started."

Master Sergeant Gibbs unlocked the front door, and held it open while the Colonel and John entered the building's foyer. Once everyone was inside, he turned and relocked the door. As they walked towards the elevators, Colonel Shaw told John that the Army's office suites encompassed the entire fourth floor of this building, only. After exiting the elevator they turned left, then left again and headed down the corridor. Each of the office doors that lined the hallway had an acronym neatly stenciled on its frosted glass window. Seeing them brought back memories of John's brief enlisted service. In fact, he was surprised that he remembered what a few of these acronyms meant. The group stopped in front of the last office at the north end of the building. The door, unlike the others, simply had "Commanding Officer, Army Worldwide Locator Assistance" stenciled on it.

Colonel Shaw unlocked the door and they stepped inside the anteroom. Upon entering, an employee or visitor, immediately met the Commanding Officer's secretary, Mrs. Shirley Patterson; according to the nameplate on the desk. Directly across from her desk were two medium-sized upholstered armchairs, separated by a small table with Army magazines neatly arranged on top. The entrance to Colonel Shaw's office was to the left of the chairs; a conference room was to the right. Pictures of the President, Vice President, Secretary of Defense, Secretary of the Army, Commanding General of the Army and Colonel Shaw adorned one wall. In the far right corner of the anteroom, the American flag and the Army flag were posted.

"Would you like some coffee, Mr. Michaels?" Master Sergeant Gibbs asked.

"No, thanks," John replied.

"Colonel?"

"No, Master Sergeant."

"Yes, sir."

"Gentlemen, if you don't mind we'll sit in my office," Colonel Shaw said.

The Colonel's office was amply decorated with Army memorabilia. There were plaques from his various duty assignments, inscribed pictures of airplanes and helicopters and their crewmembers, and the Pentagon, all neatly arranged on the walls. Behind the large oak desk was a secretaire with a laser printer and a fax machine, as well as pictures of his wife Mildred, and their children and grandchildren. Two upholstered chairs, identical to the ones in the anteroom, were on opposite sides of the room and alongside each there was a table with a lamp on it. At the far end of the room, by the window that overlooked Eisenhower Avenue, there was a small, rectangular conference table with a video teleconferencing unit.

"Colonel, before we get started I want to thank you, and Master Sergeant Gibbs, for agreeing to meet me today."

"Mr. Michaels, in any given week the Army Worldwide Locator Assistance Command receives approximately 300 phone calls requesting help. When someone calls for information we explain to him or her, the Army's policy. That is, we cannot do anything via the phone or the Internet; the request has to be in writing and signed. Additionally, we ask them to provide as much information about the service member as possible to help us help them. For example, the person's full name, last known military address, last known civilian address, date of birth, social security number if it's known, etc.," Colonel Shaw explained. "I'm authorized to override the Army's policy on a case-by-case basis, Mr. Michaels. In the last two years, you are only the third person for whom I've made an exemption."

"I certainly appreciate your willingness to help me," John replied. "For my own knowledge, would you explain what happens when a request is received by mail?"

The Colonel turned towards Master Sergeant Gibbs.

"Mr. Michaels," the Master Sergeant began, "when a letter is received in-house we research the person in our database, based on the information contained in the letter. Once we've positively identified the service member, we mail a standardized letter to their last known mailing address if it is different from what the requestor gave us, stating that the enclosed letter was sent to us for forwarding. We also notify the requestor that we've forwarded their letter.

"In our letter to the service member, we advise them that we do this as a courtesy for our veterans and that it's not the Army's policy to provide anyone with a current mailing address. It is then up to the service member, if they so desire, to correspond with that person. If the letter is returned to us as undeliverable, and that happens fairly frequently, then we send a follow-up letter to the requestor stating that the service member they're looking for no longer resides at the last known address we have on file. And we include their original letter in our reply; we don't give them the address we have on file."

"What do you do if both the requestor and the Army have the same mailing address?" John asked.

"We tell the requestor that we have the same address they do and that there is nothing further we can do for them. We also return their letter."

"Thanks for the explanation."

"You're welcome."

"Who is it that you would like us to look up?" Colonel Shaw asked.

"Sergeant Alexander Patrick Holloman."

Master Sergeant Gibbs removed a small green notebook from his shirt pocket, wrote down the name and asked John to verify the spelling.

"Sergeant Holloman received his draft notification, I believe, in late March or early April 1971. His parents' names were Sid and Mary Holloman, and the last known mailing address is 12 East 104th Street, New York, New York."

Once again John verified the information that the Master Sergeant wrote down.

"Do you know his date of birth, by chance?" Master Sergeant Gibbs asked.

"I think it was October 28, 1952; I could be a few days off, either way. I do know the month and year are correct."

"That's enough to start with," the Master Sergeant said. "Hopefully, it won't take long to find him once I've signed onto my computer terminal."

"Master Sergeant," Colonel Shaw began, "we'll wait here in my office."

"Yes, sir."

John and the Colonel were talking about the long-standing Washington Redskins and Dallas Cowboys football rivalry when Master Sergeant Gibbs returned 20 minutes later.

"Pardon the interruption Colonel, but I've managed to locate Sergeant Holloman's file in the database."

He handed a sheet of paper to the Colonel.

"Mr. Michaels," Colonel Shaw said, "the only address on file is his home of record address. I'm sorry we couldn't be of more help."

"That's quite all right, Colonel; I'm extremely grateful for you and Master Sergeant Gibbs' assistance, especially on a Sunday afternoon. It was a long shot, but I wanted to ensure I covered all avenues."

They stood and shook hands.

"Mr. Michaels, I'll escort you downstairs to the front door," Master Sergeant Gibbs stated.

"Thanks; I'm ready whenever you are."

* * * * * * * * * * * * * * * *

After returning to the hotel he stopped at the front desk to ask if he had any messages. There weren't any. Even though it was still early in the afternoon, he wanted to get to New York before nightfall so he could get a fresh start in the morning. He picked up the yellow pages, which was on the open shelf of the night table, looked up the toll-free phone number for Midland Eagle Air Express airlines and made reservations for the next available flight. When he finished, he dialed operator assistance and asked for the phone number for the New York International Resorts Hotel, in mid-town Manhattan. After making reservations, he called Dave.

* * * * * * * * * * * * * * *

"How did your meeting go?" Dave asked.

"A bust," John replied. "The only address on file was his parent's address."

"I take it you're heading to New York City?"

"Yes. I've a 4:30 flight this afternoon. I'll be staying at the New York International Resorts Hotel on 54th Street and Avenue of the Americas. I'll call you after I get to the hotel."

CHAPTER TEN

May 1, 1973

It was early evening when the flight from Hawaii landed at San Diego's Lindbergh Field airport. After exiting the plane, Alex headed directly for the Eastern Airlines counter. It would be a few minutes before the airline handlers began delivering luggage to the baggage claim area so Alex used this time to reconfirm his flight for the following day. The customer service representative reminded him to be at the airport no later than 6:00 a.m. for check-in. As Alex walked towards the baggage claim area, he had a decision to make: either spend the night in the airport sleeping on one of the plastic chairs or get a motel room. He opted for the motel. After picking up his duffel bag, he headed outside. There was a long line of taxis with their trunks and passenger doors wide open; the drivers were standing on the sidewalk waiting for anyone needing a ride. Alex raised his hand, signaling the driver at the head of the line and proceeded in his direction. When he got there, the driver took Alex's duffel bag, placed it in the trunk, and closed the door.

"Where to?" the driver asked.

"The nearest motel that has a lit vacancy sign," Alex replied, after opening the door to the rear passenger seat.

The Airport Motel, nine blocks south of the airport on N. Harbor Drive, seemed promising so the driver pulled into the pedestrian pickup/discharge area.

"Would you mind waiting a minute while I verify that they have a room?" Alex asked the driver.

"Not a problem, go right ahead chief," the driver replied.

A few moments later Alex returned.

"Thanks for waiting, how much do I owe you?"

"Five dollars," the driver replied as he opened the trunk.

Alex took a 10-dollar bill from inside his wallet, gave it to the driver and said, "Keep the change."

"Thanks, chief," the driver replied.

Alex grabbed his bag and went back inside the motel's front office. It took five minutes for the clerk to complete the registration process and show Alex where his room was located, on the motel's table map. Alex paid for the room in advance and then asked the attendant for a 5:00 a.m. wake-up call. After entering the room, Alex locked the door, dropped his duffle bag on the floor, lay down on the bed and went to sleep. He didn't bother to undress.

The early morning wake-up call from the front desk startled Alex. He picked up the phone and groggily thanked the attendant for the call. After showering and dressing, he called the front desk.

"Good morning, this is Mr. Holloman in Room 12. Would you call a taxi; I need a ride to the airport." After a short pause, Alex said "thanks" and then hung up the phone.

Alex made one last check of the room before heading for the motel office. Five minutes later, a taxi pulled up at the main entrance. Alex didn't give the driver a chance to get out and open the trunk. He opened the rear passenger door, tossed his duffle bag in the back seat, climbed in and said, "San Diego Airport, please."

* * * * * * * * * * * * * * *

As the plane taxied to its arrival berth in Dallas, passengers were informed that there were some minor changes for those who had connecting flights. Alex listened intently as the flight attendant announced some new departure gates. He had been gone two years and wasn't going to let a glitch disrupt his return home. Fortunately, none of the changes affected his connecting flight to New York City. Alex had a one-hour layover in Dallas and as he made his way through the maze of other passengers who were inattentively walking through the terminal, he thought about calling home to let his parents know he was in Dallas. He didn't.

Unlike the trip from San Diego, the flight from Dallas was half-full and Alex had a complete row of seats to himself. There was no one sitting across from him and no one sitting in front of or behind him. In a way, he was relieved that he wouldn't have to strike up a conversation with another passenger. It wouldn't be difficult for someone to realize that he was a serviceman and then potentially ask if he served in Vietnam. Talking about the war was not high on his priority list and since he had been away for almost two years, he had limited knowledge of things that had been going on here in the States. Since he would be sitting alone on this flight, he lifted up the armrests and stretched out across the three seats.

May as well be comfortable, he said to himself.

* * * * * * * * * * * * * * * *

It was exactly 4:55 p.m. when the plane touched down at Kennedy International Airport. Alex felt a rush of adrenalin surge through his body after a flight attendant officially welcomed everyone to New York City. Alex gazed out the window as the plane slowly transited through the web of airport runways and taxiways. He saw crew teams diligently loading and unloading luggage carriers, planes being refueled and service trucks that were making their rounds throughout the airport infrastructure. Eight minutes later, the plane made a wide turn and slowly headed towards its assigned terminal gate. After thanking the passengers for choosing Eastern Airlines for their travel needs, the pilot turned off the seat belt sign. Passengers hastily unbuckled their seat belts and quickly jumped out of their seats, anxious to retrieve their carry-on luggage from the overhead storage compartments. Alex had checked his duffel bag so all he could do was stand in the aisle and wait, like everyone else, for the airplane door to open and the exodus to begin. It took a few minutes, but the line began to slowly move as the passengers in the first-class section began to exit the plane.

The access ramp to the terminal building was short, but to Alex it felt like everyone in front of him was walking in slow motion. As soon as he stepped onto the ramp he heard the excitement in the voices of the people who were anxiously waiting in the arrival area. When he reached the ramp's elbow and made that short turn, he saw a crowd of people huddled around the doorway watching the passengers as they slowly entered the waiting area. Behind the crowd, Alex could hear men, women and children clamoring to their loved ones as soon as they saw them. Some passengers stopped dead in their tracks right at the entrance door, while others politely moved out of the way so everyone else could get inside.

As soon as Alex entered the waiting area he quickly scanned the crowd for his parents, but didn't see them. He stepped off to the side so he wouldn't be in the way and then slowly scanned the crowd again. Sid and Mary Holloman were standing alone, a few feet behind the crowd. Mary saw Alex first and she excitedly tugged Sid's arm with one hand, using the other to point to him. Overcome with emotion that her son was finally home, she began to cry. A moment later Alex and Sid's eyes met. Alex waived his hand to acknowledge that he saw him; Sid and Mary waved back.

Try as he might, Alex could not prevent the tears from starting to slide down his own face. As he made his way through the crowd, he could see his Mom trying, albeit unsuccessfully, to control her crying. It was a profound moment for Alex. This was the same way he remembered seeing her two years ago when he first left for basic training, and then on the morning that he returned to Fort Dix prior to leaving for Vietnam. Alex approached his mother first and hugged her. A moment later he reached over to his Dad, shook hands and put an arm around him, too.

"Welcome home, son," Sid whispered.

"I'm glad to be home," Alex replied.

The crowd had already dispersed when they finally let go of each other. With Alex in the middle, the three of them slowly walked arm-in-arm through the airport terminal as they headed for the baggage pickup area.

* * * * * * * * * * * * * * *

Alex sat by himself in the back seat of the car on the ride home from the airport. Neither Sid nor Mary wanted to talk about Vietnam so they kept the conversation upbeat, and centered on the neighborhood and the changes that had occurred during the past two years.

"How is Stella?" Alex finally asked.

"She's fine," his mother replied. "I called your Aunt and Uncle to let them know you were on your way home. Needless to say, they were very happy to hear the news, and hoped that you would come up to see them and Stella, soon."

* * * * * * * * * * * * * * * *

Ed and Carol Noone lived in the Bronx. Ed was Mary's older, and only, sibling.

"I had already planned to do that," Alex said. "I'll call them tomorrow. All I want to do tonight is unpack my bag and remember how much I missed your cooking, Mom."

"That's fine, son. I know they're looking forward to hearing from you," his mother replied.

"Does Stella know that I'm back?"

"I'm sure she was told."

"Is she still living at home?" Alex asked.

"No, she's not," replied Sid.

* * * * * * * * * * * * * * * *

Stella was four months younger than Alex. Though they lived a few miles apart, they visited each other's house on weekends and holidays. During the summer, both families would get together for outings to the amusement parks at Rockaway Beach, Coney Island and Rye Beach, and for swimming trips to Orchard Beach, Tibbets Brook and Bear Mountain.

Shortly after Alex left, Stella had gotten a job as a bank teller with First Merchants Bank and Trust Company. The branch she worked at was located at 86th Street and Lexington Avenue. After a year of traveling by subway to and from work, Stella decided it was time to look for an apartment in Manhattan. Ed and Carol were concerned about Stella living on her own, but they eventually gave her their blessing and said that the door was always open if she ever decided to move back home. Within days, she found a two-bedroom apartment on 93rd Street and Park Avenue, an easy walk to and from work, and after inquiring about the rent she signed a two-year rental lease.

* * * * * * * * * * * * * * * *

After turning onto 104th Street, Sid found a parking spot a few feet away from the three-story brownstone apartment building they lived in. A few neighbors immediately recognized Alex as he exited the car and they quickly walked over to welcome him back home. Sid, Mary and Alex conversed with the neighbors for a few minutes and then excused themselves.

Early the next morning Alex called his Aunt and Uncle.

"Hi, Aunt Carol, it's Alex; how are you?"

"Just fine, thank you; welcome home."

"Thanks. I was wondering if Saturday would be convenient to come up and visit with you, Uncle Ed and Stella."

"Saturday would be perfect, Alex. How about coming up for lunch?"

"That'll be great."

"Would you mind if I called Stella to tell her?" John asked.

"I don't mind at all. Let me give you her work number; it's 250-2500."

"Okay, Aunt Carol; thanks."

"You're welcome, Alex. I'm sure Stella will be delighted to hear from you."

"Likewise; I'll see you on Saturday."

"We're looking forward to it. Goodbye, Alex."

"Goodbye, Aunt Carol."

* * * * * * * * * * * * * * *

Alex had just finished talking with Stella, when his mother returned from the store. He told her about the conversation with Aunt Carol and the lunch get-together on Saturday.

"What are you planning to do today, Alex?" his mother then asked.

"I thought I'd walk around mid-town Manhattan and then head over to Central Park."

"Will you be back for lunch?"

"Probably not," Alex replied. "If I'm hungry I'll get something."

"But you'll be back for dinner tonight, right?"

"Yes, indeed."

"Okay son, be careful and have a good time."

"I will, Mom," he replied.

CHAPTER ELEVEN

May 5, 1973

It was 11 a.m. when Alex, Sid and Mary left their apartment.

"Sid, are we driving or taking the train?" Mary asked.

"I thought we'd take the subway; it's only one block from here. And Ed and Carol's apartment is three blocks from the subway station. I don't mind walking. Besides, there is no guarantee that we'll find a parking space on Walton Avenue."

"That's fine with me," Mary replied.

They walked in silence to the 103rd Street subway station.

* * * * * * * * * * * * * * *

The New York City subway system, first established in October 1904, is comprised of 656 miles of mainline track, for passengers. If you include the transit department work areas, that number increases to 842 miles. One of the great attributes of the subway is that it can take you to within blocks of your destination anywhere in the city.

Ninety-seven percent of the subway stations are two-story complexes and though they may vary in size, the layout, for the most part, is identical. One level consists of a manned token booth, three turnstiles and two rapid exit gates; the second level is the platform waiting area and railroad tracks. The booth is centrally located on the first level so that the Transit Authority employee, who sits behind its shatterproof glass windows, can keep an eye on the people coming and going. It's not uncommon for kids and on some occasions, an adult, to try and beat the system by hopping over the turnstile or dashing through the exit gate after a train has come to a complete stop.

The booths' don't have an outside counter where one can rest their hands while they exchange cash for a token. There is a small, dish-shaped recess under the front glass window with just enough room to place two fingers into it to facilitate exchanging paper money or coins for subway tokens. The smallness of the recess is, first and foremost, a safety issue. Veteran subway riders also know that holding their wallet or purse in their hands, while standing in front of the window, is an open invitation for a stranger to quickly come up behind them, grab it and race up the stairs two at a time and then disappear into the crowd on the street. To overcome this inconvenience, riders typically purchase a week's worth of tokens or keep their fare money in their pants or jacket pocket.

* * * * * * * * * * * * * * *

"We're in luck," Sid said, as they stepped onto the station platform. "There are a lot of people waiting so we may not have to wait too much longer for the next train."

During the weekday morning and afternoon rush hours, trains run approximately every 4 minutes. During non-rush hours, and on weekends and holidays, the trains operate on a 20-minute cycle. There are four parallel tracks that pass through the 103rd Street station. The express trains, which travel non-stop between 125th Street and 86th Street, run on the two inside tracks. The two outer tracks are for the local trains that stop at all stations on their uptown or downtown routes

They had just sat down on one of the station's wooden benches when the roar of the Number 5 train could be heard in the distance. Suddenly, there was a giant swoop of wind as the speeding five-car train exited the tunnel and hurtled into the wide-open space of the underground station. After screeching to a halt, the train doors opened simultaneously and a handful of passengers stepped out, and headed for the exit stairs. After the waiting passengers embarked, the conductor, who was in the third car, looked to his right and then pressed the control panel button that closed the doors of the last three cars. He then looked to his left and seeing no one else on the platform he pressed a second button to close the open doors of the first two cars. He then rang the "all clear" signal, alerting the engineer that it was safe for the train to leave the station. Seconds later, the train made a slight forward-jerking motion as it began its slow movement out of the station. In a matter of minutes, its speed would increase to 25 miles per hour as it traveled through the dark tunnel to the next station.

When they arrived at 125th Street, Sid, Mary and Alex exited the train and walked across the station's island platform to wait for the Number 4 train that would take them to the West Bronx. Fifteen minutes would pass before it rumbled into 125th Street. Unbeknownst to the Holloman's and the other passengers, on this particular Saturday morning, when the Number 4 train arrived at 125th Street it was still eight minutes ahead of its Saturday timetable. To adjust its schedule, the engineer and conductor had decided to remain in the station a few extra minutes. Four minutes later, the conductor closed the doors and the train started moving again. The remaining four minutes would be made up at the next stop, 149th Street, a strategic passenger transfer node during the weekday morning and afternoon rush hours.

* * * * * * * * * * * * * * *

There are over two dozen crossroads in the New York City subway system, but the two most transited ones are 42nd Street (which includes Grand Central Station on the east side and Times Square on the west side) and 59th Street. From these stations, a subway rider can crisscross through Manhattan and catch numerous other trains heading for Queens, Brooklyn and the Bronx.

* * * * * * * * * * * * * * *

After leaving 149th Street, the Number 4 train crossed under the East River and then transformed itself from an underground to an above-ground subway atop steel and cast-iron elevated structures that adhered to specific rights-of-way. For the first six blocks, the railway traveled north-west down River Avenue. It then made a slight turn and headed north on Jerome Avenue where it would continue its seven-mile route until it reached the end of its journey: the Woodlawn Avenue station. As soon as this underground to above-ground metamorphosis occurred, Yankee Stadium could be seen to the immediate left. When the train stopped at 176th Street, the Hollomans' and some other passengers got off and descended down the stairs that led to the street, below. For a Saturday in late spring, the weather was picture perfect. The variety stores on both sides of Jerome Avenue were bursting with people who were ardently shopping for bargains. As they approached the neighborhood bakery on 177th Street, Mary mentioned to Sid that she wanted to stop there.

"We can't show up empty-handed," Mary said.

"Okay, dear, we'll get some rolls and a coffee cake," Sid replied.

"I'm sure Carol already bought rolls; let's get a coffee cake and a half-pound of mixed cookies."

"Okay; coffee cake and cookies, it is."

After leaving the bakery, they continued their leisurely stroll along Jerome Avenue. Alex was walking in between his parents and half-heartedly listening as they conversed. It was not that he wasn't interested in their discussion, but his experiences in Vietnam taught him to not only listen with his ears, but also with his eyes. Sid and Mary, on the other hand, were keenly engrossed in conversation and paid little attention to any ongoing activities around them. Alex was not surprised when only he heard the distant sound of squealing tires on the black-tarred street. He cautiously looked around, but saw nothing out of the ordinary. Because the sound was short-lived, Alex couldn't determine from which direction it had originally come from. He assumed it was some smart-ass who decided to be a show-off and burn rubber after the traffic light turned green. Still, he was alerted to the possibility of a potential jackass behind the wheel of a car.

They were about three feet into the street at the intersection of Mt. Hope Place and Jerome Avenue, when Alex saw the southbound speeding car make a sudden left turn and head straight for them.

"Watch out!" he hollered, as he firmly grabbed the arms of both his parents and quickly pulled them backwards towards the sidewalk.

Alex's sudden outburst startled Sid and Mary, and they suddenly found themselves trying to maintain their balance as Alex forced them to blindly and hastily retrace their steps in reverse. Unfortunately, the heels of their shoes hit the curb causing all three of them to fall backwards onto the sidewalk. As they fell, the cake and cookies went flying over their heads. A combination of speed and inexperience caused the driver to over-compensate the turn and crash directly into the left rear side panel of a parked car on the corner. A moment later, the driver hurriedly shifted into reverse, turned the front wheels in the opposite direction and then jammed his foot down on the gas pedal in a desperate attempt to get away as quickly as possible. In his haste, he sideswiped two other parked cars on Mt. Hope Place as he erratically drove up the street.

Alex was the first to get back on his feet and he instinctively ran into the street. There was no sign of the car so he dashed back to help his parents. Sid had already gotten up and with Alex's help they took hold of Mary's arms, and helped her stand up. A moment later, both Sid and Mary began shaking uncontrollably; they were white as ghosts.

"Mom, Dad; are you okay?" Alex calmly inquired.

"I think we're both going to be very sore in an hour," Sid replied, as he began to brush his clothing with his hands.

"Wait here while I get the cake and cookies," Alex said.

"Sid," Mary began, "did you hear the car at all?"

"Honestly, no," he replied, as he watched Mary brush off her skirt. "I was listening to you and while I realized that we had stepped off the curb and into the street I didn't give it a second thought to stop and look first. I'm sorry, Mary; we could have been seriously hurt."

"Or killed," Alex said as he ambled up alongside them. "Dad, you've got to promise me you'll not do this again."

"Believe me son, it wasn't intentional. I'm very careful when crossing the street; even moreso when I'm with your Mom," he responded.

"Well," Alex said, "except for the box being slightly crumpled, from what I can see the cake doesn't look too bad. And who cares if the cookies are broke, it'll make eating them easier."

"Do you think we should call the police?" Sid asked.

"Yeah, we should," replied Alex, "a few cars have been hit and we're a witness to this fender-bender. Wait here on the corner while I go across the street to that Spanish restaurant to see if I can use their phone."

Alex had just stepped off the curb for the third time when he saw the police car, with its flashing red light, turn and park sideways on Mt. Hope Place to barricade the street's entrance.

"Someone's already called," Alex said aloud after he turned around to walk back towards his parents. "The police car must have been close by to get here this quickly," he also added.

As the police officer exited his car, a middle-aged gentleman came out from the restaurant and approached the police officer to speak with him. Alex couldn't hear the conversation, but he was sure they were talking about the accident because the man had pointed in Alex's direction and then towards the car on the corner. After conversing for a few minutes, the gentleman went back inside and the police officer walked across the street.

"Good afternoon, folks," the officer said.

"Good afternoon," Sid answered.

"Can you tell me what happened?" he asked.

"My son can tell you better than I can," Sid responded. "My wife and I were engrossed in conversation and the next thing I knew we were on our rump, on the sidewalk."

Alex turned towards the police officer and related what had transpired.

"Well, sir, your story is consistent with what the gentleman from the restaurant told me. As luck would have it, he just happened to be looking out the window and saw the entire incident. I'll need the three of you to write a statement, though," the officer said.

"Sure thing," Alex replied.

"I have paper, pens and clipboards in my cruiser," the officer said. "I'll be right back."

As Sid, Mary and Alex wrote out their statements, the officer examined the damage to the parked car on the corner and wrote some notes in his record book. He then walked up the street to look at the two sideswiped cars and did the same. When he returned, Alex gave the officer the three reports. After a cursory review, the officer asked if they felt the need to go to the hospital for a check-up.

"Other than being a little sore, we've no broken bones so I think we'll be fine," Alex said.

"Okay," the officer replied. "I won't be filing this report until after my shift ends later this afternoon. However, if someone from the investigations department has any questions, they'll contact you directly. Unless you have any questions for me, that's all I need."

"All right. Mom, Dad, you ready?" Alex asked.

"Yes, son; we are," Sid answered.

Since Mt. Hope Place was still blocked off by the police car there was no need to look towards Jerome Avenue for any turning cars. They did, anyway. The police officer walked with them, but only as far as the Spanish restaurant. When he reached its door, he opened it and went inside. When Sid, Mary and Alex reached the corner of Jerome and Tremont Avenues, they turned to their right, walked up one block to Walton Avenue and then turned right again.

Nineteen thirty-one Walton Avenue is a six-story high-rise building with 60 apartments. Its two separate wings were connected by an open courtyard. Ed and Carol lived in apartment 3B on the third floor of the left wing of the building. Normally, Sid, Mary and Alex would have walked up the stairs; today they took the elevator instead. Carol was anxiously pacing around the apartment waiting for the doorbell to ring. She had decided to dress casually, wearing a dark brown skirt, a cream-colored blouse and penny loafers. At age 54, her strawberry blond hair, which she had pulled back in a ponytail, was just starting to show tiny streaks of gray.

"Relax, honey, they'll be here soon," Ed said, when Carol walked back into the kitchen for the umpteenth time.

Ed was sitting at the kitchen table, a glass of water in his hand. He had decided that a golf shirt, chinos and loafers would satisfy his interpretation of casual wear. Unlike Carol, Ed's hair had begun to turn gray at age 50 and now, at age 54, it was completely gray.

"I know, dear," she replied. "But they should have been here by now."

Alex knocked on the door first and then pressed the door-bell button.

"That's them!" she exclaimed.

"I know, I heard the knock and the doorbell, too," replied Ed.

His words fell on deaf ears; Carol was already walking down the hallway towards the door.

"As usual, I'm talking to myself," he muttered.

"I heard you!" Carol hollered back.

Ed placed his now empty glass in the kitchen sink before strolling down the hallway towards the front door. He was extremely proud of his nephew and happy that he was finally home. The tears had welled up in Carol's eyes right after the doorbell rang and as she scooted down the hallway they began flowing down her rosy cheeks. After she unlocked and opened the door, Carol gave Sid and Mary a quick hug before turning to Alex.

"I'm so glad you're home safe," she managed to say, while trying to control her crying. "We prayed for your safety every day and our prayers were truly answered."

"I'm grateful to be home, too, Aunt Carol," he replied.

While still hugging his aunt, Alex saw his uncle standing in the doorway with a great big smile. Ed stepped out the door, gave his sister a kiss on the cheek and shook hands with Sid. Alex relaxed his hug and extended his right hand out to shake hands with his uncle.

"Welcome home, Alex."

"Thanks, Uncle Ed."

"C'mon everyone, let's go inside," Ed said.

Ed waited till everyone had entered the apartment hallway before locking the door. Carol led everyone to the kitchen and had them sit down at the table. Sid apologized for the condition of the bakery products and then recounted the incident on 177th Street.

"Is everyone all right?" Ed asked.

"Other than still being a little shaken by the event and a sore rump, we're fine," Sid said.

"Would you like some aspirin?" Carol asked.

"Please," Sid replied. "Mary needs some too," he added.

"How about you, Alex?"

"No, Aunt Carol, I'm fine; thanks. Where's Stella?" Alex then asked.

"She hasn't arrived yet; we expect her momentarily," Ed replied.

"Is she driving?" Mary asked.

"Yes," replied Carol.

They were idly talking when suddenly there was a knock on the door and the sound of a key being inserted into the lock.

"That must be Stella," Carol said. "I told her she didn't have to knock on the door, but she does anyway."

"Hi, everyone!" Stella hollered after opening the door.

"Stella, we're in the kitchen," Carol answered in a normal tone.

"Okay," Stella replied

She quickly walked down the hallway and after greeting her parents, and her Aunt and Uncle, she gave Alex a big hug.

"I sure missed you," she said and then backed up a step to take a good look at him.

"There wasn't a day that went by that I didn't think about you, too," Alex replied.

Stella noticed that Alex had lost some weight and that he looked tired, but he seemed cheerful. She was hesitant to ask about his time in Vietnam, so she decided to ask Alex a different question.

"Did you see John?" she asked.

"We crossed paths on occasion and had an opportunity to catch up on things, you know letters from home, etc." he replied. "Unfortunately, it was for only 10, maybe 15 minutes in duration. In fact, the last time I spoke with him he told me that he was three weeks shy of completing his yearlong tour in Vietnam and that he expected to be transferred soon. I told him I still had a few more months to go."

"Did John know where he would be going?" Ed asked

"No. The Army sends its soldiers to wherever they're needed at the time so I don't know where he went. I, on the other hand, wound up in Okinawa and I know he wasn't stationed there."

"I take it you haven't called his house yet?" Stella asked.

"No, I haven't," replied Alex. "I planned on calling him tomorrow," Alex said.

"John now lives in Virginia Beach."

"No kidding?"

"He was transferred to Fort Story to finish his two-year enlistment."

"What a lucky guy! What else did he say?"

"That he planned on going out on the road as a full-time professional magician."

"I figured as much."

"I'll give you his phone number later," Stella said. "Hopefully, he'll be home when you call."

"Okay."

"If everyone's hungry, let's have lunch," Carol interjected.

"We're eating in the living room," Ed said. "I've got the big table already opened up."

"Can I help set the table?" Mary asked.

"Thanks, dear, but it's already done," replied Carol. "But I could use some help in putting the food out."

"Of course," Mary answered.

"I'll help, too, Mom," Stella said.

"Guys," Carol began, "I think Mary, Stella and I can handle things."

Ed, Sid and Alex went into the living room to wait.

"I'll get the meat and cheese tray from the refrigerator," Carol said. "Mary, if you would take the condiment dish that would be great. Stella, please open the bag with the rolls and put them on a tray."

As the ladies arranged everything on the table, Carol asked Ed to get the pitcher of ice tea from the refrigerator and to fill everyone's glass. When everything was done, they sat down at the table, held hands and prayed.

* * * * * * * * * * * * * * *

"So, Alex," Ed asked, as he began to slice open a roll, "what plans do you have now that you're home for good?"

"None, right now, Uncle Ed. I plan on relaxing over the summer before I begin to actively look for work. I'm also going to call the Veteran's Administration to inquire about any benefits I may have coming to me."

"When you're ready to enter the workforce, make sure you check in with the New York State Employment Commission. I think you may be eligible for unemployment benefits while you're job hunting."

"That's good to know. I was able to save a lot of money over the past two years, but it won't last forever."

"Unemployment benefits aren't much, but it's something. And, the employment office has counselors who will help you find a job."

After a few moments of silence, the conversation changed to Stella's apartment.

"How long have you been living on your own, Stella?" Alex asked.

"About a year, now," she replied. "I found a place close to where I work; I'll give you my telephone number and address before I leave. I'm usually home by 5:30 p.m. so you can come by whenever you like."

* * * * * * * * * * * * * * *

It was nearly 4:00 p.m. when Sid, Mary and Alex decided to head back home.

"I'm going to go, too, Mom," Stella said. "Uncle Sid, I didn't see your car downstairs, so I take it you all came by train."

"We did."

"I can drive you, Aunt Mary and Alex home," she replied, "beats taking the subway."

"That would be very nice, thank you."

"It's the least I can do; besides you're not that far from my place."

Ed and Carol accompanied Stella, Alex, Sid and Mary, outside. They hugged and shook hands as they said their good-byes before getting into Stella's car. As Stella slowly pulled out of the parking spot, Ed and Carol raised their hands and waved goodbye. A few moments later the tail lights disappeared as the car turned left at the corner of Walton Avenue and Mt. Hope Place.

"Ed, did Alex look all right to you?" Carol asked.

"He looked a little haggard, but other than that I think he looked fine. Why do you ask?"

"I don't know. I mean, he seemed happy to be home and was quite talkative. Maybe it's just my motherly instinct."

"Did Mary say anything to you, about Alex?" Ed asked.

"Nothing other than that she was happy he was finally home."

"Alex just needs time to get acclimated to being a civilian, once again."

"I may ask Stella later next week; perhaps he'll say something to her."

"Carol, I think you're overreacting, but if it makes you feel better by asking Stella, then do so. Just don't be surprised if she tells you the same thing."

They walked back to the apartment building, in silence.

* * * * * * * * * * * * * * *

Shortly after they got home, Alex made a list of things he needed to do. Under the kitchen phone hung a cork memo board that had a pad of paper and a pen. He tore off a piece of paper, took the pen and sat at the kitchen table. On the paper, he wrote Monday, May 7th and drew a line under the date. He then started writing down the places that he needed to go to. First on the list was the Department of Motor Vehicles, followed by the New York State Employment Commission, the Post Office, Voter Registration Office and bank (Stella). Last on the list was a reminder to call the Veteran's Administration office. As he sat and stared at the list, pen in his hand, his mother walked into the kitchen.

"A penny for your thoughts, son" she said.

"I'm thinking about Monday and the things I have to do."

"What have you got so far?" she asked.

Alex read what he had written.

"It sounds like you have a full day planned out, son."

"I do; and I don't know if I'll get it all done. But, there's always Tuesday and Wednesday if need be," Alex replied.

Alex placed the pen back in its holder on the memo board and then folded the paper in half and placed it in his pants pocket.

"I'm going to the corner grocery store for some soda; do you want anything while I'm out?"

"No, thanks, son. Is there anything special you'd like me to cook for dinner tonight?"

"Everything you cook is special, Mom," he replied. "Whatever you feel like making will be fine."

* * * * * * * * * * * * * * *

Alex's bedroom was close to the apartment door. He had just slipped on his pants when he heard the apartment door close and the lock engaged. It was just past 6:30 a.m.; his Dad, an accountant at Empire Accounting Systems and Services, was on his way to work. Alex chose a gray button-down shirt to wear with his dark blue pants. The only dress shoes he had were the ones he was issued in Army boot camp. *I've got to buy another pair of shoes* he mumbled as he placed his wallet, keys, handkerchief and money into each of his pants' pockets.

"You're up early, Mom," Alex said, as he walked into the kitchen. Mary was drinking a cup of coffee.

"I knew you had a full day ahead so I thought I'd get up and fix breakfast for the two men of the house," she replied.

"You didn't have to do that."

"I wanted to," she said, as she got a dish and filled it with eggs, bacon and hash browns. "Do you want some coffee?"

"Yes, but I'll get it," Alex answered.

Mary sat quietly, watching Alex as he ate breakfast. Suddenly, her eyes started to fill with emotion. For a moment, time had suddenly gone in reverse and Mary found herself reliving in her mind that day, two years ago, when Alex first left for the Army. Not wishing to start crying for no apparent reason, she got up from the table and turned away from Alex.

As she placed her coffee cup in the sink she said, "Alex, remember to lock the door on your way out."

"I will, Mom. Go back to sleep, I'll take care of the dishes. I should be back home in time for dinner, see you then."

"Okay, Alex," she replied and without wishing to make a fuss she walked out of the kitchen and headed back to her bedroom, quietly crying.

CHAPTER TWELVE

June 18, 2000

New York City is composed of five boroughs: Bronx, Brooklyn, Queens, Manhattan and Staten Island. John's flight from Washington DC would be landing at LaGuardia Airport, in Queens. As the plane slowly descended, John had decided to take a taxi to Manhattan. He knew the subway would be much cheaper, but he wanted to get to the hotel as quickly as possible. After the plane docked at the arrival terminal and the seatbelt sign was turned off, John opened the overhead storage compartment door and retrieved the two pieces of carry-on luggage he had brought with him. The arrival area was crowded with family members waiting for their loved ones to step through the boarding ramp's doorway. As he slowly maneuvered through the peaceful crowd of mothers, fathers, husbands, wives and children, he fondly remembered the emotions he felt after entering the arrival area and seeing his parents, and Stella for the first time after his one year tour of duty in Vietnam had ended. Little had changed over the years.

John followed the overhead signs directing passengers to the baggage retrieval/main terminal lobby. After entering the main terminal building, he turned to the right. There was a steady stream of people entering and exiting through the six revolving doors, some 30-odd feet directly in front of him, that comprised the main entrance. As soon as John stepped outside, he saw a line of about 10 taxicabs to his left, parked in an area of the airport that's known as "the taxi loop." Since he couldn't see beyond the curve in the road, based on those already in the queue, he guesstimated that there were at least two-dozen more in the loop, patiently waiting for the line to move. On average, over 2 million people fly into or out of LaGuardia Airport each month. Anyone who wished to take a taxi to their final destination within the confines of New York City need not worry; there'll always be a line of waiting taxis.

Five Hindu men were congregated around the first taxi and although John couldn't hear them talking, from the look of things, the conversation was extremely animated. Right after he stepped outside the door they all headed back towards their cars in preparation for the coming exodus. John hailed the first taxi and waited. The driver pulled into the terminal entranceway, placed the taxi in "park" and then pressed a dashboard button to the right of the steering column that remotely popped-open the trunk. As the driver slid out from behind the steering wheel, John placed his two bags inside the empty trunk. The driver smiled and nodded his head, and then closed the trunk door.

"Good afternoon, sir," the middle-aged man cordially said, "Where are you headed?"

"Good afternoon," John replied. "I'm going to the New York International Resorts Hotel at 54th and Avenue of the Americas," John answered.

"Okay," he replied. "Traffic is not too heavy this time of day, so it should only take about 40 minutes to get there."

"That's fine," John said, as he opened the rear passenger door that was closest to the sidewalk.

After they were both inside, the driver shifted gears and slowly edged the taxi away from the terminal. If the driver looked out the rear or side view mirrors before driving away, John certainly didn't notice. It was the only subtle reminder he needed to fasten his seat belt. The service road within the airport border is LaGuardia Road. It runs parallel to Grand Central Parkway, a major thoroughfare in Queens, and at strategic intervals there are entrance and exit ramps for inbound and outbound vehicle traffic. The cab driver took the exit ramp that headed west towards the Triboro Bridge, one of three bridges, the others being the Throggs Neck Bridge and the Whitestone Bridge, which cross over the East River and connect Queens to the South Bronx. They had been on the highway for about five minutes before the driver looked in the rear view mirror and spoke to John.

"Is this your first time coming to New York City?" he asked.

"No, I'm a native New Yorker; born and raised in the Bronx." John replied.

"You don't have a New York accent."

"That's interesting you say that; many people have asked if I'm from the New England area. When I tell them I'm from New York City, they're quite surprised. They know I have an accent; they can hear it. But they're hesitant to narrow it down to one place in particular so they generalize it by guessing New England."

"Since you asked to be taken to a hotel in Manhattan, I presumed you were a tourist. That's why I asked if this was your first visit, here," the cab driver said.

"What we say and how we say it can be deceiving," John replied.

"It certainly can, especially if you were not born and raised here."

The cab driver switched on his turn signal and began to slow down as he approached an exit ramp. The overhead road sign indicated that this exit was for the Brooklyn/Queens Expressway.

Sensing the quizzical look on John's face, the driver said, "Why drive to the Bronx to get to mid-town Manhattan; the Queensboro Bridge is the best way to get there from the airport."

"I guess I've been away too long; I forgot all about that bridge. But, on the other hand, whenever I went to Queens it was primarily by subway from the Bronx."

"So, when did you leave the city?"

"1971; I was drafted into the Army," John answered.

"You were in Vietnam?"

Yes," John replied.

The driver nodded his head up and down, and then, about a minute later, began speaking again.

"Where do you live now?"

"Virginia," John said.

"Why didn't you come back to New York?"

"After I left Vietnam I was sent to Virginia."

John paused a moment.

"I live in Virginia Beach, about two and a half miles from the ocean," John said.

"Other than being close to the ocean, what else can you tell me about Virginia Beach?" the driver asked.

"The oceanfront area was originally a part of Princess Anne County, when it was first established in 1691. After rail service and electricity were first introduced there in 1888, it quickly became an extremely popular resort area to visit. However, up until 1922, you could only get there by railroad or the electric trolley. That year, a concrete roadway called Virginia Beach Boulevard was extended into the Town of Virginia Beach and Princess Anne County, from the eastern outskirts of the City of Norfolk. This new roadway extension reached all the way to the oceanfront and opened up the resort area to cars, trucks and busses. One of the more interesting facts about Virginia Beach is that it's listed in the *Guinness Book of World Records* as having the longest pleasure beach in the world and the longest bridge-tunnel complex in the world."

"How long are they?"

"The boardwalk is only three miles in length, but there's 28 miles of public beach property. The Chesapeake Bay Bridge-Tunnel complex is twenty-three miles long," John replied.

"None of the bridges within the city limits are more than 3800 feet in length."

The driver paused a moment and then added, "I've never seen a bridge that big, before."

"If you drive to Virginia Beach via Route 13, you'll have to drive across this bridge-tunnel complex. It's the only direct connection between Virginia's eastern shore and southeastern Virginia Beach."

"Do you get a lot of tourists during the summer?" the driver asked.

"We certainly do; Virginia Beach is a family-friendly resort area and has become a very popular tourist destination. During the summer months the oceanfront has all types of entertainment, many of them free of charge, including concerts. While the majority of the tourists come primarily in the summer months, January and February is also a good time to visit.

"Why visit the ocean in the winter, you can't go swimming," the driver stated.

"That's true," John answered. "But, the tourists come because humpback whales gather off the Virginia Beach shore each winter and the Virginia Marine Science Museum sponsors tours for those who want to see them up close."

"There are people who actually go out in boats to see these whales?" the driver asked.

"Yes, indeed."

"You ever go out?"

"No."

"Any particular reason?"

"Yes; whales are better swimmers."

The driver laughed.

"Virginia Beach was a nice place in the early 1970s, and still is, for that matter. That's why I decided to stay there."

"What brings you back to New York City?" he asked.

"I'm here to visit with a friend for a few days."

"When were you here last?"

"In 1973," John said.

"I came to the United States in 1980," the driver replied.

"The city has changed a lot over the years, hasn't it?" John said.

"It certainly has," the driver replied. "Not all of it has been for the good of the city."

As they drove down the expressway through South Queens, John scanned the city streets. There was very little outside activity.

* * * * * * * * * * * * * * * *

In the Bronx, dilapidated apartment buildings and run-down stores on its last legs were an everyday site. Eventually they'd be torn down, but the resultant empty lots would then become a dumping ground for trash and other items such as broken furniture, and used kitchen appliances. It was a no-win situation for the city, unless they had a construction company ready to step in within hours to begin the transformation from an empty lot to a permanent complex. There was no ongoing construction within eyesight in this part of Queens and no abandoned buildings or empty lots. There were, however, plenty of potholes on the expressway that needed filling. After 10 minutes on the Brooklyn/Queens Expressway, John was beginning to feel like a martini that was shaken, not stirred.

The cab driver slowed down as he exited the expressway at the Northern Boulevard West exit. They continued straight for about three miles until they reached the traffic circle where Northern Boulevard veered to the left to begin its southerly route. Halfway around the circle, the cab driver turned right and headed west on Queens Boulevard. It was at this intersection that John caught a glimpse of a subway train that had just departed the Queens Boulevard Station. Seeing a train was not an unusual occurrence for John; he and his friends rode the subway trains for hours and hours on many a Saturday while growing up, and he rode the subway to Catholic High, for four years. What made this particular train stand out was that there was no graffiti on any of the trains' cars.

"New subway trains?" John inquired, with a look of astonishment on his face.

"Yea," the driver replied; a smile inched across his face.

"How long have they been around?"

"The city started the transition a little over two years ago. I heard the train cars have a special outer coating that spray paint won't adhere to."

"All New York City subway trains are supposed to have graffiti on them," John said. "It's a part of the city's culture; it's what makes New York City so unique."

"Graffiti-covered trains were the only ones I've ever seen, so it's unusual to see clean ones."

"It appears that an opportune time had come to make a change and the city hierarchy jumped at the opportunity," John replied.

"New Yorkers may not like the new trains, but we'll endure the change," the cab driver answered.

Queens Boulevard dead-ends at Queens Bridge Park and the East River. As the cab driver approached the end of the road, he turned slightly to the left, following the overhead sign that directed vehicles heading towards Manhattan onto the Queensboro Bridge, which is also known by its more popular name: the 59th Street Bridge. The bridge's exit ramp ended halfway between First and Second Avenues, in Manhattan. From here, John knew that the drive to the hotel would be no more than five minutes, even with a red light or two thrown in for good measure.

As soon as the cab driver stopped in front of the hotel he turned off the meter to stop it from continuing to run up the fare, which had just hit the $52.00 mark. John removed his wallet from his pants pocket, took out three $20s and handed the money to the driver. A moment later, one of the hotel's doormen opened the passenger side door and then walked to the rear of the taxi to get the luggage from the trunk.

"Keep the change," John said.

"Thanks, mate," the cab driver replied.

"You're welcome."

The hotel doorman had already placed the bags on the sidewalk and had closed the trunk door by the time John got out of the taxi.

"Good evening, sir," the doorman said. "Have you been here, before?" he inquired.

"Not to this hotel," John answered. "But, I have been to New York City before – if that counts."

The doorman said nothing, but John did see the guy smile ever so quickly. For all John knew, the doorman was probably thinking that John shouldn't quit his day job. That would be all right if John had a day job. But he didn't. As they walked up to the hotel, the doorman gave John a quick run-down on the hotel's facilities, check out times and hours of operation for meals. When they reached the check-in counter, the doorman placed John's bags on a portable luggage truck and quickly turned on his heels to head back outside. John was ready to tip him by saying that the winter season in Puerto Rico is great, but the doorman didn't hang around long enough. Perhaps it was just as well.

I don't want the doorman to think that I'm a nut case, John thought to himself.

John politely declined bellhop services. When he asked where the elevators were located, the attendant turned to his left and pointed down the hall.

"You can't miss them," he said. "We hope you enjoy your stay with us," he then added.

"Thanks," John replied.

John's room was on the fourth floor. Once inside, he placed his bags on the bed and then picked up the room service menu that had been placed on the nightstand. The hotel had a wide selection and after glancing through it, he called in an order for the baked chicken special. While he waited for room service, John unpacked the few things he had brought with him. He didn't know how long he was going to stay, but he hoped it would not be more than a couple of days. He still had to return to Arlington to check out of the hotel, there. Additionally, even though Dave would make the necessary arrangements to pack up the show, John had to get back to Virginia Beach before that happened. He needed a few days time to rehearse the show he was planning as well as the new illusion, in case he found Alex.

John sat at the desk and jotted down some things that he knew about Alex. He needed a starting point from which to organize his thoughts so he could formulate a plan of action. This was the best approach he could come up with, albeit it was the only strategy he had at the moment.

Twenty minutes had passed.

"Room Service!" the attendant loudly announced after he knocked on the door.

John got up, walked over to the door and opened it.

"Good evening, Mr. Michaels, where shall I place this cart?"

"Good evening," John replied. "You can leave it by the desk."

"Very well, sir," the young man said. "I'll return in about an hour to pick it up, if that's all right with you."

"That will be fine," John said.

John didn't think the room service attendant would be interested in his tip about vacationing in Puerto Rico in the winter, so he gave the young man a five-dollar bill as he headed for the door.

"Thank you, Mr. Michaels."

"You're welcome."

John continued to jot down notes as he ate dinner. He had Alex's date of birth and his last known address. He also knew that Alex had a New York driver's license; he and Alex both took and passed Driver's Education during their junior year at Catholic High. He had the names of Alex's parents and Stella's parents. John also remembered Alex's old phone number and he had Stella's work phone number, too. With few exceptions, most people couldn't exist in society without creating some sort of paper trail. Obviously the more information one has the better off they'll be. And while there is no absolute foolproof way to find someone, they can be found – eventually. John realized that trying to find Alex would be difficult, but it was important to remain optimistic.

After he placed the food cart outside the door, he removed the white pages directory from the bottom shelf of the night table. Though he suspected that Alex wasn't listed, he decided to check for himself. He wanted to be sure that Alex had not used his initials only, a first name initial and full middle name, or if there was a misspelling of his last name. He struck out on all counts.

I wonder if his number is unlisted, John mumbled to himself as he closed the White Pages directory.

He picked up the phone handset, pressed the number 9 button to reach an outside line and then pressed 4-1-1 for operator assistance. When the operator answered, he asked for the phone number for Alexander P. Holloman. A moment later he hung up the phone – there was no one with that name in the New York City phone directory, whatsoever.

Well, that answers the question about him having an unlisted number.

John put the white pages back on the bottom shelf of the night table and then grabbed the Yellow Pages directory. First item on his list was the Department of Motor Vehicles. It was a long shot, but if Alex had renewed his driver's license recently it would have his current address. Unbeknownst to many people, driving records are public information. Among other things, a person's driving record will list any driving infraction such as a moving violation, etc. There were three locations listed as well as a License Express Office. John immediately ruled out the express office since he knew it was simply a place to quickly renew a driver's license. The first DMV office listed was on Greenwich Street in lower Manhattan, close to Battery Park. The second office was the Harlem Office on 125th Street and the third office was the Herald Square Office on Broadway between 33rd and 34th Streets.

John's first thought was to go to the 125th Street branch office. Four streets west and one street down was Catholic High on 124th Street. He could make a brief stop there before heading downtown to 86th Street to see Stella, at the bank. On the other hand, the Herald Square branch office was only nine short blocks south of the New York City Central Library. Most public libraries have local city directories and phone books for major U.S. cities. The library's microfiche section might contain old city phone directories that John could examine. On a hunch, he grabbed the White Pages directory again – he was looking for the nearest U. S. Post Office.

Bingo, he said aloud. *The J. A. Farley General Post Office was on 8th Avenue and West 33rd Street, two blocks west of the DMV Office.*

John's plan was starting to take shape. He'd start at the DMV office first. He knew that there wasn't a DMV office anywhere that didn't fill up within the first hour of business every day and since he only needed to ask a question, he would rather not spend hours sitting and waiting for his number to be called. If he struck out at the DMV office, he'd go to the Post Office and then walk to the public library. If nothing panned out at these places, he would then head uptown to Catholic High to say hello and see if, by chance, the school had a more recent address for Alex. Then, before leaving the school, he'd call Stella to let her know he was in town.

John had a full day's activities planned out and since he needed to get an early start he called the front desk and asked for a 6:30 a.m. wake-up call.

CHAPTER THIRTEEN

June 19, 2000

It was 7:40 a.m. when John reached the 50th Street subway entrance; the morning rush hour was still in full swing. As he waited in line to purchase some tokens, he heard the rumble of a train as it entered the station on the lower level and screech to a stop. Moments later, exiting passengers came into view as they ascended the stairs and walked towards the exit gates. Within minutes, the crowd had disappeared up the stairs leading to the street.

John knew he'd need a few tokens so he planned on buying ten. Whatever he didn't use over the next few days, he'd use when he returned the following week. It had been over two decades since he had bought tokens and he was not surprised to see that the subway fare had quadrupled in price. All things considered, the New York City subway system made traveling through the city a lot easier than trying to get around by car. And except for the elevated stations, the subway offered a temporary reprieve from the sweltering heat of summer, and some warmth from the snow and bone-chilling cold winds of winter.

John headed for the stairs that led to the station's lower level. After stepping onto the platform, he looked around; there was a large crowd patiently waiting for the train's arrival. Some people were leaning up against the wall, some stood midway between the wall and the platform's edge, and others sat on wooden benches that were strategically placed in close proximity to the stairs. A few minutes had passed before the echo of the train making its way through the tunnel began to get louder and louder. Suddenly, there was a loud whoosh and gust of air signaling the train's arrival into the 50th Street station.

As the first few cars of the train passed by, John had a momentary flashback to his days of taking the subway to school, during the morning rush hour. He had forgotten how crowded they could be and this train was packed tight. After it stopped and the doors opened, no one got out. John looked to his left and right to see if anyone had succeeded in finding an opening to squeeze in. There was no movement on the platform whatsoever. Seeing that no one was attempting to board the train, the conductor closed the doors and a few seconds later the train departed the station. *Unless there was a mass exodus at the next stop, no one would be getting on there either,* John thought.

During the weekday morning and afternoon rush hours, extra trains are placed in service to transport the thousands of riders going to and from work, and school. The next train that rumbled into the station was just as crowded as the previous one. Once again no one got off, so no one got on. When the third train arrived, the waiting passengers were relieved to see a nearly empty train. It didn't take long to fill up, though. Two stops later, at 34th Street, John exited the train and casually strode towards the stairs that lead to the heart of midtown Manhattan. Unlike the other riders who were also exiting, John wasn't in a rush. It was better to give the worker-bees the right-of-way since they needed to get to work on time.

It was a few minutes past 8:00 when John reached the top of the subway stairwell and stepped onto the sidewalk. The streets were alive. Car horns were blasting, pedestrian traffic lights were flashing "WALK" and "DON'T WALK," and errand couriers on bicycles and roller skates were darting in and around the cars, busses and trucks. Pedestrians on foot were trying to make their way in all directions. Their faces were uncompromising: no smile, no friendly greeting. Nothing. It was as if they didn't see you; but they did. However, in the rush to get to their final destination they would bob and weave around you with the ease and grace of an experienced stage dancer in order to not break their stride.

Yes; this was the city as John had remembered it. Strangely, nothing had changed except for a new generation of people. If it were not for a middle-aged gentleman whom accidentally bumped into John as he tried to maneuver his way onto the stairs, John would have continued to stand still at the top of the subway entrance.

"I'm very sorry, sir," John said.

"That's quite all right," the gentleman replied.

John stepped aside and looked around to get a point of reference. He was on 7th Avenue and 34th Street. From where he was standing he could see the Madison Square Garden marquee, two blocks down the street.

* * * * * * * * * * * * * * *

New Yorkers, and the multitude of other fans that attend the various entertainment, music and sporting events held there each year, affectionately call it "The Garden." Like the Empire State Building and the Statue of Liberty, "The Garden" is one of New York City's more famous landmarks. Originally built in 1879, Madison Square Garden would undergo three demolitions and four reconstructions over the next 89 years. The current "Garden" opened in 1968.

* * * * * * * * * * * * * * *

John turned around and headed east towards Broadway, one block away. As he walked down 34th Street, he reached into his pants pocket and withdrew the piece of paper containing the scribbled-down address of the DMV office. Above the glass and metal entrance doors, large stenciled numbers identified each building's street address. Only a handful of buildings that line the streets of mid-town Manhattan have official names. The rest are nameless high-rise office buildings constructed of steel, brick and stone, and seamlessly joined together like an endless chain of Siamese twins. These are the buildings that form the mainstay of the skyline that so adequately symbolizes the borough of Manhattan. When John reached Broadway, he turned left. As he slowly walked up the street he scanned the building numbers on both sides; he had just passed 1279-1281. The DMV office was in building 1297-1299. When he reached the fourth building, he looked at its address and then said to himself, *this is the place.* After he pushed open the door and stepped into the hallway, a private security guard stepped out from behind a portable podium to greet John.

"Good morning, sir; can I help you find an office suite?" the Hispanic security officer asked.

The officer was in his late-twenties. He was impeccably dressed in a tan and brown uniform, with brown patent-leather shoes. Attached to his left shoulder was a push-to-talk microphone handset; its cable connected to a battery pack that was affixed to his gun belt. His pistol, a black 9 mm Glock, was strategically placed on the right side of his gun belt.

"Good morning," John replied. "I hope I'm in the right building for the DMV office."

"Yes, sir, you are; DMV is on the eighth floor. The elevators are straight ahead, and to the right at the back of the hallway. When you get off the elevator, turn to your right and you'll see the DMV office directly in front of you."

"Thank you very much," John replied.

"You're welcome."

The rectangular hallway was neatly decorated with various pictures of the New York skyline, both in daylight and evening hours. As John walked down the hallway towards the elevators, he could hear the security officer greeting some other people who had just entered the building. John pressed the elevator button: a bright red light lit up indicating that the elevator was on the tenth floor. As he waited, a group of four women arrived.

"Good morning, ladies," he said.

"Good morning," they chimed back in unison and then continued talking amongst themselves.

After the elevator door opened, John stepped to the side, pressed his right hand against the door and gestured with his left hand for the women to enter.

"After you," he said.

In a few moments that empty elevator would smell better than a rose garden after an afternoon rain shower. Everyone should be so lucky!

"Thank you," they replied. "Which floor are you going to?" one of them asked.

"Eighth," John answered.

The numbers 3 and 8 were pressed, the doors closed and the elevator began its ascent. The silence was deafening, but the fragrance of the perfumed air more than made up for it. The women said goodbye as they exited and after the doors closed John was quickly shuttled to the eighth floor.

As he approached the DMV office, he saw a female employee unlocking the front doors. John looked around expecting to see a crowd ready to steamroll over him in the hopes of getting the first number of the day. There wasn't one. He waited until the woman signaled that it was okay to enter the office suite.

"Good morning, ma'am; where is the number dispenser?" John asked.

"To your left, sir," she replied.

"Thanks."

John pulled the protruding ticket from the dispenser and sat down in the front row to wait for his number to be called. A moment later a DMV employee entered the main room through a rear door that was a few feet behind the service counter. As soon as she saw John she quickly turned around, walked back through the door and turned to the left. *I think she recognized me,* John thought. *I should have used the mustache disguise from my Acme Spy Kit.* Soon, a few other employees peeked through the doorway and waved to John. He smiled and waved back. A few moments later, a tall black gentleman walked through the door and came out from behind the service counter.

"Mr. Michaels," he said, as he extended his right hand.

John stood up, "Yes, sir; that's me."

"I'm Luther Robinson, the director for this DMV office. Please excuse the actions of my employees; we're unaccustomed to having celebrities simply walk in here."

Mr. Robinson was wearing a gray 3-piece pinstriped suit, an almond colored shirt and a blue tie with red diamonds and circles. John guessed that Mr. Robinson was close to fifty, but his strong handshake would make one believe he was much younger.

"That's quite all right," John replied.

"How can I help you, this morning?"

"I'm looking for a high school friend of mine and I'm hoping that I can find him through his driver's license record."

"I see. If you don't mind, let's go to my office," he said.

"Sure."

As they headed towards Mr. Robinson's office, many of the employees said hello and a few extended their hands. John acknowledged as many of them as best he could. Mr. Robinson, on the other hand, continually asked his employees to return to their desks'. Mr. Robinson's office was neat and orderly, and moderately furnished. He grabbed one of the swivel chairs from the conference table and placed it alongside his gray-painted metal desk.

"Please have a seat, Mr. Michaels," he said.

"Thank you," John replied.

"You mentioned that you are trying to find a friend of yours."

"Yes, sir; I am."

"I do want you to know that even though information about a licensed driver is public information and can be obtained by anyone, a request should be submitted in writing to the Public Service Bureau of the Department of Motor Vehicles in Albany. Results are typically received in about two weeks."

"Two weeks is cutting things a little close for me," John replied.

Mr. Robinson was sitting straight up in his chair, intently listening.

"My alma mater, Catholic High, is having a 30th Anniversary Reunion for the Class of 1970 in less than two weeks and I'm trying to find a long-lost classmate whom, I believe, may still live here in New York City."

"Have you tried contacting a sibling, a relative or other acquaintance of your friend?"

"Yes, I have. There are no siblings and his only relative is a cousin who said that when she went to see him in January 1974, he was no longer living at his apartment."

"Does this cousin suspect foul play of any sort?" Mr. Robinson asked.

"No, she doesn't."

"I see; tell me your friend's name," he said.

"Alexander Patrick Holloman."

John watched as Mr. Robinson wrote the name on a piece of scratch paper.

"Address?"

"His last known address was 12 East 104th Street."

"Anything else?"

"His birth date is October 28th, 1952."

Mr. Robinson jotted down the information underneath the name.

"Are you sure he had a driver's license?" he asked.

"I'm certain of it. We both took driving lessons during our junior year at Catholic High and passed our driving test later that year. Like every other teenager, a driver's license was our ticket to freedom from the city's boundaries."

"I remember the feeling quite well, myself."

"I think I know him well enough to say that he would have had it renewed after his discharge from the Army, in mid-1973."

"Okay, Mr. Michaels," Mr. Robinson solemnly said. "I'll make an exemption for you. I can't guarantee anything, but I will run the name through our database and see if anything comes up."

"I understand."

Mr. Robinson turned his chair slightly to his left and then began to type some preliminary information into his desktop computer. While he waited for the computer to finish its initial processing, he placed the scratch paper to the right of his keyboard. As he entered some additional information he kept his eyes focused on the paper. He was obviously quite familiar with the computer's program and confident in his ability as a typist. In a matter of seconds, the computer had finished scanning its database. Mr. Robinson turned and looked at John.

"Mr. Michaels, the DMV records indicate that Mr. Holloman renewed his driver's license in May 1973. Unfortunately, it was never renewed again."

"Was his address listed as 104th Street?" John asked.

Mr. Robinson turned and looked at his computer screen again.

"Yes, it was."

"Damn it," John said, without thinking. "I apologize, Mr. Robinson."

"That's quite all right," Mr. Robinson said. "I can understand your frustration. I'm sorry that I couldn't have been of any more help," he added.

"It was a long shot," John replied, "but I'm grateful for your help."

John stood up and extended his hand in a gesture of gratitude. Mr. Robinson also stood up.

As they shook hands, John said, "I hope my request didn't over-extend your authority."

"Not at all," he replied, as a smile slowly inched along his face. "My position offers me some latitude, as long as I use it judiciously. I'm glad to have been of service, but sorry that we hit a dead end."

"Thanks. I've a few other ideas to pursue; hopefully, something will pan out."

"Mr. Michaels, there's a back door that leads directly into the hallway by the elevator if you'd like to exit without the fanfare."

"That would be great," John replied.

"Then follow me."

They turned left outside Mr. Robinson's office and headed down the foyer past the kitchen/break room, the restrooms and a conference room. When they reached the end of the foyer, Mr. Robinson turned the doorknob and pulled open the door. As John stepped outside into the empty hallway, he turned around and extended his hand.

"Thanks, again, Mr. Robinson."

"My pleasure, Mr. Michaels."

* * * * * * * * * * * * * * *

The post office clerk told John that all change of address forms are kept on file for six months and then destroyed. John then asked the clerk if there was any other way to verify a mailing address. After thinking about it for a moment or two, the postal clerk suggested that John mail an empty envelope to the subject's last known address with the words **Do Not Forward – Address Correction Requested** printed on the front of the envelope. The clerk couldn't guarantee its results, but told John he had nothing to lose other than the cost of an envelope and a postage stamp. John decided to take him up on his suggestion.

The clerk reached into his counter drawer, withdrew a pre-stamped envelope and placed it on the service counter. John withdrew some bills from his pocket and gave the clerk a dollar.

As the clerk counted out the change from his cash box, he told John that when he was done to jump to the head of the line and drop off the envelope. John took his change, picked up the envelope and walked over to a table filled with a dozen different mailing forms and a pen that was chained to the table.

In a small town, postal employees will often know quite a bit about the people they deliver mail too. New York City is not a small town – far from it. John doubted very much that the mailman who delivered the mail in 1973 was still on the job. He was probably sitting on a lounge chair in front of his beach house in sunny Daytona Beach, Florida drinking piña coladas and working on his suntan. Some people have all the luck.

John also struck out at the public library. While they were able to provide him with a current phone directory, they did not have any old ones on microfiche. He was batting zero for three and there was no pinch-hitter sitting on the bench as a backup relief. Bummer! It was time to call Stella to let her know he was in town, but before he did that he wanted to stop at Catholic High to say hello. And he needed to let Dave know to be on the lookout for the return of the letter-less envelope.

John headed west on 42nd Street towards Seventh Avenue. At the subway entrance there, he'd catch either the Number 1 or Number 2 train, which would take him to 125th Street. As he approached the corner of 42nd Street and Fifth Avenue, he saw a row of three phone booths on the far side of the street. Rather than waiting till he returned to the hotel later that evening John decided to call Dave, now. Vehicle traffic on Fifth Avenue was heavy. The only safe way to negate the irregular driving habits of the innumerable people on the streets of New York City was to cross at an intersection after the light turned green and the pedestrian sign lit up indicating it was safe to cross. Having grown up in the city, John learned at an early age that it was foolish to attempt to cross the street anywhere else.

On the third ring, Dave picked up the receiver.

"Dave; its John."

"Hey, boss; what's new?" he asked.

John told him what little bit he was able to do. He then asked Dave to call the hotel and leave a message if the envelope was delivered before John got back to Virginia Beach.

“Are you going to call Stella?”

“Yes, I plan on doing that, but first I’m going to stop in at Catholic High to say hello. I don’t plan on being there too long, perhaps an hour at the most. I’ll call Stella before I leave to see if she’d be interested in meeting me for lunch. It’s looking as if she may be my only hope, at this point in time.”

“It certainly sounds that way.”

“How are things going with the illusion?”

“It’s almost done.”

“Great.”

“I’m going to call the college tomorrow to let them know when to expect us,” Dave said. “I plan on arriving the afternoon prior to the reunion. It’ll only take about two hours to unload the truck, but I want plenty of time to set the various stage markers, meet with the lighting crew and the other backstage helpers, and to take care of any last minute concerns that may arise.”

“I understand. I don’t foresee us having a problem, though. We’ve done this so many times before we can do it with our eyes closed. Is anything else exciting happening?” John asked.

“Nope; everything is running smoothly at this end.”

“All right, then. If you need me, call the hotel and leave a message.”

“Okay.”

CHAPTER FOURTEEN

May 7, 1973

Alex knew exactly where the local DMV Office was located on 125th Street. For four years he walked past it twice a day on his way to and from Catholic High. As he exited the subway station at 125th Street and Lexington Avenue, he found himself walking behind a group of four high school students. Three of the guys were wearing sports coats; the other was wearing a blue sweater with the words CATHOLIC HIGH, in yellow. The stillness of the morning made it easy for Alex to overhear their conversation as he fell in step a few feet behind them. They were doing some last minute cramming for a history exam. *Probably seniors,* Alex thought to himself.

"Good morning, guys," he said. "I see you're headed to my alma mater, Catholic High."

There was a momentary lapse of silence amongst them as they decided who would be the person to respond.

"Yes, sir; we are."

The young man who answered was the tallest of the group, and the one who was wearing the sweater.

"Not that I was intentionally eavesdropping, but from the questions you've been asking each other it sounds like you're seniors. Am I right?"

"Yes; how'd you know?"

"My friends and I did the same thing," Alex said. After a momentary pause, he added, "My name's Alex – Class of 1970."

"I'm Tony," the tall guy said. "This is Alejandro," pointing to his right, "and this is Javier and Chris." They each raised their hand when Tony said their names.

"What's happening?" Alex said.

"So what brings you back this way so early in the morning, Alex?" Tony asked.

"While I was in the Army, my driver's license expired and now that I'm a civilian again I need to get it renewed. I live on 104th Street and the closest DMV office is here on 125th Street."

"When did they let you loose?"

"Last week. Listen, I didn't mean to interrupt your last-minute cram session, I just wanted to say hello."

"No biggie."

"Who is your history teacher?" Alex then asked.

"Mr. Berryman," Chris replied.

"He was my American History teacher in freshman year," Alex said. "And now that I'm thinking about it, he also taught at the sophomore level. Nice guy; lousy jokes though. Which history class are you taking?"

"Seminar on the Civil War," Chris answered.

"Mr. Berryman's history tests are fairly straightforward. They're not too hard, but they aren't easy either. If you paid attention in class and took halfway decent notes you'll pass," Alejandro said.

"Yep," Alex replied. "Well, guys, this is my stop – the DMV office."

They stopped walking.

As they shook hands, Javier said, "Why don't you stop by the school, Alex, preferably during the testing period. We may need a small distraction. You know, to pass around some answers."

Tony, Chris and Alejandro started laughing.

"I don't think Mr. Berryman would appreciate the interruption, Javier; especially during a final exam." Then, in a solemn tone of voice, Alex added, "What time is your test?"

"Alex, you're a funny guy," Javier said and then he started laughing, too.

"Peace, guys," Alex said, "And good luck on your finals."

* * * * * * * * * * * * * * * *

The DMV was closed; the sign on the door indicated office hours were from 8:00 a.m. to 4:15 p.m. Alex looked at his watch; it was 7:40. From outside the front door, he could see the large round clock that was hung on the wall behind the main counter. He compared the time on the DMV clock with his wristwatch: they matched. Alex was surprised that he was the first one to arrive. He stood adjacent to the front door so that the next person who stopped would know that Alex was at the head of the line. The lights were on inside the DMV office and Alex could see people walking to and from their workstations behind the long service counter. One employee was diligently working behind the information booth neatly arranging various stacks of papers and brochures, and a uniformed guard was systematically straightening the rows of folding chairs that made up the informal waiting area.

The car traffic on 125th Street was flowing smoothly at this time of the morning, but in an hour it would be bumper-to-bumper, with horns honking and people hollering at each other from inside their cars. This folly would go on till the evening rush hour was over, when some semblance of normalcy would resume. That is, until the following morning when it would start all over again.

At precisely 8:00 a.m., the guard walked to the front door, inserted his key into the lock and unbolted the door. He stepped back and then motioned to Alex to enter.

"Good morning, sir," the guard said, after Alex had stepped inside.

"Good morning," Alex replied. "I've a question to..."

Without warning, the guard turned his head towards the door. Alex quickly turned around, too. Another gentleman had just pushed open the door and was motioning to the woman behind him to enter.

Turning back to Alex, the guard said, "I apologize, sir. How can I help you?"

"I need to have my driver's license renewed, where do I go first?"

"You'll need to take a number at the information booth, have a seat and wait for your number to be called. Since you were first in line someone should call your number momentarily."

"That's cool," Alex replied.

The gentleman and lady followed Alex to the information booth; both took a number and then they too sat down to wait.

In the corner opposite the information booth there was a 3-foot by 5-foot information rack filled with numerous brochures. The DMV office was stylishly decorated with traffic safety posters, the seal of the State of New York and a picture of the Governor. There was another picture alongside the Governor; Alex presumed it was the head of the New York Department of Motor Vehicles.

A few moments later, a middle-aged woman walked out from the rear of the office, reset the number dispenser and after greeting everyone with a cheery "good morning," she called out the first number. Alex rose from his chair and approached the service counter; as he did he removed his wallet from his rear pants pocket.

"How can I help you this morning?" the woman asked.

Her nametag read: Mrs. Andrews. Alex thought her to be in her late-fifties. Like his mother, her shoulder length black hair had a few streaks of gray.

"Good morning, ma'am," replied Alex. "My driver's license expired and I need to get it renewed. What do I need to do?" he asked.

"May I have your current license, please?"

"Certainly."

Alex opened his wallet and withdrew his license.

As if he instinctively knew what the next question was going to be, Alex said, "I was discharged from the Army last week. That's why I wasn't able to get it renewed on time."

"That's quite all right, Mr. Holloman," she replied. "This is a common occurrence and nothing that can't be quickly fixed. Do you have your Form DD-214 with you, by chance?"

"No, ma'am; I don't. But, I do have a discharge ID card, will that do?"

"Yes, it will. May I see it?"

"Of course."

Alex opened his wallet again and withdrew the ID card he had been given when he was out-processing from active duty. Mrs. Andrews briefly looked at the front of the card and then turned it over to look at the reverse side. She made a few entries in her logbook and then handed the card back to Alex.

"Thank you," she said.

"You're welcome," he replied as he put the ID card back into his wallet. "Do I need to retake the written exam and road test all over again?"

"No, Mr. Holloman. We grant a 30-day waiver to all recently discharged servicemen and women so they can get their license renewed without having to retake them."

"That's great."

"Are you still living on 104th Street?"

"Yes, ma'am; I'm still there."

"One moment please," Mrs. Andrews said as she entered some additional information to update her records and prepared a new driver's license.

While Alex was waiting, he heard the DMV office door open and close a number of times, and the guard greeting the newcomers.

"Mr. Holloman, you're all set. Your license will expire in three years, but if you have a change of address anytime within those three years, you'll need to come back here to have your license updated again. Do you have any questions?"

"No, ma'am," Alex replied with a smile. "Thanks very much."

"You're welcome, Mr. Holloman."

Alex put his new license in his wallet, turned around and headed for the door. As he pulled it open, he heard Mrs. Andrews call out the next number.

* * * * * * * * * * * * * * * *

According to the notes on his "to do" list, both the Department of Employment and the Post Office were also on 125th Street, one and two blocks west of 7th Avenue, respectively. As he walked down 125th Street, Alex thought about stopping in at Catholic High to say hello. It was only one block out of his way, but he didn't want to turn a quick hello into a longer-than-needed visit. He had this gut feeling that, unlike the DMV office, he would be spending a few hours at the Department of Employment Office filling out paperwork for unemployment compensation. He decided to skip the school visit; he could always come back another day.

It was still quite early, but as Alex walked down 125th Street he could clearly see that vehicle traffic had already started to pick up. Many of the stores that lined the street were beginning to come alive once again, their owners ready to conduct the day's business. And there were more pedestrians out as well. Busses trudged along at a snail's pace and delivery trucks were routinely double-parking on both sides of the street to offload their products. Cars cautiously made their way around the trucks and busses, and those drivers who needed to turn on a particular corner quickly realized that a green light didn't given them sole authorization to turn. Occasionally, drivers were forced to come to a complete stop; otherwise they would have hit a pedestrian who was attempting to cross the street. It would be unfair to single out any one group in particular for the cause of the daily traffic snarls; they each had a job to do. It was all a part of life in the city and most people had learned to adapt to these inconveniences.

Unless you were with another person or were part of a group, you walked in silence. No one acknowledged anyone, unless they happened to recognize a face in the crowd. Whenever that did occur, it was not uncommon to stop in the middle of the sidewalk to hold a conversation. And for those who were walking a few steps behind, or coming from the opposite direction, well, it was their responsibility to watch where they were walking. Other than dodging a couple of mindless drivers, who were intent on turning and didn't care that they screeched to a halt within inches of hitting him, Alex's walk down 125th Street had been uneventful. As he approached the building where the employment office was located, Alex decided it would probably be quicker to do his business at the post office first. So he kept on walking.

The post office had six customer-service counter windows, but only two were currently open for business. A customer was standing in front of each window and there were two other customers standing in the waiting line. It would only be a matter of minutes before Alex would be called up to the window.

"How can I help you?" the elderly postman asked Alex.

"I was recently discharged from the Army and am living with my folks on 104th Street. I haven't had mail delivered there in two years; do I need to have a change of address card on file so the post office knows where to deliver my mail?"

"Did the Army give you a postal change of address form to complete before you were discharged?" the postman asked.

"Yes, sir; they did. I listed my parents address as the new address," Alex replied.

"Then you don't need to file another change of address now that you're back in the States. The post office on 104th Street will automatically deliver your mail to you, at your parents' address."

"Okay, thanks."

"You're welcome; anything else I can do for you today?"

"No, sir."

Alex left the post office and headed to the building where the Department of Employment office was located. Unlike the DMV and the post office, where he was able to get in and out in short time, Alex was certain that he would be in the employment office a lot longer. In hindsight, he wished he had brought along a book to read. It was then that he remembered he forgot to add the public library to his list of things to do. A voracious reader, it had been two years since he checked out a book from the library and he wanted to renew his library card privileges.

When Alex entered the employment office he was not surprised to see that there were over two-dozen people already there. One person was standing at a service counter window speaking with a representative; a few others were sitting on chairs waiting, he presumed, to be called. There was a large sign hanging over the General Information booth that read: **"Please stand behind the red line on the floor directly in front of this station and wait to be called up for assistance. Thank you."**

A middle-aged man was already at the booth and six other people were ahead of Alex. *It could have been worse; this place could have been jam-packed,* Alex thought to himself.

As he waited in line, a counselor emerged from a nearby office, walked up to the front of the room and called out a name. The person raised their hand to make the initial contact, picked up their paperwork and then headed towards the counselor. Thirty minutes had passed before Alex reached the head of the line.

"Next person in line," the gentleman behind the counter exclaimed.

"Good morning, sir," Alex said with a smile.

"Good morning," the gentleman replied. "How can I help you?"

"I was recently discharged from the Army and I want to know if I'm eligible for any type of unemployment compensation, and I'd also like some help in finding a job."

"May I see a picture identification card?"

"Certainly," Alex replied.

He gave the man his driver's license.

"I just had it renewed earlier today," Alex added.

"By chance, Mr. Holloman, did you bring a certified copy of your Form DD-214 with you?"

"No, I didn't. But, I have a discharge ID card; will that do?"

"No, we need the actual form. But that's okay; we can work around it, for now. To answer your questions, yes, you are eligible for unemployment compensation and we will certainly help you find suitable work. There are a few things you need to do. Hold on a moment."

The man got up from his booth and walked over to a four-drawer file cabinet behind him. He opened the top drawer and pulled out a handful of booklets. After returning to his booth, he put one of them on the countertop and the others into a compartment in his booth.

"You need to complete this 8-page booklet in its entirety; answer the questions as thoroughly as possible because your answers are what we will use to help you find a job. Use a number two pencil, please. When you're done, you can either mail everything to us or bring it back in person; it's your choice. And don't forget to include a certified copy of your Form DD-214."

"Where can I get it certified?" Alex asked.

"Any bank; it'll cost you about a dollar."

"All right."

"Once we have your paperwork, it'll take about two days for us to process your application."

“If I bring it back in person, do I need to stand in line?”

“No; just drop it into that box.”

He pointed to the box labeled **Completed Questionnaires** that was on the far corner edge of his booth.

“You can return to the employment office on the third day after you drop off the paperwork. At that time you will need to stand in line once again. Once I verify that your information has been entered, I’ll add your name to that day’s waiting list to speak with a counselor.”

“Sounds easy enough; thanks.”

“You’re welcome.”

The visit to the employment office was not what Alex expected. But, having never applied for unemployment benefits before, he accepted, without question, the procedure that he was told to follow. After leaving, he headed back down 125th Street to the subway station on Lexington Avenue. As he waited on the corner of Lenox Avenue for the pedestrian crosswalk light to change to green, he looked over towards Catholic High. He still wanted to stop in and say hello, but he felt it was important that he finish the things on his list, first. *The school visit can wait,* he said to himself as he crossed the street and continued on towards the subway station. *There was still plenty of time to visit, as classes would be in session till the end of the second week of June.*

* * * * * * * * * * * * * * *

Mary was quite surprised when Alex returned home so soon.

“I thought you’d be gone till late this afternoon, son,” she said.

“Me too,” Alex replied. “I was sure I would be tied up at the employment office for a few hours, but there weren’t a lot of people ahead of me. I was told that I needed to complete this 8-page questionnaire and to bring a certified copy of my Form DD-214.”

“What’s a Form DD-214?” Mary asked.

“A paper that says I was honorably discharged from the Army,” Alex replied.

“Oh.”

"Since I had planned on calling Stella to see when she and I could get together for lunch, I now have another reason for going to see her. I was told that any bank could certify this," Alex said.

"Yes, that's correct. The bank will make a copy of the original document and then stamp it as a true copy," Mary replied. "It's not yet lunch time so you may be able to reach Stella if you call now."

"Okay, I will."

Stella's phone line was busy when Alex dialed it the first time. He waited a minute before dialing it again.

It was still busy.

What the hell, he thought to himself; *I'll fill out the application questionnaire and then try calling after I'm done.* It took Alex fifteen minutes to fill out the form, sign and date it. When he finished, he picked up the phone and dialed Stella's number. It rang, this time.

"Good morning, First Merchants Bank and Trust Company, this is Stella, how can I help you?"

"Hi, Stella," Alex said.

"Hey, Alex; what's up?"

"I called because I need to get a certified copy of my Army discharge papers and I understand the bank can do it."

"How soon do you need it?" she asked.

"Today, if possible."

"If you're not busy, come over now. And if you like we can go to lunch together. Do you know where the bank is located?"

"86th Street, right?"

"Yes; right on the corner of Lexington. You can't miss it."

"Okay. It'll take me a couple of minutes to get the papers from my folder, but I should be on my way in about 10 minutes."

"Alex, I hope you're planning to take the subway rather than driving. There's no place to park anywhere near 86th Street."

"Yes; I had planned on taking the subway, Stella."

"Okay, I'll see you shortly."

After hanging up the phone, Alex headed for his bedroom. He opened the bottom dresser drawer and pulled out the olive-green folder the Army had given him on the day he was discharged. Inside the folder, in between some miscellaneous papers from his personnel file, was the Form DD-214. He placed it on his bed and then he put the folder back into the dresser drawer.

Mary was dusting the living room furniture when Alex came out of the bedroom.

"I'm going to the bank, Mom; see you later."

"Bye, son."

* * * * * * * * * * * * * * * *

It only took a few minutes for Stella to have another bank employee make a copy of Alex's discharge paper and stamp it a certified copy. Stella could have easily done it herself, but because she was related to Alex she wanted to have someone else do it, just to be on the safe side.

"There's a sandwich shop around the corner from the bank, if you'd like to go there for lunch," Stella said.

"That's fine with me," Alex replied. "How much time do you have?" he then asked.

"An hour," she replied. "I usually bring something with me from home, but this morning I decided not to. Funny how things turn out, isn't it?"

"Indeed."

* * * * * * * * * * * * * * * *

Alex ordered a foot-long ham and cheese sub with the works; Stella ordered a tuna sandwich with lettuce, tomato and mayo only. They both asked for ice tea, instead of soda. After Alex paid for their meals, they looked around for an empty booth to sit in while their subs were prepared.

"So, Alex, it's been a week that you're back, how are things going so far?"

They sat across from each other, which made it easy for Stella to maintain eye contact with Alex, as they talked.

"I'm slowly getting used to being home and waking up in my room rather than in an Army barracks. I guess, given the circumstances, everything is fine though I do feel a little antsy not having anything to do. But that's my choice to not work – just yet – until I get acclimated to being a civilian again."

"I know you said you wanted to enjoy the summer, but given how you feel do you think you may want to go to work sooner rather than later?" Stella asked.

"I'm not sure. I think that's the reason I feel antsy. I'm sure this is a normal feeling and something that will pass, in time."

"What did you get done so far, today?"

Alex told Stella about his morning adventure.

"It certainly sounds like you made some progress," she said.

"I did. In fact, I was sure it was going to be a long drawn out process, but it wasn't. I envision the long day will come about after I drop off my questionnaire and the discharge paper."

"Have you called John to tell him that you've been discharged?"

"No, not yet. I'll probably call him later in the week. Hopefully, he'll be home."

Alex stopped speaking when the sandwich shop attendant approached the booth with his and Stella's lunch order.

"Hello, Stella," Julie said.

"Hi, Julie."

As Julie placed their food on the table, Stella noticed a sudden change in Alex's facial expression.

"Julie," Stella said, "I'd like to introduce you to my cousin, Alex."

Julie had reddish-brown shoulder length hair, green eyes and was about a year younger than Alex.

He extended his hand to her and she reciprocated.

"It's nice to meet you, Alex," she said, as she began to blush ever so slightly.

"The pleasure is all mine," Alex replied as he gently shook her hand.

"Stella," Julie said, as she turned towards her, "I'd love to sit and chat with you, and Alex, but as you can see we're quite busy."

"I'll call you at home during the week, Julie. We need to plan a Saturday trip to Kleins," Stella replied.

"That'd be great, Stella." She turned back towards Alex, "It was nice meeting you, Alex; I hope you'll come back again," she said with a smile.

"I will definitely be back, Julie."

Alex turned his head and watched her walk away.

Alex was smitten with Julie, Stella thought to herself.

"So, Alex," Stella began, "you were saying something about it being a long day."

Alex quickly turned around to face Stella, his face beginning to turn red.

"I'm sorry," he said. "I…"

Stella stopped him in mid-sentence.

"You don't need to apologize," she replied. As an afterthought, she added, "She's pretty, isn't she?"

"Very," he responded.

Alex picked up his sub and took a bite from it. Stella glanced at her watch and then picked up her sandwich and took a bite also.

"Why do you believe it'll be a long day when you go back to the employment office?" Stella asked, in between bites of her sandwich.

"When I was standing in line early this morning, there were over two-dozen people already in the waiting area and only one person was called the entire time."

"How long did you have to wait?"

"Thirty minutes."

While they were eating Stella noticed that Alex would sporadically roll his eyes left and right, and occasionally he'd look over her shoulder. Because she was sitting with her back to the front door she couldn't see anyone who came in until they passed their table, or who was in the process of leaving. Stella knew it wasn't Julie that Alex was watching, because she was busy helping the other attendant prepare sandwiches and subs. Alex's unusual eye movements made Stella feel a bit uncomfortable. She was concerned that something was going on in the shop.

Stella leaned forward and whispered, "Is something happening behind me that I should know about?"

"No, nothing; why do you ask?" he quietly replied.

"Well, I've noticed that you are indiscriminately looking around the place and I was beginning to worry. Especially since I know it wasn't Julie you were looking at."

"I'm sorry, Stella. I didn't mean to make you uncomfortable. It's a habit I picked up in Vietnam."

"I understand," Stella replied. "What do you have planned for this afternoon?"

"Now that I have a certified copy of my discharge paper, I'm going to pick up the questionnaire and then head back to the employment office. I just need to drop it off and then go back in three days," he replied. "They told me it'd be two days before the information gets processed, hence the wait."

"Do you need to make an appointment or can you just show up?"

"I was told to just show up since it is first come, first served on a daily basis."

"I see."

"The smart thing to do is get there early on the day you want to speak with a counselor, which is what I plan to do."

"Good idea."

They finished eating in silence. Stella was watching Alex, and Alex was watching the room.

"That was a good sub," Alex said. "I'm definitely coming back here again."

"For the food or to see Julie," Stella innocently replied.

"Both," he answered, with a smile.

"We can come back here whenever you want to meet for lunch."

"Cool."

"I've got to get back to work, Alex," Stella said as she looked at her watch and then slowly slid out from the booth.

Alex cleaned the table and dumped the waste into the trash bin. Just before they reached the door, they turned and waved goodbye to Julie; she smiled and waved back.

Alex and Stella walked back to the bank in silence.

"Give me a call and let me know how things turn out after you've been back to the employment office, okay?" she said, as they stopped in front of the bank's door.

"I will. Tell Uncle Ed and Aunt Carol that I said hello, would you?"

"I'll call them after I get home later today," she replied.

"Bye, Alex," she said as she leaned forward and gave him a kiss on the cheek.

"Bye, Stella."

* * * * * * * * * * * * * * * *

Mary was not at home when Alex returned, but she left him a note, next to the employment questionnaire, on the kitchen table saying that she had gone to the local supermarket to buy some groceries and would be back later. Alex put the certified copy of his discharge paper on top of the questionnaire and then headed back to his room to put the original Form DD-214 back inside the folder. When he returned to the kitchen, on the bottom of his mother's note he scribbled his own saying that was heading back to the employment office and then going to the public library on 96th Street to renew his library card.

He also said that he'd be back in time for dinner.

CHAPTER FIFTEEN

June 19, 2000

John turned the doorknob and pulled open the street-level door, entering Catholic High for the first time since graduating, in 1970. Turning to his left, he walked up the dozen steps to the administration office, which was on the first floor of the school. There was a large sign, to the left of the door. In bold letters, it stated "**All guests are requested to first stop in the Administration Office.**" John complied; even though he was a school alumnus, he was a guest.

The door was slightly ajar so he knocked on the doorframe instead and then slowly pushed open the door. He stepped inside the office and stood behind the counter. Mrs. Dixon, who was sitting behind the only desk in the room, looked up and politely greeted him.

"Good morning, Mr. Michaels; I'll be right with you."

She glanced back at the piece of paper on her desk and then at her computer terminal.

"Thank you, Mrs. Dixon," he replied.

The administration office was not very big, approximately 9-feet by 12-feet, but it was large enough to efficiently conduct the everyday running of a mid-sized high school of 750 students. Inside the office, the wall to the immediate left had two windows looking out onto 124th Street. Depending on where one stood, you could also see a part of Lenox Avenue. On the wall to the right hung photographs of Brother Gregory, Catholic High's current Principal; Brother Hill, the Dean of Discipline and Mr. Tim Daniels, the Dean of Studies. Up against the far wall were two, four-drawer filing cabinets and above them, hung from the ceiling, was a neatly pruned spider plant.

"Mr. Michaels, what a nice surprise to see you," Mrs. Dixon said as she stepped out from behind her desk.

As she approached the counter she extended her hand to him.

"What brings you to the city?" she asked.

"I'm here to visit with a friend of mine and thought I'd stop in for a brief visit," he replied as they shook hands.

"We're certainly glad you did. Just a moment, let me tell Brother Gregory you're here. I'm sure he'd be delighted to see you."

"Thanks."

Mrs. Dixon walked over to Brother Gregory's office, which was diagonally across the main hallway from the Administration Office. She didn't enter, choosing instead to stand in the doorway. John didn't hear the whole conversation, but he did hear Mrs. Dixon tell Brother Gregory that "he had just walked into the office a moment ago."

"Brother Gregory," she said, after returning to the office, "is on the phone, but said that he would be over momentarily."

"I hope I'm not interrupting anything."

"Not at all. We're always delighted when alumni come by for a nostalgic visit. Are you coming to the Class of 1970 Reunion?" she asked.

"Yes, I am."

"There hasn't been a reunion gathering in a number of years, so everyone is looking forward to this one," Mrs. Dixon said.

"Indeed, we are," said Brother Gregory, who had just entered the room. "How are you doing, John?" he asked as he extended his hand.

"I'm well, Brother Gregory; thanks," John replied as they shook hands.

"Well, I'll let you two gentlemen talk," Mrs. Dixon said. "I've got to catch up on some things here."

She turned around and headed back to her desk.

"Let's go to my office, John," Brother Gregory said as he extended his arm towards the hallway.

* * * * * * * * * * * * * * * *

Almost all of the Christian Brothers who taught at Catholic High routinely transferred to other catholic high schools during the course of their religious careers. While a few remained at Catholic High until their retirement, only a select few made the transition from teacher to principal. Brother Gregory was one of the select few.

John first met Brother Gregory in September 1966, during his freshman year. In addition to teaching Algebra and Business Math, Brother Gregory was also the coach and moderator for the school's track team. He was a terrific mentor who was able to draw out the best each track team member had to give. It didn't matter to Brother Gregory if you placed second, third or last in a race, as long as you consistently gave a 110 percent effort each time you competed. He constantly reminded his students that, "in life, regardless of how well prepared we may be, we will not win every undertaking."

John remembered Brother Gregory's disappointment when, in June 1967, John told him that he wasn't going to rejoin the track team in sophomore year. Brother Gregory didn't ask why, though he did tell John that he would be welcomed back if, over the summer, he changed his mind.

* * * * * * * * * * * * * * *

John and Brother Gregory walked past a glass display cabinet that held a sampling of the many plaques and team trophies that Catholic High had won over the years. Behind some of the trophies, were laminated stories from the sports section of various city newspapers with photographs of former students who had played college and/or professional basketball. In the far left corner was a picture of a young John Michaels; he was standing underneath a woman he had just levitated with his arms outstretched in an applause pose.

The principal's office had not changed over the years. Unlike a Park Avenue CEO or other highly paid executive, there was no window overlooking the city and no extravagant anteroom to the principal's office. No one came in to redecorate when a new principal assumed the job. Brother Gregory had the same bookcase and worked from the same oak desk that his predecessors had used. The only modern amenity he had was a personal computer that was tied into the school's local area network.

Brother Gregory ushered John into his office.

"Be seated, John," he said, as he pointed to the two chairs alongside the right wall.

John waited for Brother Gregory to sit first, before he sat down.

"Thanks," John replied. "It's been a long time since I was in this office," he said. "And for a totally different reason, I might add."

"And what was the reason?" Brother Gregory asked.

"A classmate's father had passed away in the spring of 1970 and the entire senior class had asked Brother Meekin, our home room teacher at the time, if we could attend the funeral service. He wouldn't commit until he had a chance to speak with Brother Higgins, who was the Principal."

"Ah, yes; I remember – that was Steven Kellar."

"That's correct," John replied. "Brother Higgins gave his okay for the entire class to go to the funeral. However, when the service ended, I and two other close friends of Steve decided that we were also going to go to the cemetery service, as well. The three of us knew Steve's parents and we felt we owed it to Steve to be there. So rather than asking Brother Meekin's permission to go, we told him, 'we were going.' The following day, during home room, we were summoned to Brother Higgins' office. Each of us was brought in on an individual basis and asked to explain why we were absent from class the day before."

"What did everyone say?"

"We explained to Brother Higgins why we felt obligated to go to the cemetery. He said he understood our loyalty, but that our actions, however well-meaning, were still inappropriate. He then went on to explain that Brother Meekin felt that we ignored his authority by not asking his permission, which, we later learned, would have been given without any hesitation."

"If we had the wisdom that is cultivated with age bestowed upon us in our youth, I sincerely believe the world would be quite different," Brother Gregory stated.

"I agree," John replied.

* * * * * * * * * * * * * * * *

Brother Gregory and John had been talking for about twenty minutes when John said, "Can I ask a favor?"

"Certainly, John; what can I do for you?"

"I'm trying to find Alex Holloman. He is the only one from the senior class of 1970 that doesn't know about the reunion."

"I remember Alex," Brother Gregory replied, as he nodded his head up and down. "You and he were the tallest freshman track team members I've ever coached. He was a good long-distance runner, if I remember correctly."

"Yes, he was," John answered.

"What is going on with Alex?" he asked.

"For some unknown reason, no one can find him. I'm hoping that Alex may have sent a letter to Mrs. Dixon, at some point, telling her of his new address."

"I can check the school's records from my computer terminal," Brother Gregory replied.

"That would be great," John said.

John looked around the office as Brother Gregory repeatedly clicked his computer's mouse button.

A few moments later he looked up and said, "John, the address we have on file is 12 East 104th Street."

"That was his address while in high school," John replied.

"That's the only one we have listed."

"Oh well; it was a long shot. I've one more favor to ask: may I use your phone to make a local call?"

"Certainly," he replied.

Brother Gregory got up from his desk and headed for the door.

"I'll be in the administration office," he said. "If you finish before I return, come over there."

"I will. Can I dial straight out or do I need to dial '9' first?"

"You can dial straight out," he replied.

"Thanks."

John called the bank and asked the receptionist if he could speak with Ms. Stella Noone. It rang three times before Stella answered.

"Good morning; this is Stella, how may I help you?"

"Good morning, Stella, it's ..."

"Oh-my-gosh, oh-my-gosh; John Michaels is that you? Where are you; are you in town?"

"Yes, Stella, it's me; and I'm in town. I can answer your questions over the phone, but I was hoping that we could meet for lunch; unless you have a prior commitment."

"No, I don't have any plans. As a matter of coincidence, I have 'comp time' coming to me and I had decided that today would be the day to leave early. I'm so glad you caught me before I left."

"I guess I'll take that as a yes for lunch, then?" John asked.

"I'm so sorry; yes, of course we can get together. Where are you?"

"I'm at Catholic High. Where would you like to meet?"

"I still live on 93rd Street and Park Avenue. Let's meet at 96th Street and Lexington? I'll wait for you by the subway entrance; is that okay?"

"That's perfect. I just need a few minutes to say goodbye and I'll be on my way."

"Great. See you in about 30 minutes, John."

"Okay, bye."

Brother Gregory had not yet returned when John hung up the phone so he walked over to the administration office.

"Mrs. Dixon, Brother Gregory said he was coming over here, do you know where he went?"

"He did stop here momentarily and then said he was going to the cafeteria," she replied. "You can go over that way, if you like."

"Thanks, but I'll wait just outside the door."

John turned around to leave and as soon as he reached the door, he and Brother Gregory bumped into each other.

"Pardon me," they simultaneously said. Then they both started to laugh.

"Brother Gregory, I managed to contact Alex's cousin, Stella. She and I are going to meet for lunch. Thanks for the help and for taking some time to talk with me; it was certainly a pleasure seeing you again."

"The pleasure was all mine," he replied.

"I trust that I will see you at the reunion?" John asked.

"Yes, indeed," Brother Gregory answered. "The faculty and administrative staff, past and present, are looking forward to attending."

"Excellent. I'm looking forward to seeing a lot of friendly faces."

"John, I need to make my rounds before the first group of students walk in for lunch. Take care."

"Goodbye, Brother Gregory."

John turned around and said goodbye to Mrs. Dixon. When he left, he closed the office door as he found it – slightly ajar.

* * * * * * * * * * * * * * *

As John walked down 125th Street towards Lexington Avenue, he noticed that all of the stores now had steel security gates permanently mounted either under the store's sign or on the brick wall between stores. Thirty years ago, this would have been an astonishing site to see. Now it was commonplace.

When John stepped onto the 125th Street subway platform there were at least a dozen people patiently waiting for the train. *Well, I may not have too long of a wait,* he thought to himself. Five minutes later the Number 5 local train rumbled into the station and quickly screeched to a halt.

Only a handful of people boarded the train when it stopped at the 116th, 110th and 103rd Street stations. However, when the train doors opened on 96th Street, more than half of the passengers in the car John was in, exited. Many other commuters also exited. After stepping onto the station platform, John quickly fell in stride with the people in front of him. When the leader reached the turnstiles, the exiting procession, as expected, slowed to a snail's pace. The Number 5 train was long gone by the time John reached the turnstile. There was still a long line of people in front of him making their way up the stairs, and an equally long line behind him slowly inching their way towards the turnstile.

* * * * * * * * * * * * * * * *

Alex had introduced John to his cousin, Stella, in December 1966. John was supposed to be at his after school job, but he decided to hang out with Alex at his house. Stella, he learned, was a freshman at Central High School, which was five miles from Catholic High. Stella and John dated all through their high school years. She was easy to talk to and they shared a lot of common interests. All of these little nuances made them a perfect match for each other. John believed that if he hadn't been drafted, their friendship would have progressed to the next level. But, unfortunately, such was not the case.

When he returned home from Vietnam, John was given two weeks of leave. He and Stella got together every day after she came home from work. After getting settled in at his new command in Virginia Beach, he drove to New York City the first weekend he was free. For the next 10 months, John visited Stella as often as he could and when he couldn't go he'd call Stella by telephone.

One Saturday evening, while eating dinner at Brigatti's Italian Restaurant in midtown Manhattan, John told Stella that he was thinking of staying in Virginia Beach to earn a living as a touring professional magician. Stella hid her disappointment; it was not what she had hoped to hear. But she dearly loved John and wanted him to be happy so she encouraged him to pursue his dream.

Alas, their lives, it seems, were predestined to travel in different directions.

As John's magic business picked up and his tours began to get longer and longer, John's visits to Stella and telephone calls began to slow down. Eventually the weekend visits stopped, except for the few occasions when he was between tours. Their devotion to each other never faltered and John lovingly sent Stella postcards, roses on Valentine's Day and on her birthday, and lengthy hand-written letters continuously throughout the year. Stella responded similarly and through her letters, she celebrated his triumphs and cried when he failed. Through it all, Stella faithfully remained John's guiding light.

* * * * * * * * * * * * * * *

John spotted Stella immediately and he could see that she was actively scanning the exiting crowd, looking for him. It was lunchtime and there was a large crowd walking in both directions that were merging with the subway riders. Stella was about 30 feet from the subway entrance, standing close to a storefront window at a forty-five degree angle. John could have easily disappeared into the crowd to sneak up behind her, but decided not too. He kept his eyes firmly fixed on her, knowing full well that in a moment or two she would see him.

Stella was dressed in a navy-blue pants suit, her shoulder length brown hair was neatly coiffed and she was wearing black pumps. Her purse was strategically slung over her shoulder, one hand firmly grasping its two straps: there was no way she'd give it up without a fight. When their eyes met, John smiled at her. She immediately smiled back and started to edge her way through the crowd, towards him. They hugged and then she affectionately kissed him. John reciprocated.

"Stella, you haven't changed a bit," John said. "You still look like the girl I met in 1966."

She blushed and with a smile that could melt butter she mumbled, "Thank you." They stood there, still embraced, each looking at the other as if they were getting ready to part forever. Finally, tears began to well in Stella's eyes.

"I've a million questions to ask you," she said, the tears now sliding freely down her face.

As soon as Stella relaxed her arms, John instinctively followed suit. Reaching into her purse, she removed a handkerchief and dabbed at the tears.

"I see this may be a long lunch," he said. "I just hope the restaurant owner doesn't charge us rent."

"Well … maybe not a million questions," she replied and they both started to laugh. A moment later Stella said, "There's a cozy little eatery down by the corner named Silverman's Family Restaurant. The food is excellent and they have a friendly staff; does that sound okay with you?"

"Perfect," John said, "let's go."

Stella put her handkerchief back into her purse. Then she placed her arm inside John's and rested her head on his shoulder, as they silently walked down the block.

The hostess at Silverman's was excited when Stella and John walk in.

"Hi, Stella."

"Hello, Regina; how are you?"

"Doing well, thanks."

"Regina, I'd like you to meet my dear friend, John."

As Regina and John shook hands, she said to him, "Have you been here before, you look very familiar?"

"No," he replied. "This is my first time here; in the restaurant, that is. I was born and raised in New York City, but I haven't lived here since 1971."

"Hmm, I'm sure I've seen you…" there was a momentary pause in her voice, then suddenly her eyes widened, "…why, you're John Michaels, the magician!"

"That's quite profound, people tell me that all the time," John replied. "Naturally, I'm beginning to think it's true."

The quizzical look on Regina's face told John that she didn't know if he was kidding her or not.

"Pardon me," John said, "but you've something by your ear."

He reached over and produced a silver dollar, and slowly brought it into view so Regina and Stella could see it. John placed the coin into his other hand where it promptly disappeared.

"I can never figure out why it does this – the silver dollar seems to have a mind of its own," John said as he reached behind his elbow and pulled the coin from there.

He let the coin drop into his other hand again and quickly closed it into a fist.

"I got it now!" John confidently said.

But when he opened his hand the coin was gone.

"Darn it, I was so sure that time. Oh well; easy come, easy go."

Stella smiled and Regina shook her head in disbelief, not sure what to say.

Finally, she turned towards Stella and said, "Stella, we've known each other for over 15 years, you never once told me you were friends with John Michaels. What's up with that, girlfriend?"

John looked at Stella, her smile stretched from ear-to-ear.

"You never asked," she replied.

"Stella Noone, you're holding out on me. We need to talk. Next thing I know you'll be telling me you and John are running off to Las Vegas to elope."

Regina's naïve, but off-hand comment took Stella by complete surprise.

"Regina!" Stella exclaimed, as she turned to face her.

"I'm so sorry, Stella; I didn't mean to say that," Regina replied, her face turning beet-red.

"Mr. Michaels..."

John held up his hand, stopping her in mid-sentence. "That's quite all right, Regina," he said.

Regina quickly regained her composure and then asked if they wanted a table up front or a booth in the back.

"A booth would be ideal," John said.

"Sure thing; follow me," she answered.

She picked up two menus and escorted them to a booth in the far corner to afford them some privacy.

"I'll be right back," Regina said, as Stella and John sat down.

"John," Stella began, but then stopped to gather her thoughts.

"I know what you're thinking, Stella. You don't need to apologize; I know it was harmless banter. My only concern is that you're not upset, in light of what was said. Your feelings, not Regina's faux pas, are what matters to me."

"I'm fine," she replied, "really."

Regina returned shortly thereafter with silverware that was neatly wrapped inside a cloth napkin and a pitcher of ice water. After filling their glasses, she recited the lunch special: meatloaf, mashed potatoes and mixed vegetables. John ordered the special; Stella ordered a cup of vegetable soup and a tuna salad sandwich.

"Would you like something to drink, other than water?" Regina asked.

"No," John said, "water is all I'd like."

"How about you, Stella?"

"Water is fine with me, too; thanks."

"Okay. I'll be back in a few minutes with your meals," Regina said.

"Thanks, Regina," Stella replied.

Stella turned to John and said, "So tell me, what is going on in the Big Apple that brings you here?"

"I came to see you," John replied, as he placed his hands on the table.

"I'm glad you called me," Stella said as she reached across the table and took hold of John's left hand.

"Do you know about the 30th Anniversary Reunion of Catholic High's Class of 1970?" John asked.

"As a matter of fact, I do. Drew Wagner called me a few weeks ago to ask if I had a mailing address for Alex," Stella replied. "I told him I didn't and that I couldn't even tell him if Alex still lived here in the city."

"I also spoke with Drew," John said. "Ninety-nine percent of my mail goes to a post office box, by choice. Since most of it is junk, I drop it in the wastebasket at the post office on my way out. Somehow, Drew managed to get my home mailing address and that's where my invitation was delivered. During our phone conversation, I learned that Alex and four others were the only ones who had not yet been contacted. Drew also asked if I would consider bringing my show out of retirement for an encore farewell performance at the reunion."

"What did you tell him?" Stella excitedly asked.

"That I would. In fact, I agreed to do the show even before I had a chance to ask my crew. Fortunately, no one has a conflict with that date, so it worked out just fine. Other than Drew, and my crew, you're the only other person who knows. It's going to be a surprise event to cap off the evening's festivities."

"What a surprise that will be! That was nice of you to agree to perform," Stella said.

She was still holding onto his hand, so John placed his other hand on top of hers and said, "Stella, I'd be honored if you would consider going with me as my date for the evening – if you don't already have other plans for that night."

"Of course, I will," she replied without the slightest bit of hesitation and with a twinkle in her eyes.

"I'm sure Drew will find the other four guys, but I don't know if he'll find Alex," John said.

"Are you going to try and find him?" she asked.

"As a matter of fact, I've already started."

As soon as John said this, tears formed in Stella's eyes.

"But, I'm not going to tell Drew. If I can find Alex, I'd like it to be a surprise."

Regina had returned; she was holding a large serving tray in one hand and a folding table in the other. She snapped open the table, then raised her free hand up, grasped the tray and helped set it down evenly onto the folding table. She served Stella first, then John.

"Enjoy," she said, before picking up the tray and the table. "I'll be back in a bit to see if you need anything."

John picked up his glass of water and offered a toast to Stella.

"To a wonderful young lady named Stella."

Stella, blushing once again, picked up her glass and gently tapped John's.

"Thank you; I think you're wonderful, too. Cheers."

"Cheers," he replied.

As they ate, John told Stella what little he had managed to accomplish in his quest to find Alex.

"It seems so out of character for him to just disappear without saying a word to family or friends," he said. "As a magician, I've made an elephant vanish and made beautiful women," he pointed to Stella, "appear and disappear. How hard could it be to find a missing person?"

"If it were that easy," Stella began, "I would have found him, myself."

"Do you remember seeing anything unusual about his demeanor?"

"No; nothing at all. And that's what made his sudden disappearance that much more upsetting."

Seeing that they had finished, Regina stopped at the table to clear it. Before she left, she asked if they wanted dessert. They both declined, but they did ask for more water. After Regina finished refilling the two glasses, John asked for the check.

"Lunch is on the house, Mr. Michaels," she said.

"That's not necessary, Regina; I insist on paying," John replied.

John could see that Regina was very reluctant to give him the check, but she eventually did.

"Take your time, there's no rush," she said.

When Stella and John finished, they headed up to the register. Regina had just handed another customer his change and thanked him for coming.

"Regina, the food and service were superb. Whenever I'm in the city, I know where I'll be coming to get a great meal," he told her.

"Thank you very much," she answered.

Lunch was 19 dollars so John gave Regina a 20-dollar bill. After she rang up the sale, she handed him a dollar change.

As Stella and John prepared to leave, he stopped, turned around and said, "Regina, I forgot to leave a tip. I'm sorry; I don't know what I was thinking."

John took the dollar bill that Regina just gave him, clearly showed both sides of it and then folded it in half. He then folded it into quarters and then into eights.

"Regina, please open your hand," he asked.

Nervously, she lifted up her left hand and opened it. John placed the folded-up dollar on her palm and kept his index finger on it so the bill wouldn't fall onto the floor.

"Now close your hand tightly, into a fist."

Once her fingers closed over the bill, John removed his finger from inside her fist. He then turned her hand palm-down and instructed her to stand still. John showed Regina his empty right hand before reaching into his pants pocket to withdraw an Irish, 50-pence coin that he carried with him all the time. He placed the coin on top of Regina's closed fist.

"That's an interesting coin you have there, John," Stella said.

"It is indeed," he replied. "I picked it up in Ireland a few months ago. I got it from a leprechaun: a souvenir from one magician to another."

"For real?" Regina exclaimed.

"Uh-huh," John said.

He looked at Stella and winked; she smiled back at him.

"Legend has it that these coins will work their magic once a year. I think this is an appropriate time to test its magical powers," John said.

He slowly waved both his hands over Regina's fist and said, "Let the magic happen."

He picked up the coin and placed it into his other hand.

"I was told that if the magic worked..." John slowly opened his hand "...the coin would disappear until this time next year."

The coin was gone.

John asked Regina to turn her hand palm up and to slowly open it. The dollar bill was gone, but in its place was a $20 bill. Both Regina and Stella stood frozen in the moment; their eyes wide open in amazement.

"Thanks again for a great lunch, Regina," John said.

Regina nervously unfolded the bill; it was real.

"Stella," Regina said, "I like him!"

"So do I," Stella responded. "So do I."

"Goodbye, Regina," John said.

"Goodbye, Mr. Michaels; and thank you – for everything."

"Regina; please call me John."

"Okay ... John. Goodbye, Stella."

"So long, Regina; I'll call you."

"Please do."

After John opened the door, Stella put her arm inside his and they stepped out onto a not-so-crowded sidewalk. Lunch hour was over and most everyone had already returned to work.

"I hope I haven't ruined your afternoon plans, Stella," John said.

"Not at all," she replied. "I hadn't planned on doing anything except enjoying the afternoon and relaxing. Do you have something in mind?" she asked.

"Well, I was hoping we could sit and talk, somewhere. I'd like you to tell me what you remember about Alex after his return home," he replied.

"If you'd like, we can go to my place."

"That'd be great."

Stella kept hold of John's arm as they slowly walked up 96th Street towards Park Avenue.

"That was a rather interesting way of leaving a tip," Stella said as she turned her head to look at John. "I don't think Regina will ever forget that moment. I only wish I had a camera to capture the look of utter surprise at the sight of the $20 bill in her hand."

"I thought so, too. It's always a pleasure to make someone's day a bit brighter and I wanted her to know that I was sincere about returning to the restaurant."

* * * * * * * * * * * * * * * *

The pedestrian light had just turned red when they reached the corner of 94th Street and Park Avenue. There wasn't a lot of vehicle traffic and they could have easily crossed the street, but something told John to wait for the light to turn green. A young couple, in their early 20s, was standing alongside them. John could see, from the corner of his eye that the woman was staring at him with a quizzical facial expression. It was as if she was looking at a living ghost standing on the street corner. John turned his head and smiled at her. The young woman then began forcefully tugging the man's arm as she turned her head to whisper something in his ear. As she did this, he, too, looked over towards John.

Without missing a beat, John said to them, “Good afternoon, folks. It’s a beautiful day, isn’t it?”

“Say … you’re that magician guy,” the young man said. “I’ve seen you on television; you do some really wild stuff, man. Could you do something for me and my girl?”

The pedestrian light changed to green and the vehicle traffic on Park Avenue began to move once again. John and Stella remained on the corner; he had a captive audience. It would be rude to disappoint them.

“Certainly, thanks for asking,” John replied. “Let’s see, I think I have something right here.”

John reached into his pants pocket and withdrew a half-dollar and a quarter. He placed them in his open hand and pointed to the half-dollar.

“Here’s a coin that shows up in cash registers every so often,” he said as he pointed to the large coin. “The quarter, on the other hand, is much more common and it’s also what we use to keep the vending machine owners in business.”

John closed his hand around the two coins forming a slightly loose fist and then turned his hand palm-down. With his other hand, he reached into his fist, withdrew the half-dollar and placed it into his pants pocket.

“If you were watching closely,” John said, “you know what coin is in my closed hand.”

“Of course; it’s the quarter,” the guy said.

“You’re absolutely correct,” John replied as he turned his hand over and slowly opened it, showing the coin. “Now that you know what to look for, let’s try this again.”

John removed the half-dollar from his pants pocket.

“Tell you what,” he said, “I’m going to try and confuse you this time.”

John closed his hand into a fist once again, but this time he removed the quarter and placed it in his pants pocket.

“What’s in my hand now?” John asked.

“The half-dollar,” the young couple said in unison.

John opened his hand – both coins were there.

"I saw you put the quarter in your pocket and your hand was empty," the guy said. "I don't know how that quarter got back there."

John had a look of astonishment on his face.

"Hmm, that's never happened before," John said. "Maybe I should try this again."

John closed his hand into a fist and turned it palm-down, again.

"Let me get rid of the half-dollar," John said.

He withdrew the coin and placed it in his pants pocket.

"I think this coin is throwing me off track."

Before John had a chance to say anything, the young woman exclaimed, "The quarter is in your hand. I just saw it there!"

"That's quite profound," John replied.

He turned his hand over and then slowly opened it – it was empty.

"I've nothing in my hand," John said, as he showed both his hands empty.

"Whoa; where'd they go?" the guy asked.

"The quarter, sir, is right here," John said, as he plucked it from the girl's ear.

As soon as he did that the young man immediately raised his hands to both his ears, feeling for the other coin. John placed the quarter into his pocket.

"Unfortunately, the half-dollar is playing hide and seek, as usual," John said to them.

He reached behind his own elbow and slowly brought it into view.

"Ah, here it is," he said.

John tossed the coin into his other hand where it instantly vanished. He again showed his hands empty.

"Dude," the guy said, "you're amazing. Thanks."

"My pleasure," John replied, as they shook hands.

When the light changed to green again, Stella and John crossed the street. The young couple remained on the corner; they were still talking about the coin trick they had just seen.

"Do you know what's going to be even more amazing?" John said to Stella.

"No, what's that?" she asked.

"The expression on the young man's face the next time he reaches into his pants pocket and finds the half-dollar."

Stella burst into laughter.

"You really are something," she said.

"Gee, I'm glad you noticed," John answered.

CHAPTER SIXTEEN

"Come in and make your self at home," Stella said, as she opened the door to her apartment.

There was a small hallway behind the front door with a closet on each side. The hallway led directly into a spacious living room that was conservatively decorated. The furniture included a sofa, loveseat, recliner, coffee table and two end tables with lamps. Two original, contemporary oil paintings of Manhattan, with matching frames, hung on the wall.

"You've moved since the last time we got together," John said.

"I did. I had a one-bedroom apartment down the other end of the hallway," Stella replied. "When I found out this one was coming available, I made arrangements with the landlord to move into this apartment.

"I like it," John said, looking around.

"Let me give you the 50-cent tour."

"Lead the way," John replied.

From the living room they walked down the main hallway. Entrances to all the rooms were to the right. The first room they came to was the kitchen. Aside from the usual appliances, there was a table that comfortably sat four people. They went in and Stella placed her purse on the table.

"I bought a 15-inch television that conveniently fit in the corner on the far counter so I could watch the news while cooking and eating," she said.

They left the kitchen and walked a few feet down the hall to the next room, which, obviously, was meant to be a second bedroom. Unlike the kitchen, which had no door, the door to this room was kept open. Stella used it as her home office. In the far left corner of the room was a bookcase; a computer hutch and executive chair were to the left of the door. A futon couch and an end table rested against the right wall.

"This is my quiet hideaway," Stella said, as she and John entered the room.

Pictures of Stella's parents, her Aunt and Uncle, and Alex were hung on the wall above the futon. On the top shelf of the computer hutch sat a framed and autographed picture of a young John Michaels.

"I guess I owe you a more up-to-date photograph," John teasingly said. "This one is quite dated."

"Other than some gray hair and a few extra pounds, you still look the same," Stella replied.

"Flattery will get you everywhere!" John mischievously answered. "This time I'll bring the photograph in person."

"I'm going to hold you to that," Stella replied.

They stepped back out into the hallway.

"The next room is a bathroom and the last room," she said as she pointed towards the closed door, "is the master bedroom, which also has a full bathroom. It's not a Park Avenue CEO's suite, but its home and that's all that matters to me."

They turned around and headed back towards the living room, stopping in front of the kitchen. Do you want to sit in the kitchen or living room," she asked.

"Whichever is more comfortable for you," John replied.

"Let's sit in the living room. Do you want something to drink?" she asked. "I can make some coffee or you can have soda, grapefruit juice or bottled water. Which would you like?"

"Juice," John said.

Stella opened the refrigerator door and took out two, 20-ounce bottles.

"Here you are," she said, as she handed them to him.

She then opened a counter drawer and pulled out two coasters.

"We're off to the living room," Stella said. "Where do we start?" Stella asked, as she and John settled at opposite ends of the couch.

"At the beginning, of course," John replied.

"You haven't lost your knack for one-liners."

"I learned from the funniest guy in Catholic High."

"You mean Drew Wagner?"

"Yes."

"I figured as much."

"So which is better, the one-liners or the magic?" John asked.

"So far – the magic is in the lead!"

"Okay, I can take a hint when I hear it," and they both started to laugh.

John intentionally chose not to drudge up the war or his time in Vietnam. As far as he was concerned, he had no regrets about serving his country and if he had to do it again he wouldn't have changed a thing. Instead he talked extensively about life on the road as a full-time professional magician. Most of what he told Stella, she already knew from his letters. Still, though, she sat attentively and occasionally asked questions.

"During the early 1900s, the big traveling magic shows would typically take the entire summer off to rest, and refurbish the tons of equipment that were toted all over the United States and around the world. In addition, it was also a time to build new illusions and rehearse them in preparation for the 'new season's show' that began each September. We were on the road continuously, which, if you think about it, was good because it told us that people were willing to pay to see an entertaining show. And, as you know, we did have some off time, but not a complete summer."

"I always looked forward to seeing you during those short visits," Stella said.

"Me, too," John replied.

He paused a moment and then continued.

"In order to stay one step ahead of the competition, I learned to develop new material all the time and then rehearse things after the last show was over and the audience had gone home. It sometimes made for long days, but having a great crew made it all the more worthwhile. It also helps if you're having fun and we never looked at the job as 'real work.' But, when all is said and done, it was very much real, hard work."

"So why did you retire if you liked what you were doing?" Stella asked.

"I don't need the money," John replied. "I'm lucky to have found a financial manager/adviser whom I could trust to make some wise investments for me and my crew, over the years. Sure, we could have continued on for another 20 years or more, but we've worked hard, and it was time for us to sit back and enjoy the success of our work."

"What about your crew, are they okay with your decision?"

"It wasn't just my decision, it was a group decision. About three years ago, during one of our few breaks in touring, we had our annual meeting with our financial manager. After he left, I said to my crew 'What's your thoughts on us doing another three touring seasons and then calling it quits?' They asked me how soon I wanted an answer and I told them to take as much time as they needed. After all, this was not something as simple as saying yes or no. It was a major decision and I didn't want to do this without their approval."

"Evidently, they all agreed."

"Yes, they did. But not before conferring with their respective spouses."

"What would you have done if they said they wanted to continue touring?"

"We would have continued."

"After this show will you ever perform again?" Stella asked.

"Most certainly, but not as grandiose as in years' past. I love 'close-up magic,' which involves magic with cards, coins and other small items because it relies strictly on my persona to entertain people. It's a different genre than being on stage with tons of equipment."

"You mean like the magic you did for Regina and that young couple on the street corner?"

"Exactly."

"Will you ever do a big show again?"

"By all means, but only for special occasions."

"Like this reunion."

"Yes."

He took the last swig of juice and recapped the bottle.

"Do you want some more?" Stella asked.

"No, I'm fine, for now," John replied. "I've been talking long enough; it's your turn now."

Stella shifted positions on the couch, placing one leg under the other and putting a pillow behind her back.

"As you may remember, about three months after Alex was drafted, I got a job as a bank teller at First Merchants Bank and Trust Company through my friend, Susan Maynard, who was working at the 116th Street Branch."

"Do I know Susan?" John asked. "That name sounds familiar."

"I introduced her to you at my senior prom. She was dating a basketball player from Capital High School."

"Oh yeah, I remember her now. Sorry, I didn't mean to interrupt you."

"That's okay."

She paused a moment and then continued.

"I thought I was in hog heaven," Stella said. "I was earning $20 a day; $100 a week before taxes. My take-home pay was $150 every two weeks. After I had been on the job for about a year and had saved a few hundred dollars, I decided it was time to move out on my own. Needless to say, Mom had mixed feelings about me leaving. She was always saying 'A young lady should stay at home until she's married.' Dad, on the other hand, said I could live at home as long as I wanted to, but he understood that there would come a time when I would want to stretch my wings and go it alone. Of course, that didn't sit well with Mom and I'm sure he caught hell for it on a few occasions. Mom reluctantly gave in. Once I got their approval, I earnestly started looking for an apartment close to the bank. It didn't take long for me to find this place. I was quite surprised when the landlord told me the rent would be $65 a month. The electricity, at the time, was never more than $10, which together equaled one week of pay after taxes. With the apartment being so close to work, I didn't have to budget for transportation. The only other major expenses I had were for a phone and food."

"Even I caught some grief when I told my folks that I was going to stay in Virginia Beach after being discharged from the Army to pursue a full-time career as a magician," John said. "I'm sorry; that's twice that I've interrupted you."

"That's all right; I'm glad to know that it wasn't only me. I've done well over the years and learned how, and where, to invest my money. And, I worked my way up from teller to Assistant Branch Manager, my current job."

Stella paused and took a sip of juice. For the first time since meeting earlier in the day, they sat in complete silence for what seemed like an eternity. Finally, John spoke up.

"So what can you tell me about Alex? How long after he returned did you see him? Did he seem upbeat about being home for good or did he look depressed? Did he look for work right away?"

"The first weekend he was home, he, Aunt Mary and Uncle Sid came up to the Bronx to visit my folks. I arrived shortly after they did. We had lunch and talked about things in general."

"Did he talk about the war or Vietnam, at all?" John asked.

"No. In fact, the war never came up at all. You would have thought it was a taboo subject. I guess we were just grateful he came back in one piece and rather than dwell on what could have been, we simply avoided it all together."

"Considering that the war was a hot-bed issue, it was just as well to not ask questions," John said.

"I did ask him if he had seen you and he mentioned that you both crossed paths a few times and were able to talk for a few minutes. Was I wrong to not ask about the war?"

"No; not at all. Some people experience flashbacks and some don't. Some handle it easily and others, not so easily. That's why I asked you about his demeanor."

"Alex called me the following week saying that he needed to get a certified copy of his discharge paper for the employment office. He came to the bank and I had another bank teller copy and certify the paper, and then we went around the corner to a place called Jim's Sandwich Shop to have lunch."

"Was he talkative or quiet and did you notice anything unusual?"

"Thinking back, I don't remember him being any different, other than he was constantly shifting his eyes back and forth as he ate. I asked him if something was wrong and he apologized saying it was just a habit he picked up from the war. I didn't pursue the issue as I assumed he may not have wanted to talk about it so I let it go."

"That was nothing unusual. I found myself doing the same thing: constantly looking over my shoulder after I left 'Nam. It took a few months for me to stop."

"Let me get you some more juice before I relate the rest of the story," she said.

"Why do I sense that the other shoe is about ready to drop?" John asked.

"Because it is," Stella replied. "But, hold on for just a moment."

When Stella returned, she was carrying a yellowed, letter-sized envelope. After placing it on the coffee table, she sat down, uncapped her bottle, took a small sip, then took in a deep breath of air and slowly exhaled.

"Well," she started....

CHAPTER SEVENTEEN

"Alex told me that he had saved enough money to last him about a year, in case he couldn't find a job right away. His plan, after we left the sandwich shop that first day, was to return to the employment office to drop off his paperwork. He had also decided to wait till Monday of the following week, before he went back there, to meet with an employment specialist. I called him on that Monday evening to ask how things went. He said everything went well and that he was asked about his military job. I think he referred to it as his 'MOS;' does that mean anything to you?"

"Yes. MOS stands for Military Occupational Specialty; it's how the Army classifies the different jobs its soldiers do," John replied.

"He said they also asked him what other types of jobs he did while in the Army. I don't know what he told the interviewer because I didn't ask. Alex said they spent an hour reviewing his paperwork and asking questions. He was then given instructions on his obligations to look for work and how to file for his weekly unemployment compensation. We talked three to four days each week during the first month he was back and we'd also meet at Jim's Sandwich Shop every Thursday for lunch. I couldn't get him to go anywhere else. He was smitten with Julie, a friend of mine who worked there. My hunch was confirmed when he called one evening to ask me for a recommendation for a restaurant. I guess they had been dating about five or six weeks, by then. I was happy for him; he and Julie made a great couple."

"You mentioned talking with him numerous times each week during the first month."

"Yes."

"Did he just stop calling after that first month? Or do you think he started to feel more comfortable and he simply decided to reduce the calls?" John asked.

"Oh, no; we usually spoke on the phone twice a week. And, yes, I think he was beginning to feel comfortable about being home, for good."

"Well, that's a good sign," John said.

"Throughout the summer months, Alex, Uncle Sid and Aunt Mary would visit my folks, or vice-versa. Sometimes it was for lunch and other times, dinner. I think it was early July when, at the behest of Aunt Mary, Alex finally brought Julie to my folks' house for Saturday lunch. She really hit it off with everyone.

"I called Julie one Friday evening in late July and asked if she wanted to go with me to Kleins the following day. I told her I was in a clothes-shopping mood and I didn't think Alex would want to tag along with me as I walked the aisles and searched through the endless racks of clothes. She said that she had no plans till later that evening and I told her we'd be back in the early afternoon. I also told her I'd call Alex to let him know that 'the girls were going shopping.' Julie and I had a great time and she confided in me that she really liked Alex, and so did her parents. I told her that we thought the world of her, too.

"It was a great summer and for the Labor Day weekend we decided to have a family outing at Bear Mountain. We also invited Julie and her parents. Although I had met Julie's parents once before, this was the first time all the parents met. Had I not known better, I would have sworn that they all knew each other. The six of them were like old college friends who had decided to get together to reminisce about their college years.

"The day after Labor Day, Alex interviewed for a job as a courier. The job lead, he said, came from the employment specialist who was handling his case file. Alex called me after the interview was over and I asked him how things went and what the job entailed. He said the interview went extremely well and that, if hired, he would be delivering and picking up documents for various law offices, among other places, throughout the city, but primarily in and around Manhattan. Because the documents were, at times, extremely sensitive in nature, the company wanted a mature individual.

"On Thursday of that week, he called to tell me that the company offered him the job and that he would be starting work in two weeks."

"How did he react, knowing that he had gotten the job?" John asked.

"He sounded excited and was looking forward to joining the civilian work force. I then reminded him to call the employment specialist to let him know that he was hired."

"Did he?"

"Yes. The employment specialist told him that until he actually started working, he should continue to file for unemployment benefits. The following day, Alex called me at home and said he wanted to have a small celebration party in honor of him getting a job. I told him that I thought it was a wonderful idea and asked where he planned to have this get-together. He said he wanted to have it at The Trolley Car the very next night – Saturday. It would just be the three of us: me, Julie and Alex. I asked him what time and he said 8:00 p.m."

* * * * * * * * * * * * * * *

Without any formal warning, Stella stopped talking. She reached over and picked up the juice bottle and took another sip. She held onto the bottle, staring at it, deep in thought. John sat in silence, watching Stella's body language. He sensed that the other shoe was about ready to drop with a loud and thunderous thud. Stella took another sip and as she recapped the bottle she slowly took in another deep breath of air, and with one big push emptied her lungs.

"I'm sorry," she said.

"That's quite all right," John answered, as he moved closer to her on the couch.

He gently took hold of her hand; he could see that she was trying to control her emotions and not cry.

"Things were going so well," she began, "and then the bottom fell out and our world came crashing down."

She took another deep breath of air and then picked up the yellowed envelope on the coffee table.

"We never made it to the bar, that Saturday night," she said.

She opened the envelope and pulled out the folded, yellowed piece of paper.

The headline read: DRUNK DRIVER RAMS INTO MANHATTAN NEWSTAND: FOUR DEAD.

Before John had a chance to read the story, Stella burst into tears. He took the envelope and paper from her hand and placed it back on the coffee table. Then he put his arms around Stella and drew her close to him.

"Its okay, Stella," John whispered. "Its okay."

A few moments had passed before Stella was able to compose herself.

"I'm so sorry," she said.

"You don't need to apologize," he calmly said. "I can certainly understand your grief, all these years later."

Stella picked up the paper and gave it to John.

"This pretty much sums up what happened." She stood up and said, "Excuse, me; I'll be right back."

John stood up, too, and after she left the living room he sat back down. He carefully unfolded the paper and read the newspaper clipping.

Sid and Mary Holloman had just stopped at Ken Allen's newsstand, on the corner of 57th Street, on Saturday, September 8th, when a car suddenly veered off Second Avenue and crashed into the wooden newsstand.

Several witnesses stated that the driver had been driving erratically on Second Avenue for at least two miles. These other drivers watched the car weave into and out of its lane and eventually sideswipe a Yellow Cab that was double-parked on 52nd Street.

Bystanders said the driver then gunned the accelerator and sped off.

A few moments later, the driver lost control of his car, as he attempted to make a left turn onto 57th Street, and slammed head-on into the newsstand, instantly killing the owner, Ken Allen, and Mr. and Mrs. Holloman, who had just stopped to buy a newspaper.

After it demolished the newsstand, the car then crashed into the outside wall of the Lodestar Building.

The driver, who was not wearing his seat belt, was thrown through the front windshield from the force of the impact.

He, too, was pronounced dead at the scene.

John felt like someone had just sucker-punched him in the stomach, leaving him gasping for air. His hands were shaking as he carefully replaced the article in the envelope. He was numb. When Stella finally returned to the living room, she sat back down on the couch alongside John.

"Sad, isn't it? They never had a chance; they didn't deserve to die so tragically."

Words and thoughts were racing through John's mind, but none settled down long enough for him to utter a coherent sentence.

"Good gracious, what's this world coming to?" John suddenly said with exasperation. "For the life of me, I'll never understand why the lives of innocent people are needlessly snuffed out by irresponsible people who are incapable of rationale conduct."

Stella waited a moment before speaking again.

"It was about 7 p.m. when the phone rang. It was Alex. When I heard his voice, the first thing that came to mind was that he was going to tell me that he and Julie would be arriving later than the agreed upon time. He said my name and then for no reason he just stopped talking. At that point, I knew something was wrong. I thought he was suffering a flashback of some sort. In all the time he was back, Alex never once said anything about having one and if it did happen, he certainly didn't tell anyone. Alex was grasping for words and I was unable to piece together what he was saying. Finally, he blurted out that there was a NYPD Chaplain at the house who had told him that his parents were killed in a car crash at approximately 5:30 p.m.

"I was horrified. I asked Alex to tell me exactly what the officer said and all I was able to understand was that he wanted me to meet him at the 96th Street subway station. I asked the same question again and got the same answer. I wasn't sure what to do so I asked Alex to let me speak with the police officer, but Alex began mumbling something unintelligible. I was frantic; I thought for sure that Alex had gone off the deep end. Suddenly, the next thing I knew, the Police Chaplain was talking to me on the phone. He asked where I lived. I told him and he said to wait for him in front of the apartment building; he and Alex would be there in five minutes to pick me up. I thanked him and then hung up. I didn't have time to call my folks to let them know, or to call Julie.

"When we reached 57th and Second Avenue, the area was roped off with yellow warning tape. The police had already closed down 57th Street from Third Avenue to First Avenue so they could safely conduct the homicide investigation. The police cruiser we were in pulled up alongside another cruiser and after the two officers spoke we were ushered into the crime scene area. We parked about 25 feet away. Before we got out of the car, the Chaplain turned around to face us and asked that we not touch anything within the crime scene. We both nodded our heads acknowledging his instructions.

"The Chaplain, Alex and I walked in silence and as we got closer we could see that the car had already been moved back from the wall to allow the city's emergency medical response team access to the bodies. All four victims had already been taken to the morgue. A pile of crushed and broken wood was the only thing left of the newsstand; newspapers and magazines were scattered everywhere. As we watched the ongoing investigation, a Police Captain came over to speak with us. I remember him expressing his sympathy for our loss and saying that he needed a few more minutes before he would be able to tell us what had transpired.

"Within minutes of our arrival, a television crew and a newspaper reporter had also arrived and were given very limited access to the scene. I wanted desperately to call my folks to tell them before they heard it on the late news or someone else called them. I knew Mom and Dad would ask questions so it was important for me to wait until the Police Captain briefed us. I explained my dilemma to the Chaplain and asked him to run interference for me so that we got the information first. He said he would do his best and thankfully he was able to pull it off.

"After the Police Captain gave us a run down on the events that lead up to the crash, I told Alex to hold down the fort while I called Mom and Dad. Alex told me to take my time, there was nothing anyone could do and that he'd be here when I returned. As I turned around to leave, he also asked me to call Julie and tell her. I said I would.

"I guess the sound of my voice alerted Dad because when he answered the phone he immediately asked me if I was all right. They only had one phone jack in the house so I had to ask him to hold the phone receiver so both he and Mom could hear me. Mom broke down first and Dad quickly followed. John, it was the hardest thing I've ever had to do. A few minutes had passed before Dad was able to speak. He said they would leave right away. I told him the area was roped off and that there is no place to park so he said they would take the subway.

"I then called Julie. She, too, took it bad and said that if we needed anything to let her know. I thanked her and then told her that either Alex or I would call as soon as possible. By the time I got back to Alex, the television crew was talking to the police. They respected our privacy and chose not to ask us anything.

"Thinking back on it today, I'm not sure what Alex would have said to them if they had approached us. I could tell by the way he was mumbling under his breath and his sudden fidgeting that this was affecting his psyche. From that day on, Alex wasn't the same person. When Uncle Sid and Aunt Mary died, I think a part of Alex died with them."

John wanted to ask some questions, but didn't know where to begin. He'd open his mouth, as if to talk, but nothing came out.

Stella sensed his frustration, so she tried to lighten things by saying, "John Michaels, I never thought I'd see the day when you had nothing to say!"

"I'm just struggling to make sense of it all."

"I know; it's overwhelming, isn't it," she replied.

"What happened after the funeral services?" John asked. "Did Alex still seem lost and without purpose or did he snap back into reality?"

"I would say that it was a little bit of both. Some days were better than others. I made it a point to call him every other day, and Mom or Dad would call him on weekends."

"You mentioned that some days were better than others. Can you give me an example of what you mean?" John asked.

"I'd stop by the apartment after work and he would simply sit and say nothing."

"It sounds like he was in a recurring state of depression and a feeling of helplessness."

"I'd constantly make an excuse to get him to accompany me someplace. I just wanted him to get out of the house and leave the memories behind."

"How long did this go on?"

"About four or five weeks had passed before I started to see a positive change in his demeanor. I guess he finally realized that there was no changing the past and that he had to move forward."

* * * * * * * * * * * * * * *

They had been talking for a few hours when John suddenly realized that it was almost 6 p.m. He asked Stella if she wanted to go to a restaurant to have dinner.

"Would you mind if I cooked dinner, instead of us going out to eat?" she asked.

"Only if I can help," he replied.

"Certainly," she answered.

"Before we start, can I use your phone? I want to call the hotel to see if I have any messages."

"There's a phone in the kitchen."

There were no messages.

"How does chicken stir-fry, baked potato and salad sound for dinner?" she asked.

"Great!" he exclaimed. "What can I do to help?"

"I'll make the stir-fry," she said. "I'll let you take care of getting the potatoes ready for the microwave oven and preparing the salad. If you need something, let me know and I'll tell you where it's at."

"If you don't mind I'd like to talk some more about Alex."

"Fire away," she said.

"I'm estimating that it was now a few weeks before Thanksgiving, when you said that Alex started to come around."

"That sounds about right."

"Did he continue to work while all this was going on?"

"Yes."

"Did he ever say that he didn't like the job or that he wanted to change career fields?"

"No, he didn't. He told me that it wasn't hard work and there was a lot of potential for advancement. Why do you ask?"

"If he hated the job then that would have compounded his emotional state of mind. Was there any change that you know of, with his relationship with Julie?"

"I didn't notice anything different and Julie never said anything to me. From what I remember, she continued to be very supportive. I think she knew it was going to be rough-going for a while. I'm sure she would have confided in me had there been a change, however slight."

"Are you sure?"

"Yes."

"Where did Alex spend Thanksgiving?"

"It's ironic that you ask about that. We've always had Thanksgiving Dinner just like any other day; around 6:00 p.m. Julie's folks had their holiday meal around noontime. Alex went to Julie's house first and then she and Alex came over to my parents' house."

"Anything unusual happen?"

"Now that you mention it, I remember him saying that he was thinking of getting new furniture and he asked my folks if they wanted anything that belonged to his parents."

"Mom and Dad both said no; then he asked me the same question. I also said no. Alex then said that he was going to call the Salvation Army and donate the stuff."

"What did your parents say about that?"

"My father said it was an excellent idea."

"Do you remember when that may have happened?"

"It's been so long ago … perhaps mid-December time-frame, I think. Why do you ask?"

John had just finished making a salad of lettuce, tomatoes, scallions, carrots, and green and red peppers, with oil and vinegar dressing, when the microwave started beeping. After he placed the salad on the kitchen table, Stella had John set the table. She pointed to the kitchen cabinet where he would find the dishes and glasses, and the drawer with the silverware.

"I've a hunch," he replied, "but the wonderful aroma of stir-fry is causing my taste buds to salivate. Let's eat before I get carried away with questions and the food gets cold."

Stella turned on the television set and they listened to the evening news while they ate dinner. Stella was an excellent cook and John complimented her on her culinary skills.

"Trust me," she said, "while I like to cook, I do have to work out every day otherwise I'll expand like a balloon. Would you like some more?"

"No, thanks."

"How about some coffee?"

"That'll be great," he said.

While Stella made coffee, John cleared the table and began washing dishes. There was some salad and stir-fry left, so Stella retrieved two microwavable bowls from a kitchen cabinet.

"Looks like I have some lunch for tomorrow," she said, as she filled the two bowls.

When the evening news ended, Stella turned off the television set.

"Tell me about this hunch of yours," she said, as she poured two cups of coffee.

"One more question first," he replied.

"Go for it."

"Would you happen to know when your Aunt and Uncle's apartment lease expired?" he asked.

"No, why?"

"My hunch is that Alex called the landlord to tell him about the death of his parents. It's possible that the landlord may have then asked Alex what his plans were for the continued rental of the apartment. If Alex were going to stay there, the landlord would probably have wanted him to sign the lease. I think Alex then asked when the lease expired and I'm willing to wager that it was December 31st. Alex probably told the landlord that he wanted to stay till the end of the year and offered to pay the landlord the remainder of the rent through December. Alex had the money, so that wasn't an issue for him."

"And the landlord agreed?" Stella asked.

"Of course. If afforded the landlord 'piece of mind' to know that he's going to get his rent money and not have the tenant skip out in the middle of the night."

"Alex would have never done that," Stella said.

"You and I know that, Stella, but landlords don't see things that way. Their mindset is in dollars and cents, and a balance sheet that balances every month."

"You're right."

"Besides, this also gave the landlord enough time, roughly two and one-half months, to list the place and find a tenant."

"But why move?"

"That's the tough part and something I can only speculate on, from what you mentioned earlier. Here's what I'm thinking. I imagine that coming home everyday to an empty apartment only served to remind him of his parents. I think he wanted ... no; he needed to make a fresh start, someplace else. It would be the only way for him to conquer his anger, over the loss of his parents. I don't think Alex would have left home until he was ready to settle down, but this unfortunate turn of events forced his hand."

The look on Stella's face told John that she thought his theory was quite plausible.

"Did you do anything special for New Year's Eve," he asked.

"He and Julie came over to my house to help ring in the New Year."

"I presume they didn't stay the night, then."

"No. Alex would never keep Julie out all night, that wasn't his style. They left shortly after 1 a.m."

"Alex probably took Julie home, promised to call her later that day or the following day and then disappeared into the night."

"Your theory," she said, "is quite profound. Let me tell you why. I was surprised when Julie called me two days into the New Year to ask if I had heard from, or seen, Alex. I told her I didn't, but that I would stop by the apartment to check on him. She told me that she had just come from there, which was why she was calling me. She was startled to see the apartment door wide open and the place empty. She knocked loudly and within moments a painter came to the door. After talking with the guy, she realized he knew nothing about Alex; his instructions were to paint the place.

"I then reminded Julie that Alex had planned to donate all the old furniture before he bought new stuff. She remembered the conversation, but then said that Alex's phone was disconnected; that's the reason she went over to his apartment. When Julie told me about the phone, I was mad as hell at Alex."

Stella got up from the table, picked up John's cup, walked over to the coffee pot and refilled his cup. The somewhat blank expression on her face told him that she was trying to logically piece together everything John had said along with the information she already knew.

After she realized what she was doing, Stella said, "I'm sorry; did you want more coffee?"

"Sure," John replied, "why not?" And they both began to laugh.

John paused a moment and then continued.

"I believe Alex knew that neither you nor your parents would want any of the furniture," John continued. "There was also a possibility that he would not have been able to sell it all in a reasonable time, hence the reason to call the Salvation Army. Their schedule would be flexible enough to enable Alex to offload everything all at once and at his convenience."

"Like a weekend?" Stella asked.

"Exactly," John answered.

"You know, it's all starting to make sense now," Stella blurted out. "It was the weekend before New Year's Eve."

"What happened that weekend, Stella," John asked.

"I had planned on going up to see my folks that Saturday and I called Alex on Thursday evening to ask him if he wanted to go. I told him that I would come by the apartment to pick him up."

"What did he say?"

"He told me that his boss asked if he would be interested in working on Saturday and Sunday, for overtime pay."

"Did he say how long he would have to work or what hours it encompassed?"

"No, he didn't. I automatically assumed it was all-day."

"What else did he tell you?"

"That this overtime work was for a high-profile client of the company. The job needed to be done over the weekend because it was so close to the end of the calendar year."

"I'm sure he told Julie the same story so that neither you nor her would call or come by the apartment that weekend."

"You're absolutely right," Stella said. "I didn't go by there at all. In fact, the next time I saw Alex was New Year's Eve. It never dawned on me to ask him about his overtime work, and I don't think Julie asked either."

"He was probably hoping that you both forgot about it, which is what it sounds like."

"So why didn't he say anything to me, my parents or even Julie, that he was moving out of the apartment?" Stella asked.

"I don't have an answer for that; only Alex knows. Personally, if he were to walk in the door right now, I wouldn't ask him. I'd let him make the first move rather than drudge up the past. Do I think he could have done things differently? Certainly. We've all done things that, in hindsight, we wish had never happened. Unfortunately, we can't go back in time. All we can do is learn from our mistakes and hope that we've learned what not to do the next time."

"Where do you think he went?" Stella asked.

"That's a good question. My gut feeling is that he never left the city."

"I can't believe that he's managed to hide for the past twenty-some-odd years and no one has seen or found him."

"It's a big city," John replied. "Those who don't want to be found won't be found."

"Isn't that the truth!"

"Can I ask a few more questions?"

"Of course."

"When you found out that Alex had the phone service disconnected, did you call the phone company to see if they would give you any information?"

"As a matter of fact, I did. I called as a representative of the bank, making some flimsy excuse, but wanting to know if Alex had given them a forwarding address."

"What did they tell you?"

"That he didn't."

"What about the landlord? Were you able to speak with him?"

"I didn't know who the landlord was; still don't for that matter. The day after Julie told me about the painters I went over to the apartment, hoping to speak with one of them. I was going to ask for the name of their company and then call their office. I thought that once I explained why I was looking for the landlord they would give me his name and phone number. It was a good plan, but by the time I got to the apartment there was no one there. I went back the following day, during my lunch hour. Unfortunately, they had already finished the job and were long gone."

Stella stared at John for a moment as if she was reading his mind.

"As many times as I've visited Alex, I didn't know any of the other tenants in the apartment building so I didn't feel right knocking on someone's door. I'm positive my parents didn't know who the landlord was, nor did they know anyone else in the building."

"Did Alex ever tell you the name of the company he worked for?"

"No, he didn't. I only remember him telling me it was a courier job."

"A lot of companies use couriers to make deliveries around town. He could have worked for a bank, an advertising firm, a courier firm or a lawyer's office just to name a few. Oh well, it was a shot in the dark," John said.

"In hindsight, I should have sent him a postcard, knowing that it would have been forwarded, asking him to call me."

"Why didn't you?"

"I was really pissed off at him for leaving without saying anything, especially to me. We were close; I thought he'd feel comfortable talking to me if there was a problem. I guess I was mistaken."

"I don't think you were wrong, in fact, under the circumstances, I would have felt the same way. I think Alex may have needlessly put a lot of the blame on himself. Think about it, for a moment. He's drafted into the Army and goes away for two years. Then, less than six months after he returns home, his parents are accidentally killed while stopping to buy a newspaper on a city street corner. That's an awful lot of stress to deal with."

"You're right," Stella said. "I didn't think about if from that aspect."

John finished his coffee and looked at his watch; it was just after 9 p.m.

"Stella," he said, "it's getting late. I'm sure you've got to get up early for work tomorrow and I need to return to Northern Virginia tomorrow morning. I rented a hotel room in Arlington for four days and wound up only spending one day there. I need to officially check out and give them back their room key.

"I plan on catching the afternoon shuttle from Reagan National to Norfolk International and then spend the next few days rehearsing the show with my crew. I'll call you tomorrow night, about 7 p.m."

"What about your hotel room here?" she asked.

"I'm going to speak with the night manager as soon as I get back there tonight. If they'll let me keep the tab running, that'll be fine. If not, I'll check out tomorrow morning and then make a reservation for a room when I return in a few days," he replied. "If I'm going to find Alex, I'll need to do it here in the city."

They walked to the door, holding hands. When they got there he turned to Stella and said, "Thanks for having me over and for a great dinner."

"I wouldn't have had it any other way," she said.

She had a twinkle in her eyes and a smile that could brighten a dark room.

"I promise I'll call you."

"You better!" she said, and then started to laugh.

With his other hand he pulled her close. "Yes ma'am," he said, and then he leaned forward and gave her a tender kiss goodnight.

* * * * * * * * * * * * * * *

The night manager told John it would not be a problem if he wanted to keep the room, but he strongly suggested that he check out in the morning and then make another reservation before leaving the hotel. John thanked him for his frankness and went up to his room. The following morning he called Dave.

"Morning, Dave."

"Hey, John; what's going on?"

"I'm checking out of the hotel in a few minutes and returning to Arlington. I've got to check out of the Commodore Virginia Hotel. I've a late afternoon flight from Reagan International to Norfolk International."

"Do you need a ride from the airport?"

"No, thanks. I'm going to take the airport's limo service."

"Anything I can do in the meantime?"

"Yes. Call Patty, Sally and Maria and let them know that I'd like to do rehearsals tomorrow, Thursday and Friday."

"What time do you want to start?"

"9 o'clock."

"Okay."

"Thanks, Dave; see you tomorrow."

"Bye, John."

* * * * * * * * * * * * * * *

It was almost 7 p.m. when he arrived back in Virginia Beach, tired and hungry. There were no voice messages for him to listen to, but he did have a small stack of mail on the kitchen table.

He did a cursory look to see what he had and then tossed the junk into the trash bin. Nothing important stood out, so he brought what was left of the mail into his office and placed it on his desk. He'd take care of it first thing in the morning.

Stella answered the phone after it rang the second time.

"Hello, Stella," he said.

"Hey, John; did you just get home?" she asked.

"I literally walked in 5 minutes ago," he answered.

"Did you have any problem with the hotels?"

"No. The night manager recommended I check out and make another reservation, so that's what I did. As for the hotel in Arlington, they didn't say anything about my three-day absence."

"So what's your schedule looking like?"

"Tomorrow, Thursday and Friday my crew and I will be rehearsing the show and then we'll pack it up in preparation for the trip to the city, early the following week. I plan on arriving back in New York late Saturday morning and relaxing over the weekend. Then, on Monday of that week I'll start looking for Alex. I'll only have a few days to try and find him. If you've nothing planned, would you be interested in dinner and a Broadway show on Saturday night?" he asked.

"That'll be great," she said.

"Anything particular you'd like to see?"

"No; surprise me," she said.

"Okay, I'll see what I can conjure up!"

They talked for another 30 minutes before saying good-night. John told her that rehearsals might run late on Thursday, especially since they created a brand new illusion for this show and they may need to work some of the bugs out of it. But, he promised to call her on Wednesday and Friday evening, no matter what.

CHAPTER EIGHTEEN

October 31, 1973

By the end of October, Alex hadn't gotten over the loss of his parents. Every time he returned to the apartment, the memory of his parents being crushed to death by a callous driver came crashing through his makeshift defenses. He was distraught by these endless flashbacks and desperately needed to vent his anger, but he couldn't bring himself to talk to anyone about it. So he kept his feelings tightly bundled up deep inside the furthermost corner of his mind and put up a façade hoping that no one would see through it. It was the wrong thing to do.

As the Thanksgiving holiday drew closer, Alex fell deeper and deeper into despair. His last two holiday seasons were anything but festive. After he returned home in May, the thing he looked forward to more than anything else was to celebrate the holidays at home with his parents. Unfortunately, that would not happen: the two people who he wanted to be with were dead. The only family he now had was his Aunt and Uncle, and cousin. And while it would be family-like, it wouldn't be the same.

Alex rationalized that perhaps the best way for him to start over was to move out of the apartment he called home. And if that also meant ceasing contact with those closest to him, so be it. Anything that would enable him to come to grips with his anger and help give him the peace of mind he so desperately wanted was worth trying. Only after he could accept his parents' untimely death and get on with his life, would he reestablish contact with everyone.

Surely it would only take a week or two at the most, he thought to himself. He was certain that once he explained why he felt he had to "disappear," everyone would forgive him. Convinced that this was the right thing to do, he concocted a plan to quietly leave at the start of the New Year. Part of his plan was to also find a new courier job, as well.

Alex's job afforded him the opportunity to take short side trips around Manhattan, to scout out potential places to live. The options he set for himself were to find something relatively close to where he and his parents had lived, move to another borough of the city or find a place in a section of the city that was located further towards the lower tip of Manhattan. Unfortunately, the only affordable place he found was a boarding house with rooms to rent, on the west side of town. A boarding house was not high on his priority list.

Before he knew it, Thanksgiving Day had arrived and Alex still had not found a new place to live. He hated coming home to the apartment; everything he touched, every room he went into all reminded him of his parents. Whenever he saw the neighbors, they would always stop to ask him how he was doing and ended the conversation by telling him that if he needed anything to knock on their door. Alex knew they meant well and he politely answered their questions, and also thanked them for being so concerned. Unfortunately, their ongoing interest in his well-being only served to accentuate his grief so that no matter what he tried to do, he couldn't let go of the past. He had to find another place to live – quickly – so he began to reconsider his initial opposition towards renting a room at the boarding house.

Alex didn't need much in the way of personal items, other than his clothes and a few mementos. With that in mind, he set a deadline for himself: by the end of the first week in December he would either have located a new place or he would rent a room until he could find something he liked and could afford.

Although he was experiencing a temporary setback in finding a place to live, Alex was successful in locating a potential new job. The Monday after Thanksgiving Day, a fellow employee had told Alex that he heard that a new company, Mid-Atlantic Courier Services, whose headquarters was in Northern Virginia, had opened a branch office on 46th Street and was accepting job applications for experienced couriers. While Alex was making his rounds that day, he went in search of the office building where the company was setting up shop and by late afternoon he had found them. The following day, during his lunch hour, he walked into their office and filled out a job application form.

Alex had a good feeling about this potential job so he spent the remainder of the week actively looking for a place to live. Alas, he still was unable to find something affordable so on the subway ride home that Friday afternoon, December 7th, he decided to rent a room at the West End Boarding House that was located on 38th Street and 12th Avenue. At least now he could call the Salvation Army and make arrangements to donate his parents' car, the furniture and other household items he no longer wanted.

Scarcely 15 minutes after getting home, the phone rang; it was Mid-Atlantic Courier Services. A representative from the personnel department had called to ask what day would be convenient for Alex to come in for a job interview. He scheduled it for 10:00 a.m. on Tuesday, December 11th. Now that he had an interview lined up, he needed a reason to take off from work. After thinking about it for a few minutes, Alex decided that on Monday afternoon he would inform his boss that he hadn't been feeling well all weekend and that he was still feeling a little under the weather. Since he had a few hours of sick time on the books, he was going to take off the following day and go to the doctor.

* * * * * * * * * * * * * * * *

The Personnel Department manager was quite impressed with Alex, even though he had less than a year's experience in the courier business. When Alex asked when the company would make a decision, the manager told him that it would be made before the end of the year. That was cutting it close as far as Alex was concerned, but that was a chance he was willing to take. After his interview had finished, Alex headed downtown to 34th Street and 7th Avenue. From there, it was a 10 minute walk to the West End Boarding House.

* * * * * * * * * * * * * * * *

A week had passed since his interview and Alex still had not heard anything. He was hoping that the company wouldn't wait till the end of the year to make a decision and that they would call or send him a letter, at least, by Saturday, December 22nd. The following Monday was Christmas Eve and he assumed that things would slow down during the Christmas week, as well as the days leading up to New Year's Day. Though somewhat concerned that he may not get the job because of his limited experience, he remained optimistic and decided that it would be in his best interest to continue to job hunt just in case this one fell through.

When he returned home from work on December 20th, Alex found a single letter in his mailbox. It was from Mid-Atlantic

Courier Services. His hands started to tremble with anticipation as he put his keys back into his pants pocket. He grasped the envelope by the long edges and gently tapped a short edge on the palm of his hand. Holding the envelope up to the light to see where the top of the enclosed letter was, he carefully tore off the envelope's short edge, squeezed the envelope's long edges and blew into the opening. It popped open. He placed his fingers into the envelope, pulled out the letter and nervously flipped it open. The letter, written on company letterhead, read:

* * * * * * * * * * * * * * *

December 18, 1973

Dear Mr. Holloman,

Mid-Atlantic Courier Services is pleased to extend an offer of employment to you for the position of Courier, beginning on Monday, January 7, 1974. We are looking forward to having you join the Mid-Atlantic Courier Services team.

Sincerely,

Jim Powell

* * * * * * * * * * * * * * *

Alex was ecstatic. Everything was falling into place: he had found a temporary place to live and landed a new job. Now he simply needed to get his head together and fight the depression that had been trying to take over his life for the past few months. The following day, Alex informed his boss that he was resigning, effective Friday, January 4th. That afternoon, while on a courier run, Alex stopped in at the 38th Street Post Office and rented a post office box. When he got off the train at 103rd Street, Alex went directly to the Branch Post Office on 104th Street and made arrangements to have his mail delivered to his new post office box, effective January 2, 1974.

He said nothing to Stella or Julie, or his Aunt and Uncle.

Shortly after 1 p.m. on Saturday, December 29th, a Salvation Army truck pulled up in front of his parents' apartment. Six volunteers, armed with a stack of folded-flat cardboard boxes, six large rolls of brown wrapping paper and a box containing masking tape guns and extra rolls of tape, knocked on the door. Alex welcomed them in and told them that the items in the kitchen were not to be packed. Three hours later the apartment was emptied of everything except for the stove and refrigerator, which belonged to the apartment, and Alex's four suitcases with his clothes and a few personal items he wanted as remembrances of his parents. With no car, no furniture, no pots, pans or dishes and no bed to sleep on, he called a local taxi company to get a ride to the boarding house. Alex returned to the apartment the following day to finish cleaning in preparation for the checkout inspection that was scheduled for Monday afternoon, December 31st.

He thanked the landlord for allowing him to keep the apartment till the end of the lease and made arrangements to stop by his office to pick up the security deposit, the following week. He also asked the landlord if he had any 1-bedroom apartments for rent. The landlord said he didn't, but asked Alex to keep in contact with him because he expected something within the next 60 days. Alex gave him the apartment keys and they shook hands goodbye.

* * * * * * * * * * * * * * * *

The New Year was less than two hours old when Alex gave Julie a goodnight kiss at her front door and mumbled a promise to call her the following afternoon. She turned around, unlocked the door to her house and quietly stepped inside, hoping that she wouldn't wake up her parents. As Alex watched her close the front door and listened for the turning of the deadbolt lock, a feeling of guilt came over him. He desperately wanted to honor the promise he had made to Julie, but he knew he couldn't. And so, like an endless chain looped upon itself, his mind replayed the lie over and over as he began the solitary walk to the subway station to catch the next train heading downtown.

* * * * * * * * * * * * * * * *

The West End Boarding House was located on the west side of Manhattan, a part of town that was known for its street walkers, winos and young punks whose claim to fame were the gang they purportedly were a part of. While it looked like a tough neighborhood to live in, it was relatively quiet. Perhaps that was because the police routinely patrolled the area in both marked and unmarked cars. No one bothered anyone and everyone seemed to mind their own business.

The boarding house was a 4-story complex that extended from the corner of 12th Avenue and ended three-quarters of the way up 38th Street. There was only one other building on that street: the office/warehouse for the Metropolitan Aluminum Recycling Corporation.

Across the street from the boarding house was a vacant lot filled with rubble, discarded furniture of all shapes and sizes, and garbage. Not exactly a picturesque photo to put on a postcard. To the left of the lot was the neighborhood supermarket store and a row of eight, two-story, one-family brownstone homes. A few neatly pruned trees dotted the sidewalks on both sides of the street.

Ninety-five percent of the boarding house occupants kept to themselves and never seemed to stay longer than a few months. It was troubling at first, but the families who lived in the brownstone homes quickly became accustomed to the constant coming and going of the transients.

Alex's room measured approximately 18-feet by 18-feet with a small kitchenette area. There was a brown shag rug in the middle of the room, a tan colored sofa-sleeper and a matching easy chair. Two, 16-inch by 20-inch framed pictures of a country cottage were hung on the wall, equally spaced on each side of the sofa. The only window in the apartment overlooked 12th Avenue. Although his room was on the second floor, in an emergency, Alex would unlock the window, climb out onto the fire escape and drop its ladder onto the street below. It wasn't anything that he hadn't done as a teenager when he wanted to sneak out of his room, on a Friday or Saturday night, to be with his friends. Thinking back, he remembered it was easy getting out, but getting back in and not getting caught sometimes proved to be a difficult task.

* * * * * * * * * * * * * * * * *

Two days after he moved in, Alex began a daily ritual of rising early so he could walk to Central Park. He had hoped that the tranquility of the sprawling park in the early morning hours would be therapeutic. It seemed to work. There were many times when he shouted to his God that he had been robbed of the opportunity to watch his parents enjoy, what should have been, the finest years of their lives. After venting his anger and shedding a river of tears, the serenity of the park quickly engulfed him in a cloak of gentle calmness.

One morning, some 12 weeks later, Alex no longer felt the need to expel his anger or shed another tear. It had been a long and difficult endeavor, but he was finally at peace with himself; the long battle was over. He accepted that the untimely death of his parents was beyond his control and that there was nothing he could have done to preclude it.

* * * * * * * * * * * * * * * *

The months had rolled by quickly; it was now early June. Alex had called the landlord during the last week of February to inquire about an apartment, but the landlord had told him he still had nothing available and to check back in another two months. Alex was frustrated. He had hoped to move out of the boarding house five months ago, but relying on someone else to find him a place to live wasn't working out. So he resumed the apartment hunt on his own.

To compound things, he hadn't contacted Stella, Julie or his Aunt and Uncle since "disappearing" at the start of the year. In hindsight, he wished he could turn back the hands of time so he could do things differently. Now, six months later, he felt that he had thrown them an unjustifiable low blow. He desperately wanted to call them. If anything, it would bring closure for him and for those he loved. However, each time he stopped at a phone booth, he would dial the first three numbers and then pause. A moment later he'd hang up. He could offer no rationale excuse for his actions and short of apologizing he didn't know what else to say. He feared they would hang up on him before he had a chance to explain his illogical actions. Torn between two choices – call or not call – he thoughtlessly chose the latter.

* * * * * * * * * * * * * * * *

It was early, about 5:00 a.m., Alex was tossing and turning in bed when he suddenly sat upright, sweating profusely. It had been almost a year since it last happened, but Alex dreamt that he was back in Vietnam. The sound of gunfire, helicopters swooping down onto small fields to pick up wounded soldiers, planes flying overhead spraying Agent Orange and the cries of desperation from the injured asking the medics for a shot of painkiller, filled his head. He laid back down on the sofa bed, but he was unable to fall back asleep. Twenty minutes later, he got up, turned on the television and sat on the edge of the bed couch. *So much for sleeping-in, on Saturday,* Alex mumbled.

The television that came with the room looked like it had seen better days, but it worked. Alex watched whatever local channels the television received, with some help from its rabbit-ears antenna. The morning news program had just begun with a recapping of the previous night's top news stories. He paid little attention, though he did mumble a few obscenities when a story aired about a draft dodger who also happened to be running for public office.

Damn asshole, he exclaimed. *Where were you when your country needed you? Don't answer; I'll tell you. You were too busy condemning the war while you attended some third-rate university abroad; that's where you were. Meanwhile thousands of others were halfway around the world fighting for your freedom in the rice fields of Vietnam. Now you want to run for public office. I hope the people are smart enough to run your sorry ass out of town. Up yours, you coward!*

Alex stood up and walked towards the television set. *There has to be something else on, at this time of the morning,* he muttered.

He waited a moment or two as he changed channels to see if anything sparked his interest. When he ran through the entire spectrum of available channels, he found himself back at the first one, again. They had just turned the proceedings over to the weatherman. It was going to be a sunny day in the low 70s, no rain and very little humidity. When the weatherman finished his forecast, Alex headed for the bathroom to wash up. It was pointless to go back to sleep so he decided to get an early start on his morning walk.

As soon as he finished tying double knots on his sneaker laces, he opened the door of his boarding room, walked to the stairs and went down the two flights to the main floor. When he reached the bottom, he turned to the right, walked 15-feet and pushed open the first of two sets of double doors. As he stepped into the small outer hallway, he stopped momentarily to allow the door behind him to close shut. It had a self-locking doorknob that kept unwanted visitors from roaming the hallways or sleeping under the stairwell. He pushed open the outer door, stepped onto the stoop and into the early morning air. He looked around as he descended the four stairs to the sidewalk, turned to his right and with a brisk pace headed uptown towards Central Park.

Even in the summer, at this early time of the morning, Central Park was a place of solitude. Entering the park, he slowed his pace to a leisurely stroll as he followed the pedestrian path. Nothing stirred, not even the homeless who slept on benches or in the grass, empty bottles of wine still clasped in their hands and newspaper covering their tattered clothes.

A squirrel suddenly jumped onto the path, momentarily startling Alex and causing him and the squirrel to stop dead in their tracks. The squirrel turned its head from side to side, its eyes intently looking at Alex and searching for any other immediate danger. A moment later it ran towards the safety of the nearest tree and Alex resumed his walk.

It was mid-morning when he returned. The neighborhood kids were actively engaged in a game of stickball, and Alex decided to sit on the top stoop step to watch the game for a few minutes, before heading up to his room. Suddenly, without any forewarning, a car traveling faster than it should have on 12th Avenue made a sudden left turn onto 38th Street. The sound of screeching wheels, as the car turned, and a steady blowing of the horn by the driver was not enough warning to the kids playing in the street. The driver slammed his foot on the brake pedal causing the car to go into a long skid. Alex jumped to his feet, watching in horror as a young boy was struck by the car and propelled into the air. He landed with an unmistakable thud some 30-feet away, in the middle of the street. After striking the boy, the driver lost control of his car, swerved to the right and collided into a nearby-parked car.

A few seconds after he heard the screeching wheels and the continuous blare of the car's horn, Mr. Oldfield, the owner of the neighborhood supermarket, came running out from inside his store just as the young boy was struck. Mr. Oldfield recognized the clothing: it was his 8-year-old son, Mike. He hollered to his wife, inside the store, to dial 9-1-1 for an ambulance. He said nothing else, turned on his heels and ran towards his boy. Alex was already attending to the youngster when Mr. Oldfield arrived at his son's side.

"Is my son alive?" he worriedly asked.

"Yes," Alex replied, "but he's in shock and his right leg is broken."

"Are you sure? I mean he's not moving or anything. Is he breathing?"

"I'm positive, sir. I'm not a nurse, but I've had my fair share of first-aid, courtesy of the U.S. Army. He should be just fine once his leg heals."

"Thank, God."

"Has anyone called for an ambulance?" Alex asked.

"Yes, I asked my wife to do that. They should be here soon."

By now, a small crowd of onlookers had gathered in a semi-circle in the street while one man took it upon himself to watch the driver of the car. There was really no need: the unconscious driver was stuck in the front seat, pinned up against the steering wheel.

A few minutes later the faint sound of an ambulance siren could be heard in the distance. When the ambulance reached 38th Street the driver shut off the siren, but he kept the vehicle's emergency lights flashing. Two paramedics jumped out of the truck about 10-feet from the accident scene. One immediately ran towards the crowd with his treatment bag to assess the situation while the other pulled out a stretcher. Alex told the paramedic that he was the first person to reach the boy after the accident, and that the youngster was in shock and his right leg was broken. As soon as the paramedics took command of the scene, there was nothing else for Alex to do except wait for the police to arrive.

Within minutes of the ambulance's arrival, a police cruiser, with its siren roaring and its lights flashing, turned onto 38th Street. After briefly conferring with the paramedics, the officer asked if anyone witnessed the accident. Alex stated that he saw the entire incident and Mr. Oldfield said he recognized his son, but only after the car had struck him. The officer gave each of them a pad of paper and a pen, and asked them to make a written statement.

After the paramedics had stabilized Mike Oldfield and covered him with a blanket, they asked Mr. Oldfield if he wanted to ride with the ambulance to the hospital. He nodded his head affirmatively.

"Can you give me two minutes so I can tell my wife that our son is okay?" he asked.

"Okay; but only two minutes. Come to the back of the ambulance when you return."

"Thanks," he said, then quickly ran back to his store.

"It was Michael who got hit, right, Kevin?" she asked.

"Yes, honey," he replied, tears beginning to well up in his eyes. "But he's going to be fine, the paramedics told me so. We need to close the store so we can go to the hospital."

* * * * * * * * * * * * * * * *

"I only have a few seconds," Mr. Oldfield said to Alex in between breaths of air, "but I wanted to thank you for your kindness."

"I'm glad I was able to help," replied Alex.

"My name's Kevin and if there's ever anything I can do for you … anytime at all … you let me know. I know people; I have connections."

"Thanks, Kevin. Listen, I don't want to hold you up, but the ambulance is waiting. We can talk after you get back, if you want to."

"Count on it," Kevin replied.

* * * * * * * * * * * * * * * *

Alex waited till the police officer returned and then gave him his written statement. The officer quickly scanned what Alex wrote and then told him he could leave. As Alex walked back to the boarding house, a second police cruiser turned onto 38th Street just as the ambulance driver had turned on the siren in preparation for the trip to the local hospital.

When Alex reached the top step of the stoop, he turned and took one last look down the street. The police had just extricated the now conscious driver and were in the process of patting him down and reading him his Miranda rights. *That driver's one stupid bastard,* Alex mumbled to himself, as he opened the outer door and walked inside. *Life in this city can be one stupid thing after another. Fortunately, we now have one less idiot to contend with.*

CHAPTER NINETEEN

June 21, 2000

It was shortly after 8:00 a.m. when John left his house for the 20-minute drive to Pungo, a township that was founded in 1870 and annexed by the City of Virginia Beach in 1963. The area, once the site of an old Indian village, is still quite rural in appearance, much to the delight of the residents who live there. Pungo's northern border is 15 miles, as the crow flies, from the resort section of Virginia Beach, which, if you were to ask any Pungo resident, is ample space between them and the countless visitors who vacation on the waterfront during the hot summer months. Over two-dozen business establishments and specialty shops provide Pungo's residents with big-city modern amenities. And all of the businesses are within easy walking distance of each other, equally situated north and south of the area's one and only city traffic light.

In the summer of 1976, John had purchased a five-acre parcel of wooded land. After he had it partially cleared out, he had a 10,000-square-foot warehouse built on the property. There was no name over the warehouse door, only the street address. However, John and his magic crew named the place "Misdirection." Inside the warehouse there was an office, a conference room, a complete wood and machine shop, and a full-size stage complete with curtains, lights and sound equipment. The warehouse also had ample storage space for the numerous illusions and other accessories needed to outfit a touring magic show. Whenever John and his crew were in town they used the facility to rehearse new routines and build new illusions that they planned on adding to the show.

A few months after he retired from touring, John thought about selling the warehouse and moving its contents to a smaller place. There was really no need to keep such a big facility anymore, but his sixth sense was also telling him to keep the place ... just in case. So he did. Eventually, John got together with the two local magic groups and opened the Misdirection warehouse to them for their monthly meetings, and for any magician who wanted to rehearse their show on a professional-size stage. In addition, Dave had also offered his assistance to anyone who was looking to build an illusion for his or her show. For the local magicians it was a win-win situation, and for John it was a chance to give something back to the local magic community.

When John pulled up in front of the warehouse at 8:20 a.m., he was surprised to find that he was the first one to arrive. Whenever rehearsals were scheduled, Dave, Patty, Maria and Sally were usually there first. It suddenly dawned on him that he had told Dave that he wanted to start at 9:00 o'clock. John unlocked the door, stepped into the main hallway and turned on the lights. After walking into the open-bay area, he saw the new illusion in the corner next to the stage. From where he was standing, it looked great; Dave had done an outstanding job, as usual. Now all John had to do was find Alex so they could use the illusion in next week's show.

John was sitting in the office when Dave, Patty, Sally and Maria came strolling in a few minutes before 9:00 with a cardboard container holding five large cups of coffee and a bag of fresh pastries from Pungo's legendary "Sweet Tooth Bakery." They were all casually dressed in blue jeans, short sleeve shirts and sneakers.

"Good morning, John," Maria hollered as she opened the front door.

"Good morning, how is everyone doing?" John said after greeting everyone in main foyer.

"We're ready to rock and roll," said Dave.

"We've got coffee, John," Patty said.

"Excellent," he replied.

"And we also have some Danish pastries if you need a sugar rush," Sally and Patty said in unison before they began giggling.

"You two are in a spirited mood, this morning," John said.

"Why not?" Sally replied. "It's a great morning."

"And, we're excited about the upcoming show," Patty added.

Maria handed John a cup of coffee and Patty held out the bag of pastries so he could take one.

"So, tell us about your trip to New York," Sally said.

"Okay, but let's talk in the conference room."

As they drank their coffee and nibbled on the sweets, John related his adventures in New York City, and the reason for the new illusion.

"It certainly sounds like you and Stella have reconnected after all these years, if I'm reading the tea leaves right," said Maria.

"It's not like we were ever disconnected, we've always been in contact with each other, quite frequently I might add, but we've been on separate paths way too long," John replied.

"I do hope you'll introduce her to us at the reunion," Sally asked.

"If he doesn't," Patty said, "we'll just have to take matters into our own hands."

"You folks are certainly ganging up on me this morning," John replied. "And, yes, I will introduce Stella to everyone; I had already planned on doing that because I know I'd never hear the end of it."

"Amen to that," said Maria.

"Now that I've been sufficiently beat up this morning, let's talk about the show," he said.

"Gee," said Patty, "we were just getting warmed up!"

Next thing John knew the entire group began to laugh. It was certainly contagious because he started laughing also.

"John, before we get too far down the road, would you like to see the illusion performed?" Dave asked.

"You've already rehearsed it?" John asked.

"For the most part, yes," Dave replied. "I explained the workings to the girls and then we did a few run-throughs. I had to do some minor tweaking, but in my humble opinion the illusion works great."

"Okay, let me see what you've all come up with," John stated.

"What we'll do first," Dave began, "is to explain the process as we go along and then we'll perform it a second time as if it were actually being presented."

"Great," John said.

The five of them got up from the table and headed towards the stage area.

"John, get a chair and sit out in the 'audience' while I roll the illusion onto the stage," Dave said.

"Okay."

Once everyone was in position, they went through their paces. Dave was able to capture exactly what John had wanted to do, and Dave and the ladies did a great job explaining, and presenting the illusion.

"So, what do you think?" Dave asked.

"That was great, I'm not changing a thing," John replied.

"Well, then let's run through it with you," said Patty.

"Before we get started, keep in mind that performing this illusion is based on me finding Alex."

Everyone nodded their head up and down.

"Do you know who will be the MC for the show?" Patty asked.

"It will probably be Drew," John replied. "I'm planning on giving him just enough information to write his introductory script and nothing more."

There were no more questions.

"I'm ready whenever you all are," John said. "I haven't had a chance to work on the patter for this illusion yet, so for this morning's rehearsals I'll just say, 'Ladies and gentlemen: The Time Machine.' By tomorrow, I'll have something firm so when we do the final run-throughs we'll all be speaking from the same piece of paper," John said.

"That's fine," Dave said.

The five of them spent the rest of the morning rehearsing the illusion as Dave, Patty, Sally and Maria had performed it. They first did a dozen silent trial runs and then followed those up with another set of run-throughs, each with different background music selections. An illusion, by itself, is simply a puzzle. The audience isn't interested in solving a puzzle; they want to be entertained. A magician, therefore, incorporates music to help transform these puzzles into vignettes. By lunchtime John and his crew had unanimously decided on the music that highlighted the emotion of this illusion. They did one final run-through and then called it a wrap, for this part of the show.

"I vote that we break for lunch before starting the round-table discussion on the first-half of the show," John announced.

"I agree," Dave replied.

After they locked up the warehouse, everyone climbed into Dave's SUV for the short drive to the Hampton Bay Tradewinds Restaurant, which was north of the traffic light. The hostess informed them there was a 10-minute wait, so they sat down in the waiting area and looked over the menu. By the time they were seated, everyone had decided to order the daily lunch special: beef stew and noodles, a side salad, bread and butter, and coffee, for $9.95.

"Ladies," John began, "are any husbands making the trip to New York City?"

Patty was the first to respond, "George said he wanted to sit this one out at home."

Maria said her husband, Carl, wasn't going and Sally said her husband, Tom, was staying home also.

"It sounds to me like the guys are planning a weekend of golf," Dave said.

"Probably," said Patty.

"Dave, what about Melissa?" John asked.

"No, she's staying home, too. She's 'on-call' that week-end."

"John, when are you going back to New York City?" Patty asked.

"I'm going to catch an early morning flight on Saturday," he replied. "Stella and I are going out to dinner on Saturday evening and then to a Broadway play."

"Which one?" Sally asked.

"Whichever one my contact can get for me."

"Sounds like a romantic evening to me," said Maria. "What does everyone else think?" she asked.

They all nodded their heads in approval and John felt his face starting to flush.

"Gee, you all are in rare form today," he said.

"I'm glad you noticed," said Sally. "Besides, we like being nosy," she added.

"That's because we like you, John," said Maria.

"And we don't mind looking after you," added Patty.

"Thanks," he sarcastically replied.

"You're welcome," they replied in unison.

John looked at Dave. Dave shrugged his shoulders and then mumbled something about not getting caught up in the middle of this conversation. John gave him a 'gee, thanks for helping a friend out' look and Dave, unable to contain it any longer, started to laugh. Eventually, so did John.

* * * * * * * * * * * * * * *

When they got back to the warehouse, a little over an hour later, Dave and the ladies headed towards the conference room for the round-table discussion on the first half of the show. John grabbed a stack of notepads and pens from his office and returned to the conference room, placing everything in the middle of the table. Patty grabbed the entire pile and passed out a notepad and pen to everyone.

"John, do you have anything special planned for the show's first half," Dave began, "or do you want to get our input first?"

"Both," John answered. "Let me tell you what I came up with and then you folks jump in and tell me what you think. Once we all agree, we'll move on to the next item. Is that okay with everyone?" he asked.

Dave and the ladies agreed.

"First up is the opening set," John began. "My suggestion is 'The Enchanted Garden.'"

"I think we ought to consider 'Oriental Mysteries,'" Maria offered.

"I second that," Patty added.

"Any other suggestions?" John asked.

Sally thought about it for a minute and then said, "I agree with John's recommendation."

"What do you think, Dave?" John asked.

The ladies looked at him.

Dave opted to stay neutral, saying, "I think either opening would be great. But to be fair, I think we should flip a coin; if Patty, Sally and Maria agree."

They did.

Dave stood up, reached into his pocket and withdrew a handful of change, and dropped the coins onto the table.

"We'll use a quarter. Maria, since you spoke first you call it once I flip it in the air. 'Heads' is Oriental Mysteries and 'tails' is The Enchanted Garden. Is that okay with you?" Dave asked.

"Yes," she replied.

Dave picked up the quarter with his right hand and then flipped it into the air. Maria called 'heads'. Dave let the coin hit the table; it landed on its edge and spun around in circles before coming to rest, 'tails' side up.

"Fair enough," Maria said. "It's The Enchanted Garden routine. Can I make a suggestion, though?"

"By all means," John answered, "that's why we're having this meeting."

"The reason I suggested Oriental Mysteries is because I think it would be great to start this particular show off by having you magically appear in a puff of smoke, rather than simply walking out from stage left at the music's intro."

"Maria, that's a great idea!" Dave exclaimed. "I can easily redesign *The Gateway Illusion* to resemble a garden archway so it ties in with the routine's overall theme."

Patty and Sally were nodding their heads in agreement of Maria's suggestion and Dave's idea, and then everyone turned towards John.

"Great idea; I like it … let's do it," John said.

"What's next?" Patty asked.

"I thought we'd do an audience participation routine in front of the closed main drape, which will give everyone time to clear the stage and prepare it for the next illusion. The routine I planned on doing is *The Money Auction/Million to One Wish.*"

John waited a few moments for some feedback; there was none.

"No comments?" he asked.

Sally spoke for the group, "That routine is fine."

"Next up," he said, "is a choice between *The Zig-Zag Lady* or *Piece-by-Piece* or *The Girl without a Middle.*"

Everyone recommended *Piece-by-Piece*.

"We're back out in front of the closed main drape again," John began, "but I was thinking of doing something a bit different, this time. I thought we'd present a medley of illusions, starting off with the *Linking Rings* followed by the *Linking Hoops*. Then we'll open the main drape and pick up the tempo with three larger illusions."

"Which ones did you have in mind, John?" Dave asked.

"I've thought of two: *The Neon Light Saber Illusion* and the *Asrah* illusion, but I'd like some input on the third," John said.

"John, we need to re-think the *Asrah* illusion," Patty said.

She paused a moment.

"The *Asrah* is a combination of a floating lady and a dis-appearing lady. You've made one of us disappear, but haven't brought the person back. As a closing illusion it's great, but in the middle of the show it doesn't work."

"That's a good point," Dave quipped.

"I suggest that we present the *Neon Light Saber Illusion*, the *Temple of Benares* and the *Aerial Levitation*," Patty said. The nice thing about the Temple is that you've made the lady disappear and then reappear, using one illusion instead of two. As for *Aerial Levitation*, I like that one better than *Asrah*."

"Dave's right, Patty; you've made a really good point," John said. "What does everyone else think?"

Dave, Sally and Maria agreed.

"Okay, those are the three we'll use."

John paused a moment.

"Okay, we're ready to wind down so I think we should do one more audience participation routine and one more illusion before we wrap up the first half."

"I like *Markers*," Sally said.

"Good choice, Sally," Maria replied.

"Okay, what about the final illusion?" John asked.

"What did you have in mind, John," Dave asked.

"I think we should do the *Body X-Change* as the final illusion of the show."

"I think that's a great closing routine," Maria said.

John looked at the others; they were all nodding their heads in agreement.

"I really appreciate everyone's input," John began, "I think we've put together a solid show that everyone will truly enjoy."

John looked at his watch: it was 2:45 p.m.

"Let's call it a day and meet back here tomorrow morning at 8:30 a.m."

* * * * * * * * * * * * * * * *

The following morning Dave suggested they use *The Gateway Illusion* as is and then on Saturday, he'd re-design it for the show. John agreed. They also decided to rehearse the audience participation routines in the morning and the larger illusions in the afternoon, after they had lunch. Though it had been quite some time since their last show, everyone's timing was right on the mark and at 4:30 p.m. they called it quits for the day.

"Right after I get home, I'll be making reservations for everyone at the New York International Resorts Hotel on 54th Street and Avenue of the Americas, for next Thursday, Friday and Saturday. Patty, Sally and Maria, I'll get you an early afternoon flight on Thursday with Midland Eagle Air Express Airlines. It's a 90-minute flight to New York so by the time you pick up your luggage and get to the hotel you should be able to register. And speaking of the New York City airport, I'll also make arrangements with the airport limo service to take you all to the hotel. I'll have them hold up a sign with my name on it."

John turned towards Dave and asked, "Are you leaving on Wednesday or Thursday?"

"I'm going to leave about 3:00 a.m. on Thursday morning. I expect to arrive at the college by 11:00 a.m."

"Why not leave on Wednesday afternoon and stop for the night in Dover, Delaware?" John asked.

"I don't mind driving in the early morning hours," he replied.

"Okay. When are you packing up the show?"

"On Tuesday," Dave replied.

"Ladies, if you have any luggage that you don't want to carry, bring it to the warehouse so Dave can pack it up with the show. If anyone needs me, I'll be leaving here in about 30 minutes and plan on being home for the remainder of the day. Tomorrow, we'll set the show up from top to bottom and do complete run-throughs."

Dave, Sally, Patty and Maria said goodbye to John and left to go home.

* * * * * * * * * * * * * * *

Friday's run-throughs went off without a hitch. They worked through lunch and, at 1:30, called it a day. There was no need for them to continue rehearsing; they were ready.

"Patty, Sally and Maria, I'll meet you at the hotel on Thursday afternoon. Dave, I'll meet you at the Crestwood College Linwood Hall Auditorium, on Thursday around noon. Hopefully, I'll have found Alex. Have a great weekend and a safe trip, everyone."

They each wished John a wonderful time at the theatre on Saturday night.

* * * * * * * * * * * * * * *

As John turned down the street where he lived, he saw the mailman pull away from the curb in front of his house. After he parked his car in the driveway, he walked back to the curb and opened the mailbox. Inside was a single letter. John could tell right away that it was the one he had sent from the post office in Manhattan a few days earlier. He quickly pulled it out and read the computer-formatted, yellow strip of paper that was pasted on the bottom of the letter; it contained a forwarding address.

Bingo, he loudly exclaimed.

CHAPTER TWENTY

May 29, 1975

It had been well over a year since Alex had last spoken to the landlord who managed the apartment where his folks had lived, so he decided to visit the landlord's office in person. Alex had been actively looking for an apartment, but the ones he did find were either too far way or the rents were extraordinarily high. Neither option suited Alex; he knew there were reasonably priced apartments in the city. It was just a matter of asking for help in finding them. The landlord remembered Alex and after some small talk Alex asked him if he had any apartments for rent. Anticipating a negative answer, Alex was elated when the landlord said that one would be coming available on September 1st. The current tenants were expecting their first child and were moving into a two-bedroom apartment in the same building. Alex expressed his interest in the soon-to-be-vacant apartment by asking where it was located and how much the rent would be.

The apartment building was on 53rd Street, close to 11th Avenue and DeWitt Clinton Park, and if Alex was willing to sign a two-year lease, the rent would be $72 a month. Alex had some idea of the neighborhood, having previously made some courier deliveries to that area. It was definitely better than where he was living at present and the monthly rent was only ten dollars more than what he was paying at the boarding house. Alex liked what he heard and with a handshake agreed to rent the place, sight unseen. He had no reason to mistrust the landlord and he was confident the place would be cleaned, freshly painted and ready for occupancy on September 1st, as promised. The landlord asked Alex to come back at the end of the week, when he would have the rental lease ready for signing.

Shortly after Alex returned to the boarding house later that afternoon, he stopped in the supermarket for some groceries and to tell Kevin, his only friend, that he was moving uptown. Kevin was not surprised to hear those words; he had seen countless people come and go over the years. He knew that Alex had an opportunity to get a fresh start and Kevin respected Alex's decision to move.

"If you ever need anything," Kevin began, "you let me know. I still owe you a favor for helping my son after he was hit by that car last summer."

"You don't owe me anything," Alex said, picking up the grocery bag. "I would have done the same for anyone else."

* * * * * * * * * * * * * * *

It was hot and humid on the morning of September 1st, when Alex made one last check of the boarding house room he had called home for the past 20 months. All his personal items were packed … he was ready to move. Alex carried his four suitcases down the stairs, two at a time, and placed them outside the boarding house rental office on the first floor. He knocked first, and then turned the doorknob and walked inside.

"Good morning, Mr. Holloman," the receptionist said, as soon as Alex stepped inside.

"Good morning, Mrs. Anderson," Alex replied, leaving the door open.

"Have you got everything from your room?" she asked.

"I believe so," he replied.

"We're sorry to see you leave, we've enjoyed having you as a tenant."

"Thank you," he answered. "Could I use your phone to call for a taxi?"

"Certainly," she replied, "help yourself."

After he hung up, he removed the room key and front door key from his pocket, and placed them on Mrs. Anderson's desk.

"Almost forgot these," Alex said.

Alex had already lugged his suitcases down to the sidewalk and was waiting for the taxi when Kevin stepped out from inside his store and crossed the street.

"If you're in the neighborhood, stop in to say hello," Kevin said as he extended his hand to Alex.

"I will," Alex replied, as he reached out and gripped Kevin's hand.

"And remember, if you ever need help...."

* * * * * * * * * * * * * * *

Alex had jumped on the music bandwagon right after the British invasion began in February 1964. His parents would have nothing to do with this "new style" music and when Alex asked for a guitar for Christmas they said "maybe." Alex knew that meant "no," so he decided to do the next best thing: he would begin collecting rock n' roll records. Two days before he left for Army basic training, he carefully packed up his entire collection; it filled six medium-sized boxes. After loading them into the trunk of his parents' car, he drove to his Aunt and Uncle's apartment in the Bronx, and gave the entire collection to Stella.

A month after Alex had moved into his new apartment, he decided to begin anew his music collection. Alex went to Walter's Music World on 48th Street and 5th Avenue. It was the place where he had bought all his records as a teenager. Alex climbed the three steps up to the entranceway, pushed open the door and stepped into the largest music shop in all of New York City.

Entering Walter's Music World was like walking inside a toy factory for adults. In addition to the enormous selection of music CDs and cassettes, on the walls hung 6-string and 12-string electric and acoustic guitars, and 4-string and 5-string electric bass guitars in all shapes, styles and colors. Also hanging on the walls were banjos, mandolins and ukuleles from every manufacturing company imaginable. Walter's Music also sold other musical equipment such as drum sets, organs, wind and brass instruments, orchestra equipment, amplifiers and PA systems. In addition, they had shelves of sheet music, instructional books, songbooks and all the other incidentals an amateur or professional musician would ever need or want.

Each time Alex went to Walter's Music he'd first swing by the guitar displays before heading for the CD racks. Rather than randomly buying CDs he remembered having as vinyl long-playing records, he decided to start with the letter "A" and slowly work his way through the alphabet buying only those CDs he wanted. Six months after moving into his apartment, on his next weekly trip to the music store, Alex inquired about buying a guitar and taking lessons. As far as he was concerned, it was never too late to learn to play, even if it was only for his own enjoyment.

The employees at Walter's Music World were not the type of salesmen whose sole interest was to continually move the store's merchandise at the expense of its clientele. They took as much time as was needed to talk with their customers by first asking what type of music they liked and whether they already knew how to play the instrument they were looking to purchase. If the musical instrument was for a child, they asked which school the child attended. Once they understood the customer's needs, they were able to offer professional advice to help the customer make an educated purchase. Walter's Music was, first and foremost, all about personal service; it's what kept them in business for the past 30 years, and made them stand head and shoulders above the other music stores in New York City.

It didn't take long for Alex to find a 6-string acoustic guitar that he liked and felt comfortable with. He spent many Saturday mornings at the shop learning how to read music by sight and to play by ear. And every day after work, Alex would spend a few hours practicing what he had previously been taught. He poured his energy into learning; after all, he had a lot of catching up to do. In two years time, Alex became quite proficient as a guitarist. Even old-man Walter, the store owner, was impressed with Alex's drive and determination, so much so that he offered Alex a part-time job teaching beginning guitar lessons, on Saturdays. Alex gratefully accepted the offer; perhaps his life-long love of music would rub off on someone else.

* * * * * * * * * * * * * * *

On September 29, 1984, almost six years after teaching his very first class, Alex told Walter that he needed a temporary break from teaching guitar classes. While Alex had thoroughly enjoyed his Saturday teaching job, the time had come for him to turn the reins over to someone else. Walter reluctantly accepted Alex's resignation and told him that the door would always be open for him to return as an instructor whenever he was ready to have another go at it. Alex thanked him and then agreed to stay on till the end of December to give Walter enough time to find a new instructor.

* * * * * * * * * * * * * * *

It had been over 11 years since Alex had left 104th Street and not once did he ever have a desire to return there. However, that all changed in mid-July 1985. Alex had just left the 96th Street public library and was walking back to the subway station for the trip back to his apartment, when, for no apparent reason, he suddenly changed directions and began walking uptown. Something had triggered the resurrection of a deeply buried emotion that had been quietly residing in Alex's subconscious all these years. *But why now,* he wondered. He had, long ago, overcome the anger that had been slowly trying to gain complete control over his life. Whatever sentiment was still lurking around in a far corner of his mind, it needed to be released. So rather than avoiding it and hoping this feeling would quietly go away, he decided to tackle it head-on. The sooner he did, the sooner it would end, for good.

When Alex reached 104th Street and Lexington Avenue he turned right and headed east towards First Avenue. With his hands in his pants pockets, Alex slowly walked down 104th Street scrutinizing the apartment buildings and storefronts on both sides of the street. Structurally, nothing had changed, but it was all but impossible to not notice the metal security gates that protected storefront windows and doors, and the litter that was strewn about the street, piled up against the curb or on the sidewalk itself. As he approached Third Avenue he thought about what he would say if he saw someone he knew. A simple "hello" would suffice and if the conversation continued beyond that he'd play it by ear.

The traffic light was red when he reached the corner of 104th Street and Second Avenue. As he waited for the light to change to green, he felt a rush of adrenalin pulsing through his body and his heart began beating faster. He could see the front of the building where he grew up, a few hundred feet away from where he was standing. Alex removed his hands from his pockets: they were clammy. He took a deep breath and slowly exhaled. Alex needed to quickly regain control of his emotions and not let the unknown play havoc with his mind, as it was now trying to do once again.

A minute later the traffic light turned green. *It's now or never,* he mumbled to himself. *Either cross the street and put an end to this once and for all, or turn around and go home with your head hung low.* Alex looked in all directions and seeing no cars, he stepped off the curb and made a dash for the opposite side of the street before the light changed back to red. He had come this far; there was no way he was going to turn back now.

For a Saturday afternoon, there were only a handful of kids playing outside. And for every child outside, there was also a parent watching every movement on the block with eagle eyes. As Alex casually strolled down the street towards First Avenue, he could feel the stare of these parents. He was, after all, a stranger to them. This was certainly not the way he remembered growing up in this neighborhood. Back then, parents rarely took up residence outside their apartments while their children played on the sidewalk. Sadly, those days were long gone.

As he walked past the apartment building where he had lived, he noticed its front door had been marred with graffiti. *What a shame,* he thought to himself. *Of all the buildings on the block, this was the only one someone had intentionally chosen to mark with yellow, green and red spray paint.*

Since his departure in January 1974, 104th Street had undergone a radical transformation, much like a caterpillar that transforms into a butterfly. However, unlike the butterfly whose beautiful color is a wonder to behold, the East 104th Street neighborhood was colorless and dour, in spite of someone's half-baked attempt to showcase their lackluster skill with a few cans of spray paint. When Alex reached First Avenue, he turned right and headed back downtown. He had seen all he wanted to see of 104th Street. The adage, "You can never go home again," seemed quite apropos.

* * * * * * * * * * * * * * *

The ensuing years melted away faster than a snowball on a hot summer afternoon. In June 1999, Alex received an inter-office E-Mail from the Human Resource Department of Mid-Atlantic Courier Services. It was advance notice that a formal letter was being mailed, later that day, telling him that in January 2000 he will complete 25 years of service with the company. It seemed like it was only yesterday that he had first started working for this company.

The E-Mail also said, "All permanent, full-time employees completing 25 years of continuous service were eligible for retirement and a company pension. A retirement application package is available for all interested applicants in the Human Resource Office."

* * * * * * * * * * * * * * *

While the thought of being eligible to retire with a pension was tempting, Alex would have to carefully weigh his options on whether retirement was the right choice to make, at this time. At age 48, he still had a minimum of 14 years before he could even apply for early Social Security benefits. A retirement check, no matter how generous, would not be equivalent to what he was currently earning every two weeks. If he opted to retire, Alex would have to embark upon a second career or raid his savings account each month to maintain his current comfort level. The more he thought about it, the more determined he was to forgo retiring and to continue working.

* * * * * * * * * * * * * * *

Other than going to work, an occasional movie, a weekly visit to Walter's Music World and a semi-monthly trip to the 96th Street public library, if anyone were looking for Alex there was a better-than-average chance you'd find him at home. He had planned on having the phone line activated in his apartment shortly after moving in, but he always put it off to another day. By the summer of 1999, that "other day" was still nowhere in sight. Similarly, he intentionally let his driver's license expire since he didn't own a car. If he needed to get around town he took the bus, the subway or simply walked. Alex was the perfect example of a free spirit hippie whose only ambition was to enjoy a carefree and stress free life. And by all accounts he was doing just that.

CHAPTER TWENTY ONE

June 23, 2000

The address on the forwarding letter, which John had sent from New York City, indicated it was a post office box. The box number was unimportant at this point, the key to the puzzle was the Zip Code: 10018. John was going to wait till after he returned to New York City on Saturday to follow up on the forwarding address, but he realized that by the time he got there and checked into the hotel, all of the branch post offices would be closed. He decided to call the Princess Anne Station.

The postal clerk that John spoke with told him that the 10018 Zip Code was for New York City's Midtown Station, located at 223 W. 38th Street. John asked for the phone number and after copying it down, he thanked her for the help. Now all he needed was a pretext for calling there. He sat back in his chair and stared at the phone, as if that were of any help. It wasn't, but it was the only thing he could think of at the moment. As he shifted his gaze back to the envelope, he noticed his keys on the desk. John picked them up and as he put them in his pants pocket an idea suddenly came to mind. He picked up the phone and called the Midtown Station Post Office.

"Good afternoon, sir. My name is Alex Holloman; I'd like to speak with someone about my post office box, please."

"Certainly, Mr. Holloman; hold on a second."

"Thanks."

A moment later, a gentleman who identified himself as 'Tom' answered.

"What can I do for you, Mr. Holloman?"

"Tom, I just realized that I lost my key ring, which, in addition to my house and car keys, also has my post office box key on it. I'd like to put a hold on my mail delivery until the box can be refitted with a new lock and I can get a new key, please."

"Mr. Holloman, what's your box number and have you picked up your mail today?"

"The box number is 143 and, no, I have not picked up my mail today," John replied.

"Please hold on while I get your file."

"Sure; thanks."

So far so good, John thought. He didn't particularly like the idea of claiming to be Alex, but this was the only thing he could think of doing.

"Mr. Holloman, it's Tom; umm, I have a slight problem. You don't have Box 143; it's assigned to someone else. Are you sure you gave me the right box number?"

"Yes; I'm looking at yesterday's mail as we speak, and ... oh, shoot. Tom, I just realized that I've called the wrong Post Office Branch; I apologize. I'm a bit frazzled right now, having lost all my keys."

"That's quite all right, Mr. Holloman; I can certainly understand your concerns."

So much for the change of address lead, John mumbled, after he hung up the phone. *I wonder how long ago Alex had Box 143?* On his "to do" list, John wrote a memo to visit the Midtown Station Branch Post Office. His gut feeling was that Alex had been living in close proximity to this post office. In fact, for all John knew, Alex may still be living close by, except now his mail is being delivered to an apartment building's mailbox. *But, if that were the case why didn't I get the right information from the post office? Surely their records are continually updated.*

John leaned his chair back to think. *Perhaps Alex recently moved from that area. That would explain why the post office still had him listed as having that box number. Oh well,* he mumbled. Underneath the branch post office memo, he wrote a note to call the electric company and visit the voter registration office.

John had also thought of another option to pursue, that being to check the courthouse records for real estate purchases, but he quickly discounted the idea. He couldn't think of any place in Manhattan that would be for sale other than luxury apartment suites and, unless Alex had somehow come into a large sum of money, those places were definitely out of Alex's price range. John was reasonably sure that Alex was renting an apartment somewhere in Manhattan.

The last thing he wrote on his list was to drop by Crestwood College to say hello and to leave the hotel's number in case they needed to contact him.

* * * * * * * * * * * * * * *

John called the hotel to reconfirm his reservation and to make four additional room reservations for Thursday, Friday and Saturday nights. He then called Midland Eagle Air Express Airlines to reconfirm his flight and to make reservations for Patty, Sally and Maria. When he finished, he called the ladies at their homes to give them the hotel and flight information, and then he called Dave, who, he correctly assumed, was still at the warehouse. It was still too early to call Stella so John set about packing his luggage.

John was on his way to the den when the phone rang. He took the call in the kitchen.

"Hello," John said.

"Hi, John, it's Drew; how are you?"

"Hey, Drew; I'm well, thanks. What's up?"

"I just wanted to touch base with you once more and to ask if you needed anything."

"Everything is on track," John replied. I'm leaving for the city tomorrow and my crew will be arriving on Thursday. I planned on stopping in at the college on Monday to look over the stage and support areas, and to make sure they're ready for us. I'm just doing some precautionary follow-up, based on past experience."

"I understand," Drew replied.

"I do appreciate your concern and the offer of assistance."

"Not a problem, always glad to help. Since you're leaving tomorrow, I'm sure you've a million things to do so I won't hold you up.

"I'm certain that this will be a memorable reunion and one will be talked about for years to come," John said.

"I hope so," Drew replied

* * * * * * * * * * * * * * *

It was almost 7:00 p.m. when John finally called Stella, as he had promised to do.

"Hi, Stella; its John," he cheerfully said.

"Hey; how are things going?" she asked.

"Rehearsals went really well. Considering that my crew and I haven't done a show in quite sometime, our timing was right on the mark. We've got a terrific show planned for the reunion."

"Any hints you're willing to divulge?"

"You mean about the show?" John asked.

"Uh-huh," was her reply.

"The new illusion worked flawlessly in rehearsals."

"I can see that I'm not going to get any insider gossip from you," she said and then started to laugh. "Regardless, I'm excited about seeing the show. Just thinking about it brings back fond memories of your going away party at The Trolley Car, in 1973."

"That was a fun night, wasn't it?" John said.

"It was. What's the plan for tomorrow?"

"I'm due to arrive around lunch time."

"Do you want me to come pick you up?"

"That would be great."

"What airline are you flying in on?"

"Midland Eagle Air Express; the flight number is 427; coming from Norfolk International Airport."

"Shall I meet you at the curbside car pickup area or inside at the arrival terminal gate?"

"Come inside. I need to make some reservations with the airport limo service for my three assistants who are arriving on Thursday afternoon."

John and Stella spoke for about an hour and at no time did Alex's name come up. Had it, John didn't know whether he would have said anything to Stella about the post office box. He didn't want to keep it a secret from her, but there was really nothing she could do. And he certainly didn't want her to drive around downtown Manhattan this late in the evening.

Right after he and Stella finished talking, John called Brian Watson, a journalist friend whose job was to attend

Broadway plays and other entertainment events, and to write reviews of them for the *New York Mirror*. John met Brian about 20 years ago when Brian was working in Baltimore, Maryland. Brian had attended John's show and he wrote a feature article about John for the *Baltimore News*. The story was so well received that Brian was subsequently reassigned to the newspaper's entertainment division. Some ten years later, Brian was offered a job in New York City and he jumped at the opportunity.

"Howdy," John said when Brian answered the phone.

"John Michaels, you scoundrel; where are you?" he asked.

"I'm at home in Virginia Beach. How are you and Mary-anne?"

"We're doing well," he replied. "What's up?"

"I'm coming to New York City tomorrow and was wondering if you knew of any theatre that may still have open seats available."

"What play are you interested in?" he asked.

"You're the expert; whatever is available."

"How many tickets you need?"

"Two."

"So what's going on in the Big Apple that's bringing you here?"

"I'm attending the 30th Reunion Anniversary of Catholic High's Class of 1970. And, I'm bringing the show out of retirement for an encore performance."

"You sly dog! Let me call you back in 10 minutes," Brian said.

"Okay, thanks. Bye."

* * * * * * * * * * * * * * *

Brian got two orchestra tickets for the Saturday evening performance of CATS!

"John," Brian began, "the tickets will be at the Crown Theatre's box office. I didn't give them your name so all you need to do is tell the person manning the booth that you're my friend from Virginia Beach."

"Thanks, Brian," John said. "How much do I owe you?"

"Nothing," Brian replied.

"Brian, you and I both know that nothing is free."

"Well, there is one caveat to these tickets."

"Okay, now we're getting down to the brass tacks," John said.

"You know how it is, John ... it's the unwritten rule of business associates," Brian sarcastically replied.

"Okay, partner; I'm listening."

"Maryanne and I want you to come by the house on Sunday afternoon for dinner and to bring your date along, too."

"Okay, I can do that; what time?"

"Umm, let's plan on 4 o'clock; how's that?" Brian asked.

"Perfect," John replied. "Thanks for the tickets, Brian."

"You bet! See you on Sunday."

John had the sneaky suspicion this visit was going to turn into another feature article. It's always nice to have your name in print, as long as they spelled it correctly.

* * * * * * * * * * * * * * *

The flight to New York City was uneventful and the plane touched down a few minutes prior to high noon. John saw Stella as soon as he entered the waiting area. She was dressed in gray slacks, a white blouse and black leather flats. When they got within arm's reach they embraced and kissed.

"Where to first?" she asked.

"The limo service in the main terminal," John replied. "I don't want to hold up an airport concierge while I take care of some personal business. Besides, it'll be a few minutes before the airplane handlers begin unloading the plane."

It took all of 10 minutes for John to make arrangements to have a limo driver pick up his assistants on Thursday and then again on Sunday. He paid for the limo services in advance and then he and Stella headed for the Baggage Claim. The automated conveyor belt had already begun pushing out luggage at the designated pickup area on the lower level when they arrived. Now it was just a matter of waiting for John's four bags to make its way to where he and Stella were standing.

* * * * * * * * * * * * * * *

After John completed his check-in process, he asked the attendant to reconfirm the other four reservations he had made.

"Will you need assistance taking your luggage to your room," the young lady asked.

"The only thing I'll need is a cart," John replied.

The attendant stepped out from behind the counter and walked over to a large door across the hallway. She opened it and pulled out a bellhop cart.

"It sure is a nice suite," Stella said as she walked through the two rooms. "Did you get the same type of rooms for your crew?" she asked.

"Yes. Their rooms are a few doors down from this one," he replied.

Stella had just finished opening the window blinds when John exited from the bedroom.

"Done already?" she asked.

"Yes indeed. Having done this many times over the years, I've got the unpacking part down to a science. I wish the packing-up part were easier though."

"What's on the agenda?"

"I thought it was supposed to be a surprise?" John said.

"I need about an hour to get ready; you know, change clothes, etc."

"You look fine," he replied in a somewhat serious tone, trying his best not to grin.

"This is okay for walking around town, but…"

That's all it took before John burst into a wide grin.

"John Michaels … I should have known better!"

"Have a seat," John said as he pointed towards the table by the window in the front room. "I have some news to tell you."

John began by telling Stella how he got the tickets to the show and the dinner arrangements for Sunday afternoon. Then he told her about the letter that led to a post office box that Alex had used, at one time. There was a look of utter astonishment on Stella's face and it took her a moment to gather her thoughts.

"There's no way to know how long he had this post office box?" she asked.

"Probably not," he replied. "I was going to make a trip over there on Monday, but if you're up for an afternoon adventure we can do it now."

"Yes, I would."

"I don't think it will take too long so we should be done in plenty of time to get you back to your apartment."

"That's fine."

After John and Stella stepped outside the hotel's main door, John asked a doorman to hail a taxi. Within seconds, one pulled up in front of the hotel. After they were seated, John asked the driver to take them to the Midtown Station Post Office at 223 W. 38th Street. On any given weekday, it would take 40 to 50 minutes to drive the one-mile distance. On a Saturday afternoon, the ride took less than 10 minutes. The post office was on the west side of 38th Street, close to Tenth Avenue.

"Where do we go from here?" Stella asked after the taxi departed.

"I'm not sure," John replied as he looked around. "Other than what looks like warehouses and a few small businesses there's not much around here. I didn't see anything residential on the way over, so let's gamble a bit and walk towards Twelfth Avenue. From there, we'll wing it."

They walked hand-in-hand down 38th Street.

"Stella, other than Alex's hobby of collecting records do you know of any other pastime or social activity he may have had?" John asked.

"No; music was his sole passion."

"That's what I thought."

"Two days before he left for basic training, he drove up to the Bronx to say goodbye to us. Much to my surprise, he brought his entire record collection."

"What did he say?"

"He said, 'I won't need these anytime soon; I'd like you to have them'," Stella replied. "I was shocked. I then told him that I'd return the collection to him once he got back home, but he said not to worry about it because he'd start his collection all over again."

"Do you still have the records?"

"Yes; they're still packed in the boxes he brought them in."

When they crossed Eleventh Avenue, John saw some brownstone homes on the left side of the street and further down, close to Twelfth Avenue, he saw a large supermarket sign.

"I didn't expect to see residential houses around here, or for that matter, a supermarket," John said. "Let's cross over to the other side of the street."

As they reached the first brownstone building John saw a sign on the large building on the opposite side of the street.

"I mistook that for some sort of warehouse," he said to Stella, as he pointed towards the large building. "Actually, it's a boarding house."

"I'd have never guessed that this place existed," Stella replied.

"Unless you had a reason to be over here on the West Side, you wouldn't have known about it. I didn't even know it was here."

"Do you think there are more boarding houses close by?"

"That's a good question; I don't know. I'm going to stop in the supermarket for a drink; are you thirsty," John asked.

"Yes, I am."

"Let's get some soda."

"Okay."

As soon as they entered the store, a gentleman, who John thought was probably about 60-years-old, greeted them. He was wearing a smock and his name, Kevin, was embroidered on the right side.

"Good afternoon, folks. Can I help you find something?" he asked.

"Soda," John replied.

"The chill refrigerators are towards the back of the store," Kevin said as he pointed in the general direction.

"Thanks," John replied.

When they got back up front, John commented to Kevin that he was quite surprised to see a supermarket here on the west side of the city.

"I was really hesitant about buying this place in the late 60s, but, thankfully, business has been really good," Kevin said. "In addition to the private homes that you walked past, there's the boarding house across the street. It's a big place, that boarding house, and it has been the primary source of my business over the years. The people living there have to eat, too. I don't carry every brand name product, but one brand is as good as the other."

"Was the boarding house here in the 60s?" John inquired.

"Yes it was, and so were the residential houses," Kevin replied.

"They look new," John said.

"That's because the owners take extremely good care of their property."

"That makes sense," John answered.

"It's important, especially if an owner should ever decide to sell the house. No one wants to buy a run-down place."

"You're absolutely right," John said. "By the way, is that the only boarding house around here?"

"Yes it is."

"How much do I owe you?" John then asked.

"Two thirty-two," Kevin replied.

As John reached into his pants pocket, Kevin said, "Have you been in here before, you look very familiar?"

"No, sir; this is my first time here," John replied, as he gave Kevin a five-dollar bill.

"I'm sorry; I must have you mixed up with someone else. I've met a lot of people, and watched them come and go from this neighborhood over the past 37 years. It's a wonder I still recognize my own family," he said with a laugh.

"No problem at all, sir," John said.

"Thanks folks, come back again," Kevin said as he handed John his change. "Have a great day."

"Thanks," John answered.

Outside the supermarket, John and Stella turned to the left and slowly walked past the vacant lot, stopping on the corner of 38th Street and Twelfth Avenue.

John turned to Stella and said, "If I were a betting man, I'd bet that Alex was a tenant at that boarding house in 1974."

"What makes you so sure?" she asked.

"Convenience," John replied. "Hold onto that thought for a moment and I'll tell you why. First, though, I want to hail a taxi."

As Stella stood on the sidewalk, John ventured a few steps into the street and looked in both directions. There were not too many cars on Twelfth Avenue and just when John was about to suggest that they walk back to Tenth Avenue, a taxi appeared on the horizon. He raised his left hand over his head and waved it in the air to get the driver's attention. When the driver flashed his high-beam lights, John dropped his hand and stepped back up onto the sidewalk, next to Stella.

* * * * * * * * * * * * * * *

Fifteen minutes later they were in Stella's car and driving up Fifth Avenue, enroute to her apartment.

"Tell me why you think Alex was living at that boarding house," Stella said.

"Let me preface my answer by telling you something about the magic community first, because I think it will help you understand my thought process. When a new magic trick or illusion is seen for the first time and magicians are not sure how it works, they will converse amongst themselves to try and ascertain 'the secret.' Ideas are suggested, discarded and sometimes hotly debated. The only thing gained is that they agree to disagree. Over the years, I've learned that if you want to successfully hide 'the secret' to a particular magic trick or illusion, you publish it in a book. Now that may seem odd, but it's the truth. Why, because magicians will read the book and once they learn how the trick was accomplished they promptly forget about it."

"Are you implying that Alex was in plain sight all along, but was invisible to everyone?" Stella asked.

"Well, not exactly invisible," John replied, "but, yes, he was in plain sight all the time. But only if you knew where to look for him," he added.

There was very little traffic on Fifth Avenue and they also managed to hit every green light after leaving the hotel. As soon as they turned onto 93rd Street, Stella noticed a driver getting into his car to leave. She switched on her turn signal to warn other drivers that she intended to park. A few moments later she backed into the spot and turned off the engine.

"Why the boarding house and not another apartment?" she asked, as she turned to face John.

"I can only speculate on that," John said. "At some point in time after the death of his parents, Alex decided to leave the apartment and move on with his life. Why he feels the need to move is something only he can answer. Anyway, while he's walking around Manhattan he takes advantage of the unique opportunity his job affords and looks for a place to live. Unfortunately, when he made his decision to move away, time may not have been on his side and as it got closer to crunch time he's got to make a decision he can live with, knowing full well that this is only a temporary fix. One day, by sheer coincidence, he makes a delivery on the west side of Manhattan and accidentally finds this boarding house. Do you remember me saying that this place offered convenience?"

"Yes, I do."

"It was the supermarket owner, Kevin, who unknowingly confirmed my hunch when he said that most of his business came from the tenants in the boarding house. As we left the store, I took another look at it and realized that it's a really big place, just as he had said. Unlike a large apartment building that may have 80 to 100 rental units, this boarding house probably had at least four or five times the number of rental units. A majority of the units are probably studio rooms, which would be all that some people would want, or need. In addition to the low monthly rent, what makes this boarding house attractive is that there is a supermarket directly across the street and a post office one block away. These two businesses offered convenience to both the transients as well as the families who live in the brownstone houses. No one had to walk very far carrying large bags of groceries and everyone could have their mail delivered to a post office box."

"Do you think he would remember Alex if he saw a picture of him?" she asked.

"I doubt it. With the amount of people who have come and gone in that neighborhood over the years, no one person would stand out in his memory unless it was something really poignant."

"Well, it was just a thought."

"And a good one, too," John replied. "Come on, let me walk you upstairs to your apartment and then I'm going to head back to the hotel to change clothes, too."

"Do you want to take my car?"

"No, I'll take the subway."

"What time can I expect you?" Stella asked as she unlocked the door to her apartment.

"Five-thirty," John replied. "I'll call you before I leave the hotel," he said before giving her a kiss goodbye.

* * * * * * * * * * * * * * * *

They had an early dinner at Gino's Italian Restaurant on 46th Street and Broadway, and since the Crown Theatre was only two blocks away on 48th Street, they opted to walk.

It was close to midnight when John brought Stella back to her apartment.

"Would you like to come in and stay for awhile? I can make some coffee?" Stella asked as she unlocked the apartment door.

"Can I have a rain check, Stella?" John replied.

"You most certainly can," she answered. "What time can I expect you, tomorrow?"

"How's 10:30 sound?"

"That's perfect; I'll have brunch ready."

"I'm looking forward to it."

After a goodnight kiss, John waited till Stella closed and locked the door before leaving.

CHAPTER TWENTY TWO

June 25, 2000

At 3:30 p.m. the following day, John and Stella left for Brian's house. They took the subway, since Brian lived two short blocks east of the Union Square-14th Street subway station. It had been about three years since John last saw Brian and his wife Maryanne. They had driven down to Virginia Beach to attend a benefit show at the Bradford Hawkins Theater. After John introduced Stella to Maryanne and Brian, the two ladies went off for a tour of the house. Brian and John headed for the family room to talk. John told Brian about the Class of 1970 Reunion and his attempt to try and find Alex. As John suspected, Brian was taking notes.

"You'll have to let me know if you find him, John," Brian said. "I'd like to have a happy ending to cap off this human interest story."

"I'll certainly let you know, Brian; one way or the other."

* * * * * * * * * * * * * * *

John and Brian had been talking about an hour when they were summoned to come to the dining room for dinner.

"Brian, how did you get your big break in the very competitive entertainment reporting industry?" Stella asked.

"I went to see a Yankee magician whose tour happened to bring him to Baltimore, Maryland. After I got home that night I wrote a feature article for the newspaper I worked for and submitted it to the entertainment editor," he replied. "He liked the story and shortly after it was published I was offered an opportunity to transfer divisions."

It took a moment, but Stella finally realized that the magician Brian was talking about was John.

"How was his show, back then?" Stella then asked.

"Really good," Brian replied. "He's definitely gotten better over time," he added.

"Thanks a lot, partner," John said.

"Anytime," Brian responded with a straight face.

Maryanne and Stella laughed.

* * * * * * * * * * * * * * *

After dinner, they moved to the living room to talk while having coffee.

"I saw your guitars and 1960s memorabilia collection in your music room, Brian. I must say I'm very impressed," Stella said.

"Well, thank you, Stella. Are you a 60s aficionado?"

"Yes, I am. My cousin, Alex, wanted a guitar right after he saw The Beatles on television in 1964. My Aunt and Uncle weren't fond of this new music and when Alex asked about the possibility of getting a guitar, the answer he received was 'maybe.' He took that as a 'no' and decided to collect records instead."

"I think there were a lot of parents who were against getting their children a guitar. Mine were, at first. But, they eventually gave in and they bought one for me as a Christmas present in 1965."

"Everything I know about 60s rock n' roll, I learned by helping Alex organize and catalog his records. Before he left for the Army, he packed up his entire collection and gave it to me."

"Do you still have them?"

"Yes I do. When John asked me about the records, yesterday, I told him that I didn't open or unpack the boxes Alex gave me. It was always my intention to give them back after Alex returned home. Unfortunately, I never got the chance."

"Wow! You definitely have some real treasures. I'll have to make a mental note to one day do a story on 1960s collectors. Would you be interested in being a part of it?"

"I'd love to; thank you for asking."

John was happy to see Stella in the spotlight, instead of himself.

It was just past 9:00 p.m. when they exchanged goodbyes with a promise that it wouldn't be another three years before John, and Stella, came back to visit.

* * * * * * * * * * * * * * * *

"So what plans have you made for the next few days," Stella asked as they rode the train back to 96th Street.

"I'm going to stop in at Crestwood College tomorrow to say hello and to check out their theatre. I also need to make arrangements to have a run-through with the college's stage crew on Thursday evening."

"I see."

"Monday, Tuesday and Wednesday evenings are open, unless I get a last minute call. Thursday, as I mentioned, is D-Day for my crew and me. We'll be tied up most, if not all, evening doing last minute checks. And, somehow, in between all this, I'm going to continue to look for Alex."

"So there is hope that I'll get to see you?" Stella asked.

"Of course," John said, "as long as you don't get tired of seeing me."

"Not a chance," she replied with a smile.

"Drew told me that we can arrive no earlier than 4:00 p.m. on Friday. The reunion officially kicks off at 4:30, followed by dinner around 5:30, and the "unknown" entertainment at 7:00 p.m. I was planning on picking you up at 3:30. Is that all right?"

"That's perfect. I'm taking vacation time on Friday and Monday."

"I can come and get you earlier if you'd like," John answered. "I plan to arrive at the auditorium around noon to check on things."

"No, 3:30 is fine."

"So be it," John said.

CHAPTER TWENTY THREE

June 30, 2000

John made arrangements with Tri-State Limo to pick everyone up at the hotel at noon, on Friday, and take them to Crestwood College on 68th Street and Park Avenue. At 3:00 p.m. that afternoon, the limo would return for John, take him uptown to Stella's apartment on 93rd Street, and then bring them both back to the college. Sensing that it would be close to midnight when they'd be leaving for the evening, John arranged to have two limos return to the college at 11:45 p.m.

The company that Drew had hired for the reunion, *A Catered Affair*, was already on site when John, Dave, Patty, Sally and Maria arrived at the college. They entered the Linwood Hall Auditorium through the main doors and carefully made their way to the stage, being careful not to get in the way of the catering crew who were busy arranging the tables and chairs, and strategically hanging wall decorations.

"So what do you think, John?" Dave asked as he looked around.

"It's going to be a full house; that much is for sure. And I'm looking forward to seeing old friends and former teachers, and catching up on what everyone is doing."

"What time do you expect Drew to arrive?" Dave asked.

"Around 2:30; that's what he told me."

"Does he know to contact Mr. Fisher, the college's chief of security, if something comes up?"

"Yes; he's been coordinating with him since day one. I'm sure he'll have his hands full once he gets here, so I wouldn't worry about him coming up on stage or going backstage. I plan on going outside ahead of time, in case the limo is early, so I'll remind him as soon as he gets here."

After they walked up the three stairs leading to the stage, they turned left and headed for the performers' dressing rooms.

"Keep walking, I'll catch up in a moment; I'm going to close the main drape," Dave said.

After they finished making some last minute stage preps for the opening routine, John headed for the men's dressing room to change clothes. It was just past 2:00 p.m. The big illusions were already in place and ready to be rolled out when needed. The only thing left to do was a final check of the lighting and sound system. Once that was done, Dave and the ladies could sit back and relax till it was time for them to change clothes.

"I'm heading outside to await Drew's arrival and the limo," John said, after re-entering the performers' backstage room. "Barring heavy traffic, Stella and I should arrive no later than 4:15 p.m. My plan for later on this evening is to excuse myself from the table about five minutes before Drew heads for the stage."

"Okay, John," Patty replied. "Don't worry about us, if we need something we'll contact Mr. Fisher."

"Great; see you all later."

"Bye," they said in unison.

* * * * * * * * * * * * * * *

Five minutes after John stepped outside the auditorium, a taxi pulled up and Drew and his wife, Judy, got out. Drew was wearing a gray three-piece suit, white shirt and red tie, and Judy was in a wine-colored sleeveless gown. He still had a stocky build, but the flattop haircut he had worn throughout high school was replaced by a head full of slightly graying hair.

"You're early," Drew said as he and Judy climbed the stairs.

"I had nothing else to do and since I was in the neighborhood I thought I'd stop in and take a look around," John replied.

"John, this is my wife, Judy."

They shook hands.

"It's a pleasure to finally meet you, John. Drew talks about you all the time."

"I hope he hasn't bored you with stories about our four years at Catholic," John replied.

"Only a few," she answered with a smile.

"I can only wonder which ones and how much embellishment was tacked on for good measure," John said.

"Thinking back, the stories were rather funny," Judy replied.

Sensing it was now or never, Drew jumped into the conversation.

"I take it that you are leaving to pick up Stella?" Drew asked.

"Yes, I am. I told her that I'd be at her place by 3:30 p.m. My ride should be here shortly. By the way, I didn't see any signs on the tables, Drew. Are you planning on having any special seating arrangements?"

"I was only going to reserve one table for Brother Gregory, Brother Hill, Mrs. Dixon and her husband, and Mr. Daniels and his wife."

"That's a good idea. From what I've seen, each table seats 10 people. Who else is going to sit with them?"

"Judy and I. And, if you don't mind, I'd like you and Stella to join us," Drew said.

"Thanks; I'm sure Stella would like that. Well, here's my ride," John said, "they're early, but that's okay with me."

Drew and Judy turned around and watched as a limo slowly turned into the main entrance driveway.

"I thought I'd surprise Stella."

"I'm sure she'll be delighted with your choice of transportation, John," Judy said.

"Would you hunt down the head caterer, Judy, and ask her to put a 'Reserved' sign on the table closest to the stage. I'm going to walk with John to the limo."

"I can do that," she answered. "Do you want to sit on the left or right side of the room?"

"The left side – as you walk in."

"All right," she replied.

"I should be back in about an hour, Drew, if traffic is not too heavy. Judy, I'm looking forward to chatting with you when I return. I'm sure you have a few stories you can tell me about Drew."

"Thanks a lot, John," said Drew.

"Fair is fair," Judy replied. "So, yes, John, I have a few funny stories I can share with you and Stella."

"Great; I'm looking forward to it," John replied.

* * * * * * * * * * * * * * *

As they walked down the stairs, Drew turned to John and asked, "Is there anything you or your crew need?"

"No, we're all set. The main drape is closed so hopefully that'll be enough to let everyone know not to go up there."

"I don't think anyone will, John."

"Neither do I; it's just a precautionary measure on our part."

"I'll keep an eye on things," Drew added.

"Thanks. Does the caterer know to deliver some meals backstage?"

"Yes, but I'll remind them again. Do you want the caterer to serve your crew first and if so, who should they contact?"

"That would be great if they can do that; have them ask for Dave."

"Okay, I'll tell them," replied Drew.

* * * * * * * * * * * * * * *

Traffic heading uptown was heavy, which made the going slow at times, but the driver still managed to get to 93rd Street, with five minutes to spare. The driver slowed to a stop, double-parked the limo and then turned off the ignition.

"I'll get the door," John told the driver.

"Very well, sir," the young man replied.

"I should be back in about 15 minutes."

"Yes, sir," he answered.

Once inside the apartment building, John took the elevator up to the third floor. When he reached Stella's apartment he rang the doorbell and waited. No one ever opens their front door until they've first looked through the one-way peephole. Though she was expecting John, Stella checked anyway. Moments after ringing the bell, Stella unlocked the door and ushered John inside. He headed directly for the living room as she re-locked the door.

"I just need to get my purse and I'll be ready to go," Stella said as she headed for the kitchen.

Stella was wearing a midnight blue, silk chiffon evening gown, diamond earrings and satin silver-colored shoes. Her shoulder length brown hair was loose in soft curls.

"Stella, you look absolutely stunning," John said after she had returned from the kitchen.

"Thank you," she replied. "And you look quite distinguished."

"I had a choice between the blue dungaree bib overalls or this; I flipped a coin and the suit won out," he replied with a straight face.

"John Michaels, you're a nut," she laughingly answered. "I'm ready, if you are. And, no, you don't have to flip a coin to see if we should leave now or wait five minutes."

"Then I guess I don't need this," he said as he reached into the air and produced a silver dollar at his fingertips. He placed the coin into his pocket and said, "Okay; let's go."

Stella smiled, shook her head back and forth and said, "I should have known better."

She then leaned towards John and kissed him.

"Gee, if I had known that producing a silver dollar would be this rewarding, I'd have produced a handful."

"See, even I can surprise you with a little bit of magic," she answered.

"And you certainly did!"

John waited until Stella had locked the door and put her keys in her purse, before reaching out and taking her hand. The limo driver was standing behind the car when John and Stella emerged from the apartment building. As soon as he saw them, he walked around to the driver's side and opened the rear passenger door.

"A limo?" Stella asked.

"Of course," John replied. "It's a memorable occasion and I'm with a beautiful lady. I didn't have to flip a coin to determine the best mode of transportation."

The traffic heading downtown was no different than it was going uptown. On the ride back to the college, John told Stella about his conversation with Drew and Judy, and whom they would be sitting with that evening.

"How will you get away from the table before Drew introduces you?"

"Five minutes before Drew heads for the stage, I'll go to the men's room. There's another door to the backstage area in the main lobby. Unless you work at or attend the college, you wouldn't know about this door. By the time everyone at the table realizes I haven't gotten back, Drew will have already introduced me and the show will have begun."

"That's pretty sneaky, isn't it?"

"It comes with the job."

There was no red carpet or paparazzi standing on the sidewalk when the limo arrived back at the college exactly at 4:00 p.m. Then again, John wasn't expecting any. But knowing Drew's wry sense of humor, it wouldn't have surprised John if a crowd of strangers were recruited to stand around and cheer as the limo arrived. There weren't any.

* * * * * * * * * * * * * * * *

When John and Stella reached the top step, Drew and Judy greeted them.

"Hello, Stella," Drew said, "it has been a long time."

"Drew?" Stella inquisitively asked.

"In person."

Stella gave him a hug and then said, "What happened to the flattop?"

"It went out with thc other 1960 fashions," he answered. "Stella, I'd like to introduce you to my wonderful wife. Judy, this is Stella Noone, Alex's cousin."

Stella and Judy shook hands.

"It's so nice to finally meet you, Stella."

"Likewise," Stella replied.

"Congratulations," Drew began, "you are the first couple to arrive for the reunion. And in case you were wondering ... there are no door prizes."

"What good is being first, then?" John asked.

"Absolutely nothing," Drew answered with a laugh.

"John, our table is up front on the left; you can't miss it. There's also a bar to the right as you enter. We've got a large tab so use it while it's still available. Once it runs out, it's cash all the way."

"All right. Well, Stella, shall we go inside?"

"By all means. I'll see you inside, Judy; I'm looking forward to talking with you," Stella said.

"Why do I feel that that conversation will be about me?" Drew said.

"Because it will be," Judy replied. "I'm sure Stella has a few good stories that I haven't heard before."

Drew looked at Stella; she smiled and shrugged her shoulders.

"Hey, this is what reunions are all about," John said.

"Thanks a lot, John," Drew replied.

"Anytime," John answered.

John took Stella's hand and they walked into the auditorium.

"Do you want something to drink?" John asked.

"Whatever you're having, I'll have," she answered.

"Do you have ginger-ale?" John asked the bartender.

"Yes, sir."

"Two, please," John said.

As they headed towards their table, Stella asked, "Are you at all nervous about tonight's show?"

"Yes and no. Yes, because it's been a while since my crew and I have done a live show; but, no, in that we're comfortable with the show we've got planned for this evening. On the other hand, though, this is not an unknown group; the audience will be composed of people I've known since 1966. Once the music starts everything will fall into place."

At the table, John pulled out a chair for Stella and waited for her to sit before he pulled out the chair alongside her, and sat down.

"Before I forget; when the show is over please come back-stage. I want to introduce you to everyone."

"I'd like that, John; I will."

At 4:15, the auditorium came alive as members of the class of 1970 began drifting in. John and Stella got up from their table and began to mingle with the arriving guests. By 4:30, there was a crowd lined up outside the main door waiting to enter. Drew and Judy stayed outside to greet everyone, which was why the line was moving slowly. But, this personal touch made everyone feel welcome. As more and more people came in, they looked around the room before heading towards a table or stopping at the bar, first. By 5:00, the last of the 300 plus guests had entered the auditorium, found a table to sit at and then they, too, began mingling with the other partygoers.

* * * * * * * * * * * * * * * *

Drew looked at his watch: it was 5:20. He excused himself from the group he was talking with and headed towards the front of the room. He stood on the floor in front of the stage, reached into his jacket pocket and removed a whistle he had brought with him for this special occasion. He blew two short bursts and waited while the spirited conversations slowly subsided and everyone had turned towards the stage.

"Good afternoon, ladies and gentlemen, and welcome to the 30th Reunion of the Class of 1970. In case you're wondering, yes, this is Brother Kernan's whistle from gym class. I've waited 30 years for this occasion just so I could use it."

Everyone started laughing.

When the laughter ended, Brother Kernan edged his way towards the front of the group and said, "I've often wondered what happened to that whistle. Mister Wagner, report to me after the reunion for detention."

Brother Kernan returned to the group he was with as the crowed burst into laughter, again. Drew waited for the laughter to subside before continuing.

"This isn't the first time I've gotten detention from Brother Kernan," Drew said. "I quit counting three months into our senior year."

Once again, the group started laughing.

"Folks…" Drew began.

He paused a moment and then began speaking.

"Folks, before we get started I want to thank everyone once again for coming to the reunion. There were a number of classmates who couldn't attend because of other commitments and there are two others whom … well, their absence is quite different. The two guys are: Bobby Marcellas, the All-City handball champion, and Alex Holloman, our senior-year class president. Many of you may not know this, but Bobby was killed in Vietnam in 1971."

Some of the guests began talking in hushed voices so Drew paused for a moment.

"About seven months after he was discharged from the Army in 1973, Alex vanished without a trace. I have been looking for him on and off for the past 26 years, but have had no luck in finding him. I wish I could tell you more, but I can't because, frankly, I don't know any more than what I've just told you."

Drew paused to take a deep breath.

"Okay … I know you'd like to continue socializing, but the caterer is ready to begin serving dinner. If you would – please return to your tables and be seated; thanks."

After everyone was seated, Drew turned towards Brother Gregory and asked him if he would lead everyone in prayer, before dinner was served. When Brother Gregory had finished, Drew signaled the lead caterer to begin. Dinner began with a garden salad, followed by the main course of roasted tenderloin of beef, vegetable casserole with a lemon-garlic sauce and twice-baked potatoes. Following a dessert of a mixed berry sorbet, coffee and tea was served.

The main topic of conversation between Brother Hill, Mr. Daniels, Mr. Dixon, Drew and John centered on the success of the school's basketball teams, and the 30-year rivalry between Catholic and Glenwood Memorial. They all agreed that both high schools have been quite successful in that many of the seniors who played basketball had won full college scholarships and a few went on to play professional basketball. Mr. Daniels reminded everyone that, aside from the sports scholarships, there were many other outstanding students who were recipients of various scholastic scholarships. He then said that over the past 30 years, 92-percent of the graduating seniors had gone on to college.

Judy, Stella, Mrs. Dixon and Mrs. Daniels were listening to Brother Gregory relate some of the antics of the senior class of 1970.

"There were two especially memorable events," Brother Gregory said. "The funniest one was the Freshman Halloween contest. A couple of seniors had cornered the freshman class, on the stairs outside the third floor hallway, while they were on their way back to their classrooms from lunch. These two seniors told the kids that Catholic High had a long-standing custom for the freshman class to dress up for Halloween. The five best-costumed freshmen, as judged by the Junior Class, would be exempt from taking mid-term exams. The freshmen were instructed to stop in the administration office before they left school that day and ask Mrs. Dixon for the sign-up sheet."

"I had a line of students that started from inside my office and wound its way in to the cafeteria," Mrs. Dixon interjected. "To this day, I still don't know who started that rumor. Brother Higgins, who was principal at the time, said that that was a first for him."

"Knowing how much of a prankster Drew is, I wouldn't be a bit surprised if he was one of those two seniors," Judy stated.

Drew, engrossed in a different conversation, heard his name being mentioned and turned towards his wife.

"Yes, Judy; what did you need?" he asked.

"Nothing, Drew," she replied; "nothing at all."

Drew shrugged his shoulders and turned back towards the others.

"Brother Gregory," Stella began, "what was the other event?"

"That would be the rumor that the annual spring boat ride to Rye Beach, in upstate New York, was canceled and that refunds were being handled by Brother Meekin, but only during his homeroom class period. I was in the classroom next to his and from the corner of my eye I saw, through the door window, a rather large standing-room-only crowd in the second floor hallway. Concerned that something terrible had happened, I opened the door and had to push my way through the crowd. As soon as I did, the seniors began laughing hysterically. It took almost 30 minutes to clear the hallway and the stairs, and to get everyone back into their classrooms. Of course, no one could identify who had said that the boat trip was canceled."

John was relieved that at no time during the course of their meal did Alex's name come up. He wasn't sure what he would have said, if asked. John passed on the dessert, but did ask the server for some more ice water. When he finally looked at his watch, it was 6:52 – time for him to leave. He excused himself from the table saying that he was going to the men's room. When Stella looked in his direction, he winked at her. She smiled.

After he pushed open one of the door's leading out into the hallway, John turned right and headed for the door that led to the theatre's workshop. He had plenty of time to get to the stage since Drew had mentioned that he wanted to take about five minutes to again welcome everyone to the reunion. Precisely at 7:00, Drew excused himself from the table and walked towards the stage. He climbed the stairs on the left side and stood behind the podium that had been strategically placed a few feet from the stairs. He placed his hand inside his jacket pocket and withdrew some slightly wrinkled papers. After smoothing them out as best he could, he turned on the podium's microphone and began speaking.

"Ladies and gentlemen, may I have your attention please."

Other than Stella, no one at the table realized that John had not yet returned; everyone was looking at Drew and waiting for him to begin speaking.

* * * * * * * * * * * * * * *

Dave and the ladies had already made their final checks and when John entered the stage the four of them gave him a thumbs-up – everything was ready. He gave a thumbs-up in return and headed directly towards center stage to wait for Drew to finish talking, and for the main drape to open.

* * * * * * * * * * * * * * *

"Ladies and gentleman; may I have your attention please."

The noise slowly simmered down and when the room fell silent, Drew began.

"Thank you. For the record, Brother Kernan has reclaimed his whistle, hence the reason I'm up here on stage."

The audience's cheer resulted in Drew's momentary silence.

"Now we're negotiating on the detention charge," Drew added.

Once again, there was a loud cheer followed by a chant of "no detention, no detention." After a few seconds of this, Brother Kernan stood up. The group quieted down and Brother Kernan officially absolved Drew with a blessing, which brought a round of applause from the crowd.

After the applause ended, Drew continued, "Thank you, Brother Kernan. I'm sure it has been an exciting afternoon for all of us and as you finish your dessert I'd like to take this opportunity to say a few words. I promise to keep it short."

All right, Drew, John muttered to himself. *Don't ramble on; this is not the debating club where you have to win over the audience to see things your way.*

"We have some special entertainment for your enjoyment this evening. Our own John Michaels has agreed to come out of retirement and present an encore performance from his full evening magic show."

Upon hearing this announcement, everyone in the room turned their heads to look towards the table where John was sitting, only to find he was not there.

"Stella, did you know about this?" Judy whispered.

"Yes, I did, Judy," Stella whispered back.

"Drew did a wonderful job of keeping it a secret. I had no idea John would be performing tonight," she said.

"Don't worry, folks," Drew said. "John is already backstage and is waiting for me to finish."

As soon as Drew said that, the entire group stood up and began applauding. It took a few moments, but everyone finally sat back down.

"I'm not sure if you were applauding because John was backstage or the fact that you're waiting for me to finish speaking," Drew said.

Once again, the crowd stood up and applauded. As soon as the applause began to die down, Drew continued.

"Okay, I can take a hint."

The audience laughed.

"I'm sure many of you have seen John's numerous television performances. Tonight, he performs live, for us. He's promised some new and novel illusions in addition to some of the things you've seen him present on national television. Additionally, John has a special illusion for tonight's show. He told me he created it especially for our reunion and after tonight it will never be performed again. Believe me, I've tried to coax it out of him, but he kept ignoring my questions. So without further ado, ladies and gentlemen please join me in a round of applause as we welcome ... John Michaels."

Drew turned off the microphone and pushed the podium towards the side curtain. Standing in the corner behind the closed main drape, Dave grabbed the podium and pulled it out of view. As soon as Drew stepped off the last step, the lights were slowly dimmed, the music began playing and the main drape was opened. The stage was set with a botanical garden backdrop that stretched from one end to the other. On each side of the stage were two self-contained water fountains that were sprouting water about a foot into the air. In the center of the stage stood a wood and metal garden archway; Patty and Maria stood on each side, slightly forward. Sally stood about three-feet to the left of Patty, holding a wicker basket in her hands.

Suddenly, the music stopped, there was a drum roll and the sound of two cymbals crashing together, then a puff of smoke and John magically appeared inside the garden archway. He paused there for a moment, and then stepped out and bowed to acknowledge the audience's applause. When the music began again, John handed Patty his walking stick. She then took two steps backwards while John and Maria took three steps forward. He removed the glove on his left hand, turned to his left and handed it to Maria. He then turned back towards the audience, removed the glove on his right hand and tossed it into the air; it changed into a bouquet of flowers. After he caught the bouquet, he handed it to Maria; she then headed off stage.

As Maria walked away, Sally approached. John turned to his right and began a continuous production of miniature flowers from the fingertips of both his hands, dropping each one into the wicker basket that Sally was holding. After the last flower fell into the basket, a bouquet of flowers suddenly appeared in John's hands. He handed it to Sally; she placed in into the basket, and then turned and headed off stage. John turned towards the audience and posed with his arms outstretched.

As the audience applauded, Patty walked up and stood alongside John. He turned towards her and gently removed the black-colored scarf she was wearing around her neck. He curled the scarf around his right hand and into a small ball, and then tossed it into the air. As it fell, it transformed into a rainbow-colored scarf. John gave the scarf back to Patty and then she gave him the walking stick. While Patty loosely tied the scarf around her neck, John tapped both ends of the stick on the stage floor. He twirled it in his right hand and then held it up vertically; his left hand on top and his right hand on the bottom. A moment later the black walking stick visually changed colors, first to yellow and then to green; and then it transformed into a bouquet of long-stem flowers. John handed the bouquet to Patty, who then headed off stage.

Maria and Sally returned and stood on each side of John. Maria was holding a 14-square-inch black bag that had a large round hole cut through it on both sides. In her right hand she held three large silk handkerchiefs: red, blue and yellow. Sally was holding three large, white feather wreaths. After Maria gave the bag to John, he placed his right hand, from back to front, through the cutout hole and wriggled his fingers. After removing his hand, he opened the bag and turned it towards the audience so they could see inside. He then turned the bag right side up and motioned for Sally to place one of the wreaths inside the bag. Maria then placed the blue silk through the cutout opening letting its ends hang down loosely. While John held onto the bag, Sally reached in and slowly removed the wreath, which had now changed its color to blue. The other two white wreaths also changed colors to red and yellow, respectively.

John removed the three silks from the wreaths and gave them to Maria. He then opened the bag and Sally placed the three wreaths into it. Maria then placed all three silks through the cutout hole, letting their ends hang down loosely. While John held the bag, Sally reached in and pulled out a giant blue, red and yellow wreath. John opened the bag and turned its opening towards the audience: it was empty. He handed the bag to Maria and then turned around to grab the three silks that were hanging on the wreath. They struck a pose and the audience applauded.

As Maria and Sally left the stage, John did a short juggling act with the three silks. After he caught the last silk in his left hand, he placed it into his right hand, with the other two. He then reached inside the three silks and produced a dove delicately perched on his left forefinger. John made a slow, soft upward swing of his left hand and the dove flew out into the audience and circled around before landing back on John's forefinger.

Patty and Sally had since returned and they stood on each side of John. Patty had rolled out a table with a birdcage on it; Sally was carrying a clear plastic tube with black caps. John gave Patty the three silks and then he walked around to the rear of the table. He opened the top of the cage, placed the dove on a wood perch and then closed the lid. He then walked towards Sally and as soon as he was within arms distance, she handed him the clear tube. John removed a cap and Patty placed the three silks into the tube; she then headed off stage. John replaced the cap and then he tossed the tube into the air so it flipped over and over, end for end. After he caught it, he reached into the tube and pulled out a parasol. He pressed the button on its handle and it sprung open: its cover was red, blue and yellow. He handed the empty tube and the parasol to Sally, who then headed off stage.

Maria returned once again; she was holding a silver-colored tube atop a wooden base in her right hand. She relaxed her grip on the tube as John placed his hand on it and lifted it up. Inside was a clear plastic tube. He carefully placed the silver tube back over the clear one and then let it drop down onto the base. He clapped his hands twice in rapid succession and then lifted the outer tube: inside the inner tube was a dove. John handed the outer tube to Patty, who had since returned to center stage. With her hands firmly holding onto the wooden base and the clear tube, Maria turned it sideways so John could reach inside with his fingers to retrieve the dove. Free of its confines, the dove flapped its wings while it rested on John's right forefinger. As Patty and Maria walked off stage, John placed the dove alongside the other one in the cage.

Sally returned to center stage with a butterfly net that was attached to a long metal pole. She handed it to John and then she put her right hand over her eyes and slowly turned her head side-to-side. A moment later she tugged John's left arm and then pointed her left-hand forefinger in the air. John looked up and then swung the pole high in the air; nothing. Once again Sally pointed to another spot in the air. John swung the pole and a dove magically appeared inside the net. He let the pole slide down through his hand and then tilted it on an angle so Sally could reach into the net and remove the dove.

Twice more, when John swung the pole, a dove appeared inside the net. After the last one was placed into the cage, he handed the pole back to Sally. As she headed off stage, Patty returned carrying a large silk-foulard that was neatly folded into a small package. She placed it on top of the birdcage and then opened it so all four sides were covered. Stepping behind the table, John grasped the cage by its sides and carefully picked it up. John waited until Patty had pulled the table away before taking a few steps forward. He looked to his left and then to his right, and then he tossed the foulard-covered cage up into the air. The cage had vanished. After catching a corner of the silk foulard, he struck a pose and the audience applauded.

Maria returned carrying a large flat, plastic tray in her hands. On top of the tray was a collapsed rectangular cardboard box. John picked it up, showed both sides and then popped it open. He placed his hand through the opening and then placed the open box onto the tray. He waved his hands over it and when he lifted the box up, an aquarium, complete with water and fish, was on the tray. As the audience applauded, Sally and Patty emerged from stage right, and together with Maria and John they took a collective bow.

* * * * * * * * * * * * * * *

John walked towards the front of the stage as the main drape closed behind him.

"Could I have the house lights turned up, please?" John asked.

After the lights came on, he said, "I think we should give Drew a round of applause for his steadfast work in organizing this 30th Reunion of the Class of 1970."

The audience stood up and turned towards Drew and gave him a standing ovation. Once the applause began to subside, John began speaking again.

"Mr. Landers," John said, "I'd like to borrow a bill ... a piece of paper money ... would you be kind enough lend me a $10,000 bill?"

All eyes were on Mr. Landers as he stood up. He pulled one of his pants' pockets inside out signifying that he had no money and then sat back down. The audience laughed.

"Ladies and gentlemen, I think Mr. Landers could use a little encouragement."

The audience started chanting *Bill, Bill, Bill, Bill*. Realizing that he wasn't going to be let off the hook, Mr. Landers reluctantly stood up, again. This time the audience began applauding.

"Mr. Landers, now that you're standing up, would you mind coming up on stage to help?" John asked.

The audience cheered as he slowly made his way up to the stage.

"Since you don't have a 10,000-dollar bill in your wallet, I guess this also rules out asking for a 100, 50, 20, 10 or five-dollar bill. Is that a fair assumption?" John asked.

Mr. Landers nodded affirmatively.

John paused momentarily and then said, "How about a single? Surely you have a dollar bill in your wallet?"

Mr. Landers reached into his back pocket, withdrew his wallet, took out a dollar bill and handed it to John.

John took the dollar and said, "This is your dollar; you didn't borrow it from someone else, correct?"

Mr. Landers nodded affirmatively.

"Mr. Landers, I don't remember you being this quiet in our English class," John said as he folded the bill and placed it in his front pants pocket.

"Times have changed, John," he replied. "Besides, I have this sudden urge to check my jacket for a stick of chewing gum!"

The audience roared with laughter when they heard this. For some it brought back memories of that day in Freshman English class and for the others it confirmed what they heard John had done.

"Well, before we continue perhaps you may want to check your pockets now," John replied.

He did … there was no gum, but before he would allow John to proceed he checked his pants pockets, as well. The audience laughed.

"Okay, John, you can continue now," Mr. Landers confidently said.

"Thank you for that vote of confidence and thanks for loaning me a dollar. I'll pay you back at the next reunion … five years from now."

As John said this, he grasped Mr. Landers' left arm and began to slowly escort him towards the stage stairs. As he did, he dropped an unopened pack of chewing gum into Mr. Landers' left jacket pocket. No one saw it.

John suddenly stopped walking, smiled and said, "I'm only kidding, Mr. Landers. Let's go back to center stage."

John removed the dollar from his pocket and held it up, in his left hand, for everyone to see.

"Mr. Landers, would you be interested in learning a trade secret on how to double your money?"

When Mr. Landers nodded affirmatively, John folded the bill in half.

"There you are; we've been partners only a minute and I've doubled your money!"

The audience laughed. Once things quieted down, John continued.

"Mr. Landers, I'd like to take a moment to talk to you about inflation. In today's economy, this dollar is not worth a dollar; it's worth a lot less. I'll tell you what; let me give you a quick lesson in economics to prove my point."

John turned and faced the audience.

"I have Mr. Landers' dollar bill – John waved it up and down – and I will give it to the first person who comes up and gives me 75 cents."

Brother Gregory was the first one out of his seat. He walked up to the stage, reached into his pants pocket and withdrew a handful of change. He selected three quarters and gave them to John. In exchange, John gave him the dollar bill.

"See how easy that was, folks," John said. "Now, I have Mr. Landers' 75 cents and I will give it to the first person who comes up and gives me 50 cents."

Mr. Landers reached into his pants pocket for some change.

"It wouldn't be fair to let you buy your own money, Mr. Landers. Thanks, anyway."

Steven Kellar, who was captain of the junior varsity track team, ran up to the stage and made the money exchange with John.

"So far, so good, Mr. Landers," John said.

John then sold the 50 cents to Drew for a quarter and then sold the quarter to Jose Cabrera, for five cents. Jose was the only student to ever have the distinction of being president of the Spanish Heritage Club for his entire four years at Catholic High.

After the last transaction was completed, John said, "As you can see, all that's left of Mr. Landers' dollar is 5 cents; a concrete example of how inflation really works and the value of a dollar in today's economy."

John turned sideways and gave the nickel to Mr. Landers.

"Mr. Landers, you have just learned a lesson in inflation that cost you 95 cents. On behalf of the Class of 1970, I'd like to thank you for coming up and helping me today."

The audience applauded and John paused a moment.

"Money is not the only thing affected by inflation, Mr. Landers." John turned back towards the audience and continued,

"Even the magic books, magazines and tricks that magicians buy also cost more. Here's a perfect example."

John reached into his inner jacket pocket and withdrew an envelope. He showed the front of it to Mr. Landers as he read aloud the printed words, *Magic Wishing Cards*.

"This is what I paid a dollar for," John said to the audience as he opened the envelope and removed two 3x5 index cards. "The owner of a magic shop that I've frequented many, many times over the past 25 years told me he found this at the bottom of a box of old magic tricks he had in his warehouse. He wasn't sure anyone would buy it, so one day he offered it to me for the princely sum of one dollar. To be honest, Mr. Landers, I don't see anything magical about these index cards, do you?"

John turned sideways, handed the two index cards to Mr. Landers and then turned back towards the audience. A moment later Mr. Landers gave the index cards back to John.

"Would you mind checking the envelope, also?"

As Mr. Landers inspected the envelope, John said, "The directions that were inside the envelope said that the owner would be granted one wish; a once in a lifetime opportunity. That person could wish for a million dollars, a trip around the world, the lottery's winning numbers ... anything they wanted."

After Mr. Landers returned the envelope, John put the index cards inside and closed the flap, tucking it into the envelope.

"The only thing the owner of this envelope had to do was to make a wish and then tap the envelope three times."

John pretended to make a wish and then tapped it. As he was about to open the envelope, he stopped and looked directly at the audience.

"This is silly," he began, "I don't know why I bought this in the first place, nor do I know why I'm boring you with a fantasy tale."

He paused a moment.

"I guess it was just wishful thinking on my part."

John turned towards Mr. Landers and said, "I hate getting bad news so would you mind looking inside this envelope for me? If something's inside, don't say anything ... just give me a thumbs-up sign."

He handed the envelope to Mr. Landers and then John turned back towards the audience.

"They say you should never reveal what you wished for because…"

The audience suddenly began laughing, so John stopped talking. Mr. Landers was giving John a thumbs-up sign. John turned to face Mr. Landers.

"I'm sorry Mr. Landers; I know that there are two index cards in the envelope, I should have been more specific. If there's anything other than the index cards in the envelope, then you can give me a thumbs-up sign."

John turned back towards the audience.

"You know what I wished for? I wished that I had my dollar back."

The audience began laughing again. John turned towards Mr. Landers: his right thumb was pointing up.

With a look of surprise, John said, "You mean there's something other than index cards in the envelope?"

Mr. Landers nodded affirmatively.

"You're kidding me, right?"

Mr. Landers shook his head back and forth.

"That's not possible, Mr. Landers! What could possibly be inside the envelope other than two index cards?"

Mr. Landers pulled out a dollar bill.

"I don't believe it … I just don't believe it," John said in a dejected tone of voice.

Mr. Landers handed the dollar bill and the envelope to John.

"Of all the things I could have wished for … I had to ask for a lousy dollar."

Mr. Landers suddenly leaned towards John and whispered in his ear.

"Ladies and gentlemen, Mr. Landers just reminded me that I borrowed a dollar from him a little while ago and now would be a good time to repay the loan."

The audience began to laugh.

"Looks like I'm about to lose another dollar," John said.

He then turned towards Mr. Landers.

"Here you are. By the way, you can keep the nickel as interest for the temporary loan of your dollar. Thanks for coming up to help. Ladies and gentlemen, please give Mr. Landers a round of applause as he returns to his seat."

John waited till Mr. Landers was about 15 feet from the stage stairs before calling his name.

"Mr. Landers…"

He stopped and turned around. When he did, the applause quickly ended, too.

"Mr. Landers, I was wondering if … well … you mentioned chewing gum a few minutes ago. I was wondering if I could have a stick of your chewing gum, please. I promise not to chew it till after the show is over."

Instinctively, Mr. Landers put both his hands into his jacket pocket. The look on his face was priceless as he withdrew an unopened pack of chewing gum and held it up for everyone to see. The audience chanted *Bill, Bill, Bill, Bill,* once again. Mr. Landers walked back over to John with his hand extended. They shook hands and then Mr. Landers gave John the entire pack of gum.

"Ladies and gentlemen: give it up for Mr. Bill Landers," John said.

The audience gave him a standing ovation.

* * * * * * * * * * * * * * * *

As the music began to play, the house lights were lowered and the main drape was opened. A large three-section box, painted navy blue with black trim, was in the center of the stage. On the front of the box a yellow profile silhouette of a lady extended from top to bottom. Patty emerged from stage left just as John turned around. When they reached the illusion, John first opened the side door. Then he opened the "window door" in the top and bottom sections, and the front door of the middle section so the audience could watch Patty as she stepped inside. Maria entered from stage right, pushing a silver-colored vertical bar rack with four large stainless steel blades resting on it. John waved to Patty and after she waved back he closed and locked all the doors.

John picked up a blade, stepped in front of the box and inserted it under Patty's head. It effortlessly slid all the way through to the back. He placed a second blade under the first one. The third and fourth blades were inserted just above Patty's knees. John walked to the left side of the box and pushed the bottom section to the right, separating Patty's lower torso from the rest of her body. He then walked around to the right side and pushed the top portion to the left, separating Patty's head from her body. Standing in front once again, he re-opened the top and bottom window doors revealing Patty's head and feet. He then swung open the front door of the middle section; there was an audible gasp when the audience saw that Patty's body was gone. John leaned into the open space and waved his arm up and down. He then walked around to the back of the illusion, lowered the middle section's rear wall and leaned into the open space so the audience could see him.

Without waiting for the applause to subside, John raised the rear wall and locked it back in place. He closed all the doors, and then pushed the top and bottom sections back to their original positions. As he removed each blade, he gave it to Maria to place back on the rack. John then walked to the side of the box and opened the door; Patty stepped out unharmed. With Maria on his right and Patty on his left, they walked arm-in-arm to the front of the stage amid the applause. After the main drape was closed behind them, Patty and Maria headed off-stage in opposite directions.

* * * * * * * * * * * * * * * *

Once again, John asked to have the house lights turned up.

"Ladies and gentlemen, people have often asked me if there is one particular trick that I like best. It's a difficult question to answer because everything that I – no make that, everything that my wonderful assistants and I – perform, whether it's an illusion or one-on-one with a member of the audience, is special and unique in its own way. What I thought we'd do for tonight's show is present a few of our hallmark illusions. We'll start with one of the oldest illusions in magic history, the linking rings, and we'll end with the always-popular levitation of a beautiful woman."

John turned slightly to his right and placed his right arm in between the closed main drape sections. Sally placed two gold, 14-

inch diameter rings into John's hand and then returned to the side wing area to await her cue after the main drape was opened. Holding the rings firmly in his hand, John brought his right arm back into full view and then turned towards the audience.

"Maestro; music please," he said.

John placed one of the rings into his other hand and then twisted both hands back and forth, showing two separate rings. Following that display, he meticulously linked and unlinked them in a carefully choreographed routine. At the conclusion, he placed his arm in between the main drape sections to exchange the two small rings for two hula-hoop-sized rings. Once again, after showing them separate, he linked and unlinked them in a series of clear-cut moves. He finished just as he started: with a ring in each hand.

As the music tempo picked up, the main drape was opened. John walked to the side wing area and handed the two rings to Dave. As soon as Dave took them, John took one step sideways, grabbed the neon light saber illusion and pulled it towards center stage. As he did this, John turned the cabinet completely around so the audience could see all four sides. When he reached center stage he positioned the illusion sideways, so its rear wall was facing stage right. Attached to the outside rear wall were an 'On/Off' switch and a 6-spoke, 24-inch diameter ship's wheel made of hardwood and brass. John removed both side doors and placed them on the floor so the audience could see inside the illusion. He then spun the ship's wheel, clockwise. An inside panel with 48 neon light bulbs moved forward on its tracks and emerged through matching holes in the front wall.

John flipped the power switch on; the bulbs illuminated the entire stage. He then spun the ship's wheel counter-clockwise, pulling the inside panel back to its original position. Just before it reached the halfway mark, John stopped and turned the power switch off. After the inside panel was pulled completely back, John replaced the far side door and secured it in place. As he did this, Sally entered from stage left. With John's help she stepped inside the cabinet and then turned and stood facing the front panel.

John spun the wheel again, stopping when the inside panel came to within a few inches of Sally's back. He then picked up the other side door, mounted it in place and secured it. Stepping behind the illusion, he turned the power switch on and then resumed spinning the wheel. The lit bulbs harmlessly pierced Sally's body and exited the front wall. John turned the illusion completely around to show the audience that Sally was inside. With the illusion again facing stage right, he flipped the power switch to the 'Off' position and spun the wheel to retract the inside panel. He removed the front side door and then extended his hand to help Sally as she stepped out; together they struck a pose. After John replaced the side door, Sally exited to the right while John pushed the illusion off stage, in the opposite direction.

He grabbed the Temple of Benares illusion and spun it around as he walked towards center stage. Patty followed a few steps behind John; she was pushing a 2-foot-tall rectangular box containing eight cutlass swords. John unlatched the hook that secured the two rooftop panels in place and carefully let them fall to each side. He held his hand out for Patty; she took hold of it, placed one foot into the temple and then lifted her other leg up and placed it inside, too. She slowly lowered her body down into a comfortable cross-legged sitting position. After John closed the two rooftop panels and locked them, he removed a sword from the box and with careful aim, and a lot of finesse, he inserted it into the temple. Then, in rapid succession, he inserted the remaining seven swords into the temple through the sides and the rooftop. He then opened the two front doors to reveal a temple full of swords: Patty was gone. After closing the two doors, he removed the swords and unlatched the rooftop panels; Patty stood up and with John's help she climbed out. John and Patty walked towards stage left. When he got to within a few steps of the stage wing, he forcefully pushed the temple so it would glide back on its own, out of sight.

John stepped to his left and grabbed the metal handle that was attached to a rectangular utility platform cart, on which rested two bar stools and a wooden plank. As he pulled the cart towards center stage, Maria entered from stage right; they met behind the cart. A moment later they each picked up a stool and then walked around to the front by going in opposite directions. After placing the stools on the stage floor, John turned around, picked up the plank and placed it across the top of the stools. Maria sat down and then John placed his hands on her shoulders and helped her lie down. Standing behind the stools, midway between each one, John made continuous upward gestures with his hands, as if he were lifting up the air, and a second later Maria began to slowly ascend upwards.

He then headed towards stage right and grabbed the hula-hoop that Dave was holding. Returning to center stage, John raised the hoop up and proceeded to pass it over Maria's body, starting at her feet. After the hoop passed over her head, John set it on the floor and pushed it so it rolled off stage. As he made a downward gesture with his hands, Maria began to descend.

He stepped back behind the stools, took Maria's hand and helped her sit upright. With John still holding her hand, Maria stood up and then they headed towards the front of the stage. Patty and Sally emerged from stage left and right, respectively, and joined them. Once there, the four of them held hands and took a collective bow.

* * * * * * * * * * * * * * * *

John stepped in front of the main drape as it closed behind him.

"Could I have the house lights turned up again," he asked.

He waited before continuing.

"Ladies and gentlemen, the dictionary defines premonition as the act of predicting the future before it ever happens," John began.

He reached into his inside jacket pocket and withdrew a manila envelope.

"Earlier this morning, I placed a prediction inside this envelope."

John glanced into the audience looking for a volunteer. Michael Murphy, the only Catholic High student to ever bowl a perfect game, was sitting at the second table. Walking to the front of the stage, he asked Michael to hold the envelope.

"Please don't look inside until I ask you to and ignore anyone who tries to bribe you to open it … unless they make you a substantial monetary offer you just can't refuse."

Michael nodded his head up and down, and then returned to his seat. Peering out into the audience on the opposite side of the room, John asked Joel McIntyre, the varsity basketball team captain, if he would mind helping with an experiment in extrasensory perception. He agreed and as he made his way up to the stage from the back of the room, John prompted the audience to give Joel a round of applause.

"Thanks for coming up Joel," John said. "I have two decks of playing cards in my pocket and in a moment I'm going to have you select a card from each deck. To help the people in the back of the room, I want you to write your selections on a dry-erase board."

As John said this, the main drape was opened.

"Step back this way, please, Joel."

John reached into his right, outside jacket pocket, withdrew the two decks of playing cards and placed them on the table. He picked up the blue deck first, removed the cards, cut the deck three times and then spread the cards from hand-to-hand.

"Joel, please reach in anywhere and take a card," John said.

He pulled out the 10-of-Clubs.

"Put the card on the table," John began. "Using the pen on the dry-erase board ledge, write the word *blue* in large block letters on the top left side and draw a line under it. Then write the number '10' under the word so everyone can see it." After Joel did this, John said, "Alongside the number write a large 'C;' this will represent the word 'Clubs'."

When he finished, John picked up the red deck of cards, cut this deck three times and then spread the cards from hand-to-hand.

"Joel, I'd like you to once again reach in and take a card."

This time, he pulled out the 5-of-Diamonds.

"Write the word *red* in large block letters on the right side of the dry-erase board and draw a line under it. Then write the number '5' under the word so everyone can see it. Alongside the number write a large 'D;' this will represent the word 'Diamonds'."

John waited.

"Now that you've selected two cards," John began, "we're going to take this one step further and mark these two cards with a very unique identifier."

John reached into his left, outside jacket pocket and withdrew a third deck of cards.

"These are E.S.P. cards," John began. "Dr. Joseph Rhine, an American psychologist, developed them in the early 1900s as a means to test a person's psychic ability. There are five symbols: Square, Star, Wavy Lines, Cross and Circle; and five of each symbol, a total of 25 cards."

John spread the cards from hand-to-hand face-up so Joel could see them. He squared up the deck, turned it facedown, cut the deck a few times and then asked Joel to remove two cards. The first card Joel pulled out was the 'Square;' the second one was the 'Circle.'

"Draw a square completely around the '10C' and a circle around the '5D' on the dry-erase board."

John picked up the 10-of-Clubs and the Square with his right hand, and the 5-of-Diamonds and the Circle with his left hand. He then walked towards the front of the stage.

"Michael, did anyone try to bribe you to open the envelope?"

Michael shook his head side to side, as he said, "No."

"Very well, for the very first time, please open the envelope. Inside are two large cards; hold a card in each hand, raise both hands up high in the air and show both sides of the cards to everyone, please."

The audience gasped when they saw that the two cards Michael was holding matched in value, color and E.S.P. symbol, the two cards in John's hand, which also replicated what Joel had written on the dry-erase board.

John retrieved the two cards and the envelope from Michael and after thanking him, had him return to his seat. After placing everything on the table, he turned towards Joel and said, "Thanks for coming up to help. Ladies and gentlemen, please give a round of applause to Joel and Michael."

* * * * * * * * * * * * * * * *

"Ladies and gentlemen, we have a brand new illusion to show you; I hope you like it."

The main drape opened to reveal Maria standing next to a square platform resting atop a five-foot high, open frame structure. Mounted on top of the platform was another open frame structure, six and one-half feet high. John and Maria pushed a set of stairs towards the structure and when the two pieces were snugly resting against each other, they firmly attached the stairs to the platform with sliding bolts.

Maria headed back off stage while John climbed up the stairs. After stepping inside the open-frame structure, he turned to his right, leaned over and grasped the handle of a white window shade. He raised it up and locked it in place, then turned around and raised the rear shade. After locking this one in place, he raised and locked the left side's shade, creating a three-sided makeshift box. Maria returned with a half-panel that was covered with the same white material. She stopped directly in front of the platform and raised the panel over her head. John took hold of it and then stepped back into the box. Facing the audience, he carefully inserted the half-panel into the running tracks of the open structure and made sure it smoothly slid up and down. John let the panel slide down, covering his lower body.

The half-panel, the audience quickly realized, would, depending on its position, only conceal John's lower body or his upper body – but not both at the same time.

As soon as the music began to play, John raised the half-panel up, locked it in place, and then he thrust his arms out through cutout holes on the left and right sides of the box. Scarcely a moment later, another set of arms began to slowly emerge alongside John's, even though only one body and one pair of feet were plainly visible inside the box. The four arms began moving up and down in synchronized movement to the beat of the music. They then began to slowly retract back into the box. After they were completely inside, the front panel was unlatched and allowed to slide down. John had disappeared; Sally and Patty were inside the box.

Sally removed the front panel from its tracks and handed it to Maria; she placed it on the floor. When the music stopped, Patty, Sally and Maria simultaneously pointed to the back of the auditorium.

John bellowed, "Here I am!"

Every head in the audience turned around. John victoriously raised his hands in the air to symbolize the successful exchange and then he quickly trotted up towards the stage to join Patty, Sally and Maria, who were now standing together at center stage. The audience rose to their feet for a standing ovation. When John reached the stage, the four of them held hands and bowed; the audience began to applaud louder.

* * * * * * * * * * * * * * *

John stepped forward as the main drape was closed behind him. When the applause began to subside, he asked to have the house lights turned up, again.

"Thank you. Thank you very much. Ladies and gentlemen," John said, "there will be a 15-minute break while the stage is cleared and readied for the show's finale."

As the music began playing; John turned around and stepped through the break in the main drape. As Drew climbed the stairs, Dave pushed the podium back out into view. Drew maneuvered it into position and then turned on the microphone.

"Wasn't that something, folks?" he said.

The audience started applauding again.

"John's truly amazing. If the finale is anything like the first half of the show we have just seen, we are in for a real treat."

With nothing else to say, Drew turned the microphone off and pushed the podium towards the curtain. Once again, Dave grabbed it and pulled it from view.

* * * * * * * * * * * * * * *

"It's one thing to see magic performed on television, but when you see it presented in person, it's simply amazing," Drew said to everyone at the table.

"I agree," Mr. Daniels said. "John has certainly mastered the art of magic."

"Stella, do you know what John has planned for the second half?" Judy asked.

"No, I don't. We didn't talk about the show at all. In fact, the only thing I asked him was if he was nervous about coming out of retirement to do an encore performance."

"What did he say about that?" Mrs. Dixon asked.

"He said that he was a little bit nervous, but that once the music started everything would fall into place, just as he and his crew had rehearsed it."

"Well, he certainly didn't look nervous to me," Mrs. Dixon said.

* * * * * * * * * * * * * * *

At the 14-minute mark, the music started playing softly and a recorded announcement bellowed out, **ladies and gentlemen, the show will resume in one minute.** Right at the 10-second mark, the house lights were slowly dimmed and another announcement made: **ladies and gentlemen, here is Mr. John Michaels.** The main drape was opened and sitting center stage was a 6½-foot tall, three-foot square wooden box painted fire engine red. The word "BELIEVE" was stenciled on the front of the box. From stage left John headed out towards center stage and stopped at a point just in front of the illusion as the music gradually faded out.

"Ladies and gentlemen, tonight for the first time anywhere, I'd like to present another new illusion, The Time Machine."

John paused a moment.

"For years, scientists have searched for ways to travel through time. While many said it was impossible, they should have asked a magician. After all, that's what we do – the impossible."

The audience laughed.

"Tonight, I will tempt the unknown forces of the universe by entering The Time Machine to return to a time in history's past. In order to prove the authenticity of such travel, it is my intention to try and bring something back from the past – our past; to the future – today – right here, right now."

He paused for a moment and then looked directly at Drew.

"I promise not to bring back anyone's homework or test grades."

Everyone in the audience began laughing. Right after the music began, Dave and Maria emerged from stage right, and Patty and Sally from stage left. They approached the ominous box and took their positions: Dave stood behind the box, Patty and Sally on each side and Maria in front. They grasped a handle that was affixed to each panel, while their other hand unlatched the bolts that held the panels in place. With precision timing they slowly stepped backwards, allowing the panels to fall away from the frame. The two side panels and the rear panel were lowered down to a 45-degree angle while the front panel was lowered all the way to the floor.

"Empty as a politician's promise," John said.

The four panels were raised up and locked back into place. Maria opened the door on the front panel and John stepped inside. He turned towards the audience; Maria closed the door and then locked it. Dave, Patty, Sally and Maria then turned the box completely around, stopping when the word, BELIEVE, was facing the audience once again. Simultaneously, the four of them took two steps backwards and waited for the music to stop. When it did, they approached the box again, grabbed a handle, unlatched the bolts and slowly lowered the four panels as they had done before. There was an audible gasp from the audience when they saw that the box was empty; John had vanished.

A moment later, the four panels were raised up again and locked back in place. Maria then unlocked the door on the front panel and it swung open. John stepped out and headed towards the front of the stage. As the audience applauded, Maria closed and locked the door. John waited for the applause to subside.

"Thank you very much, ladies and gentlemen."

He paused a moment.

"As I mentioned at the onset of this illusion, I have brought something back from the past with me."

John placed his hands into his jacket pockets, earnestly probing for *that something.*

After a moment of fruitless searching he stopped and said, "I must have accidentally dropped it inside The Time Machine."

As soon as he said those words, he turned around as if he was going to walk back towards the illusion, but he didn't move. Dave, Maria, Patty and Sally unlatched the bolts holding the four panels together and slowly lowered them down all the way so that they rested on the stage floor. There was another gasp from the audience when they saw a man standing inside the box with his back to the audience. John quickly spun around and looked directly at Stella. As soon as he made eye contact with her, John placed his hand over his heart and then extended it towards Stella, and followed that by throwing a kiss in her direction.

"Ladies and gentlemen," John began, "I'd like to introduce a good friend of mine ... and someone you all know."

Stella stood up, at the table.

"Oh ... my ... gosh," she said, as tears began to rapidly cascade down her cheeks.

"Please help me welcome – Alex Holloman, a member of Catholic High's Class of 1970."

Alex slowly turned around to face the audience. He carefully stepped off the illusion's platform and headed towards the front of the stage to stand alongside John. The audience gave John and his crew, and Alex, a standing ovation.

* * * * * * * * * * * * * * * *

The main drape was immediately closed behind John and Alex, and the house lights were turned up. John turned towards Alex and they shook hands. John then turned back towards the audience, waved goodbye and then stepped through the main drape, leaving Alex alone at center stage with the audience still standing and applauding. A moment later, with tears in his eyes, Alex turned and walked towards the stairs to greet friends he hadn't seen in 30 years, and to hug a cousin he so dearly missed.

Stella ran towards Alex. They embraced.

Stella, Alex whispered, *I'm so very sorry for what I did to you, Aunt Carol and Uncle Ed. It was terribly wrong and I have no excuse for it. I can only hope that, one day, you can find it in your heart to forgive me.*

Alex, Stella whispered back, *you are the only family I have; you're back and that's what matters most. Come to my apartment after the show.*

I promise you, I will, Alex replied.

The reunion attendees gave Alex and Stella a few minutes to have a private moment together, and then the entire group got up from their tables and headed towards them both.

"Alex," Stella began, "I'm going backstage to catch up to John. I think you'll be in good hands with these well-wishers."

"I think so too, Stella. Go ahead; I'll be here when you and John come back out."

Stella gave Alex another hug before leaving.

CHAPTER TWENTY FOUR

By the time John stepped behind the main drape, Dave, Patty, Maria and Sally had already reattached the four panels to the illusion frame, and had repositioned The Time Machine alongside the other illusions that needed to be repacked in their respective road cases.

"Guys, it was a great show. Thanks for your hard work," John said, as he approached the group.

Patty, Sally and Maria gave John a group hug and then the five of them headed towards the performer's backstage room.

"I'm going to wait for Stella, here by the workshop door," John said. "I'll see you in a bit."

* * * * * * * * * * * * * * * *

After climbing the stairs, Stella walked towards the middle of the stage and then gently pushed the main drape to find the opening. Tears were beginning to well in her eyes once again. After parting the drape, she stepped behind it and turned to the right. Just beyond the wing curtains she saw the side wall; she turned around. The oversized floor-to-ceiling double-doors, which, when closed, formed a movable stage wall, had already been pushed open. As soon as she saw John in the doorway, she ran towards him; tears had begun streaming down her cheeks. When she got within arms distance, she opened her arms to embrace him. He lovingly embraced her.

"I can't believe you found him," she managed to say while trying to regain control of her emotions. "How did you, uh, I mean, when and where did you find Alex?" Stella asked.

"Did you have a chance to speak with him," John asked.

"Yes, but only for a few minutes. The next thing I knew, everyone had gathered around us. I told him I was leaving him in good hands while I came to look for you. But you haven't answered my question," she said.

"What did he say about that?" John asked.

"He thought it was a good idea."

"I'll tell you how I found him on the way home tonight. First, I want to introduce you to my crew; the people who really make all the magic happen. They've been with me so long they're family."

John took Stella's hand and the two of them headed to the performer's backstage room.

"I must look terrible," Stella said, wiping the tears from her face.

"You look beautiful," John answered. "Besides, I'd be really concerned if you weren't crying. The backstage room is through that door at the end of the hallway," John said, pointing towards it.

Dave, Patty, Sally and Maria were sitting on the two couches in the room, drinking cokes and talking about the show, when John and Stella walked in. They stood up.

"Stella, this is Dave."

"It's nice to finally meet you, Stella," Dave said. "John talks about you all the time."

"It's nice to meet you, too Dave," she replied as they shook hands.

"Indeed, he does!" Patty, Maria and Sally said in unison.

"Is that right?" Stella replied, as she turned her head looking first at the ladies and then at John. "We will have to sit and talk; I'm curious to know what stories John has been telling you," Stella added, as she turned back towards the ladies.

"And my three lovely ladies: Patty, Maria and Sally," John said as he pointed to each of them.

Stella shook hands with each of them.

"I'm honored to finally meet you all," Stella said.

After pausing a moment, she continued.

"You all were fantastic. I don't think there was a dry eye in the house when the box opened and Alex stepped out. I know; I'm still somewhat overwhelmed by it."

"Thank you," the four of them said in unison.

"We're glad to have been part of the reunion," Dave added.

"John," said Dave, "why don't you and Stella head back out to mingle with the other guests. We'll take care of things back here."

"When have I ever not helped after a show?" John asked.

"We insist," Dave replied. "It's a class reunion, John. I'm sure there are some guests who would like to talk with you and Stella, now that the show is over."

From the corner of his eye, John saw Patty, Maria and Sally nodding their heads in agreement.

"Looks like I'm being overruled," John replied.

"John doesn't always follow orders, Stella," Dave said, as he turned to look at her. "There are times when you have to pull rank and exercise your authority," he added, with a smile.

"Thanks a lot, Dave," John answered.

"You're welcome," replied Patty, Maria and Sally in unison.

With an innocent look on his face, John turned to the ladies and said, "You all don't have to agree with Dave, you know."

"We don't mind," Patty answered.

Stella began laughing and a moment later so did Patty, Maria, Sally and Dave. Eventually, John did too.

"John, let's plan on meeting for breakfast in the hotel's dining room around 8:30 tomorrow morning," Dave said. "And bring Stella with you."

"What do you think, Stella?" John asked.

"Sure, I'd love to. Thank you for inviting me, Dave," Stella replied.

"Our pleasure," Dave responded. "Okay, John, you're excused, so get on out there. Don't worry about us, Stella. We planned ahead and have already packed up all of the smaller things we used during the show. The illusions just need to be packed in their road cases and that won't take much time at all."

"Well, that being the case," John began, "when you're done, please come out and join the party."

"Okay, we'll do that," Dave replied.

"Stella, I think that's my cue that I'm supposed to leave."

"It was nice meeting all of you," Stella said.

"Likewise," Sally replied.

Stella and John walked back towards the stage. It would have been quicker to enter the auditorium through the main door, but John didn't want anyone to know about the lobby door to the theatre workshop. They returned to the table where they had been sitting only to find that everyone had already gotten up to mingle. The only things left at the table were ladies' pocketbooks, and men's suit jackets carefully folded over the backs of their chairs.

"I guess we'll be going to bar for the rest of the evening. Do you want something to drink?" John said.

"Are you going there now?" Stella asked.

"Yes, I am. I want to get some water before we start making the rounds. Do you want something to drink?"

"A glass of white wine would be wonderful," Stella replied.

John and Stella made their way to the bar and after talking with the bartender for a few minutes they spent the remainder of the evening talking with teachers, and old classmates, many of whom Stella remembered from the get-together at The Trolley Car, back in 1971. Dave and the ladies finished packing up the last illusion a few minutes before 10:00 p.m. They each picked up a bottle of soda and walked out to the auditorium following the same route as John and Stella. It didn't take long before they were approached by some of the reunion attendees congratulating them on their performance and asking about the show. Around 11:15 p.m., the reunion started to wind down as the crowd started to leave. It was 11:30 when Alex finally caught up with John and Stella to say that he, too, was going home.

"Alex, you're welcome to crash at my place, if you'd like," Stella said. "I'm going to meet John for breakfast tomorrow morning, so you can sleep in. Perhaps the three of us can spend the afternoon together."

"I don't live too far from here, Stella," Alex replied. "But, thanks for asking."

"However, can we, the three of us, get together tomorrow evening for dinner?" Alex asked. "I know a great restaurant on 49th Street."

"That sounds wonderful," Stella replied. "When and where do you want to meet?"

"How about 6:30 p.m., at your place," Alex replied. "Is that all right?"

"Perfect," Stella replied.

Alex turned towards John.

"I don't know what to say, John, except … thanks," he said as he held out his hand.

"You're welcome," John said, as they firmly shook hands.

Alex then turned and gave Stella a hug and a kiss.

"See you all tomorrow," he said.

Stella and John watched as Alex headed for the main doors in the lobby and then stepped out into the night.

"I hope he comes by," Stella said, tears starting to flow down her cheeks.

"He will," John said. "I guarantee it."

It was almost midnight before the last few reunion guests, which included Drew and Judy, Stella and John, and Dave, Patty, Sally and Maria, walked out the auditorium and into the night.

"Drew, the reunion was terrific," John said.

"Thank you," he replied. "I didn't get a chance to say it earlier, but I want to thank you, and Dave, Patty, Maria and Sally for making it a great success."

"Drew, it was our pleasure," Dave answered. "We're glad to have been a part of it."

"John, I owe you one," Drew said

"You don't owe me anything, Drew."

"I don't suppose you're willing to tell me how you found Alex, after all these years?" he asked.

"It's a long story, Drew. I'll give you a call during the week and fill in the missing pieces."

"I'll look forward to it."

Drew turned to Stella and said, "You must come up and visit Judy and I."

"I would love to," Stella replied. "I'll call Judy and we'll set up something."

"Please do," Judy answered.

As they reached the bottom of the stairs, two limos turned into the parking lot and slowly made their way towards the front of the auditorium.

“Here are our rides,” John said. “I’m taking Stella back to her apartment; I’ll be back at the hotel within the hour.”

John turned towards Drew.

“Since you and Judy came in a taxi, why don’t you guys get into the limo with my crew? It’s kind of late to be flagging down a taxi.”

“Are you sure it won’t be a problem, John?” Judy asked.

“Positive; just tell the driver where you’re staying.”

“Thanks, John,” Drew said.

“My pleasure.”

CHAPTER TWENTY FIVE

As the limo headed up Fifth Avenue, Stella turned towards John and said, "Tell me how you managed to find Alex."

"It was the culmination of a couple of things and a lot of luck," John replied.

Stella was giving John the look that implied *I hear you, but you're going to have to do better than that*. John knew the look when he saw it; he had 25 years experience working with three ladies.

"Before I did anything on Monday, I called Crestwood College. After I introduced myself to Mr. Fisher, the chief of security, I asked if I could spend a few minutes that morning or afternoon with the stage crew. Mr. Fisher told me that the auditorium was going to be occupied all day and he asked if I could reschedule this for the following morning. I agreed and we made arrangements to meet at the college at 7:30 a.m. The next thing I had on my list was to contact the electric company."

"Why them?" Stella asked.

"Unlike the boarding house, if, as I strongly suspected, Alex had moved to an apartment, he would have had an electric bill to pay each month. However, there was one important question that I needed to know first. Was Consolidated Power & Electric a state-owned or a privately-owned company?"

"What difference does that make?" Stella asked.

"If they are a state-owned entity, all its records are accessible to the public for free. However, if it was a private entity, then the company is under no obligation to furnish records to the public or answer questions about any of its customers."

"Are they state-owned or private?"

"Their office manager told me that they were a privately-owned company. I then asked her to transfer me to their legal department and after talking to one of the paralegals I was told that they would not entertain any inquiry unless it came in writing from a lawyer's office, and they had an opportunity to review the request."

"It sounds like they weren't very sympathetic."

"Here's the underlying issue: if they made an exception, regardless of how well-meaning it is, the company risks' opening Pandora's Box."

"I understand your point. I didn't know about the public versus private issue though; that's interesting."

"The only other place that I could think of checking was with the Voting Registrar's office; these records are open to the public. I got their phone number and street address from the white pages, and gave them a call. Unfortunately, they would not provide any information to me over the phone. They did say that were I to show up in person they would gladly help me. There are two offices in Manhattan: the main office, which serves all of New York City, and the voting registrar's office for the borough of Manhattan. Initially I was going to go to the Manhattan office, but decided at the last minute to go to the main office, which is close to Battery Park. It was a fairly simple process to locate Alex, since everything is computerized. However, the only address they had on file was 104th Street. The record showed that he registered shortly after his discharge from the Army, hence the address. Evidently, he never bothered to change his address after he moved. It wasn't even lunchtime and I was already batting zero for two. After leaving the main office I headed back to the hotel to strategize a new plan of action."

"What did you come up with?"

"Absolutely nothing."

Stella began to laugh.

"I finally decided to take a stroll around midtown Manhattan and play tourist. I was hoping that this would help me think."

"Did it help?"

"Not one iota. My lunch consisted of a hot dog, a bag of chips and a soda from one of the street vendors."

"Some lunch," Stella said.

"Yeah, tell me about it."

"What happened on Tuesday?" Stella asked.

"I left the college around 8:15; I was on my way back to the hotel when I decided to visit my friend Nate Howard, who owns the largest magic shop in New York City. I got there shortly after he opened the shop, for the day. I told Nate what I was doing and the dead ends I had encountered. He asked me if I would mind working behind the counter as a demonstrator for a few hours. Seeing the quizzical look on my face, he said working on something else would help clear my mind. I told him I tried that yesterday, to no avail. But, Nate is a great guy and I didn't mind helping him, so I did. And I had a lot of fun! About an hour, maybe an hour and a half later, Nate and I were talking about the types of music that some of the up-and-coming magicians were using in their acts. Needless to say, we had an interesting and sometimes spirited conversation."

"I take it that means you both agreed and disagreed. Is that a fair assessment?"

"We agreed about 99 percent of the time, so I wouldn't say we were always at odds."

"I'm sorry, I didn't mean to interrupt you, but when you said you had a spirited conversation that intrigued me since I know you are pretty laid-back."

"I am laid-back. I've always encouraged magicians to be original because that's what will set them apart from their competition. By noontime I still hadn't thought of anything so I told Nate that I was going to head back to the hotel. Nate wanted to pay me, but I wouldn't consider it. So, instead, we compromised: he offered to buy lunch. After Monday's extravagant lunch, Tuesday's had to be better."

"Was it?" Stella asked.

"Oh yeah! Nate called a local delicatessen and had them bring over a tray of lunchmeats, cheeses and assorted breads. About two hours later, as I was getting ready to leave, for the second time, I asked Nate where he sent magicians in search of sheet music. He rattled off the names of a few places, but said that most people wind up going to Walter's Music on 48th Street and 5th Avenue. As soon as he mentioned that place I knew I had heard the name before, but couldn't remember where or when."

"That's where Alex bought all his records!" Stella exclaimed. "I didn't know they were still in business."

"Yeah, they're still in business. Have you ever been to the store?"

"Only once; Alex and I went there one Saturday afternoon in the summer of 1965."

"Maybe that's why I remembered the name; I may have heard Alex mention it in high school. Do you remember anything about the place?"

"Not much, other than they had racks and racks of record albums, 45s, and music books and sheet music. I also remember them having a couple of electric guitars that were a part of a window display."

"That was the other clue that fell in my lap."

"What, the guitar?"

"Precisely."

"What do you mean?"

"As I walked back to the hotel that afternoon, I started thinking about the comment you made to Brian about Alex's love of music. Instead of going back to my hotel room, I decided, instead, to go to Walter's Music to have a look around. Many people continue their childhood hobbies as adults, so I was hoping that Alex might have returned there as he began to rebuild his music collection.

"When I got there the first thing that grabbed my attention was the store's operating hours, which was stenciled in big letters and numbers on the front door. On Mondays, Tuesdays and Thursdays they were open from 9:00 a.m. to 4:00 p.m. On Wednesdays, Fridays and Saturdays they were open from 9:00 a.m. to 6:00 p.m. Sundays they were closed."

"I'm not sure I follow you about the store's hours of operation."

"Under the premise that Alex still frequented this music store, I tried to put myself in his shoes by asking what day or days he would go there."

"And your answer was…?"

"While he could have gone there any day the store was open, in all likelihood there were only three probable days during the week that Alex would have gone there: Wednesdays, Fridays and Saturdays."

"Obviously, you chose a specific day; which one?"

"Actually, I had narrowed the choice down to two days – Wednesdays or Saturdays, or both."

"Why those two days and not Fridays?"

"First let me tell you why I ruled out Fridays."

"All right."

"If I had a regular 9 to 5 job, come Friday I would be more interested in going home to relax after a long work week, rather than poking around the music store even though they were open late that day."

"I can relate to that," Stella said.

"Exactly. So now that I had narrowed the choice down to two days, the decision became a bit more problematic. Specifically, how do I choose one day over the other and, more importantly, why? I didn't have an answer to my question so I decided to walk around the store for a few minutes. I had never been in there before, but I could see why they're so successful. They have it all: a full complement of goods to help the beginner as well as the professional and everyone else in between. There is a wide selection of musical equipment, music books, sheet music, CDs, everything -- and a friendly and knowledgeable staff. After I left the store, I headed back to the hotel. By the time I opened the door to my room I was still somewhat clueless. The only two options that readily came to mind were to flip a coin, or hope that something profound would jump out at me. I wasn't ready to flip a coin and the only profound thought that came to mind was that I was making this harder than I needed to."

"Which day did you ultimately choose?"

"Wednesdays," John replied.

"Really? I was thinking you were going to say Saturdays."

"The first thought that popped into my mind about Saturdays was that it is typically a day when everyone is out shopping. When Alex decided to drop from sight, he may have avoided running around town on Saturdays for fear of being seen."

"But he could have just as easily been seen during the week," Stella said.

"That's true. But, logically, he had less chance of that happening because 99 percent of the people work indoors, in an office building. His job, as a courier, required that he pay strict attention to those around him as he made his way around town. If he did manage to glimpse a recognizable face in the crowd, he could easily duck into a store or turn around and quickly walk to the nearest street corner and head in another direction before anyone had a chance to see him."

"But couldn't he have done the same on Saturdays?"

"Possibly, but it probably wasn't something that he was willing to risk."

John could see, from the expression on Stella's face, that she was rapidly putting everything into perspective.

"Let me tell you what solidified my choice of Wednesdays."

"Please, do. It's not that I don't see your point, I do and I agree, but I'm curious to know what piece of the puzzle I seem to be missing."

"Deliveries," he replied.

"Deliveries?"

"Correct."

"Now I'm really lost."

"From a businessman's viewpoint, Saturdays are probably the biggest day of the week as it relates to sales. Why, because of the sheer volume of people who spend the day shopping. It's always in the storeowners' best interest to have their shelves stocked on a continuous basis. But, it's imperative that they be stocked to the brim for the weekend shoppers. For example, if you went to the grocery store on a Saturday, intent on buying food for the coming week, only to find that the shelves were somewhat empty, would you go to another store?"

"Yes, I would."

"Precisely. That is, unless you planned on shopping at two or more grocery stores, based on their weekly specials. Any store that isn't prepared for an influx of customers willing to spend their money is not going to stay in business very long. Wednesdays' late operating hours got me thinking. Why is the shop open late this particular day? The only answer I could come up with is that Wednesdays' is delivery day for Walter's Music. This gives the store adequate time to prepare for the weekend. Of course, if the delivery truck arrived early in the morning, there was a good chance that they could have some or all of the new stock in place by early afternoon. Hence the reason they stay open two extra hours in the middle of the week. Now, let's look at this from another point of view. As a long-time, loyal customer, Alex knows when the new stuff arrives at the store. He can avoid the Saturday crowd by shopping on Wednesdays, which means he gets first dibs on the new CDs. I realize that this sounds like a stretch, but it was the only thing that made sense to me. So based on that hunch, I headed over to Walter's on Wednesday afternoon, arriving there at 4:30 p.m."

"And what did you find?"

"My hunch was correct. Some employees were busy unpacking boxes and setting up new displays. The remainder of the employees doubled up helping the customers. I walked around for a few minutes and then decided to hang around outside the place, but across the street. If Alex were to come by, I didn't want him to see me first; I preferred it be the other way around."

"Just to be on the safe side," Stella added.

"Precisely," John said. "Lo and behold, about 5:30, Alex came strolling up the street. I turned around so he wouldn't see me and I watched him, through the reflection on a storefront's window, walk into Walter's Music. My first thought was to wait for him to come out, but I quickly changed my mind. I turned around, crossed the street and walked into the store. He wasn't hard to spot; he was thumbing through a display shelf filled with CDs. He was definitely preoccupied, probably because he knew that he had limited time to spend in the store before they closed.

"I quietly snuck up right behind him and said, 'There's no saying whom you'll meet in this store.'"

Startled, he looked up from the display shelf to see who was talking to him. He immediately recognized me and we shook hands."

"What did he say to you?" Stella asked.

"He asked what brought me to New York City. I told him that it was a long story, but in a nutshell, I was looking for him," John replied.

John paused a moment.

"He then asked how I knew he'd be here at the music store and I said that it was purely luck."

"Was he glad to see you?" Stella inquired.

"Yes, he was."

"I said that if he wasn't in any rush, could we get some coffee and talk. He told me that he had no particular place to go and that there was a coffee shop around the corner."

John paused again.

"As we walked towards the exit, an older gentleman approached us. It was the owner, Walter, so we stopped. Alex introduced me and as we shook hands, Walter said that I looked familiar to him, but his curiosity was piqued when he saw me talking to Alex. Walter then told me that he has known Alex for almost 40 years and that Alex never once told him that he knew me."

"What did Alex say?"

"He looked Walter in the eyes and said, 'you never asked.'"

"That's Alex," Stella giggled.

"Alex told him that we went to the same high school, we were in the same classes, and that he was responsible for introducing me to his cousin, Stella. Walter then told me that Alex used to teach beginner guitar lessons here at the shop, many years ago. So I asked Walter if Alex was a good guitar player and instructor."

"What did he tell you?" Stella asked.

"He said Alex was as good a player and teacher as I was a magician."

"Wow!"

"Walter then turned to Alex and asked him when he was coming back to teach guitar lessons. Alex said he'd call him next week. Walter's reply was 'That's all I've been hearing from you for years.' So Alex promised that he would call him and Walter said he was going to hold him to that promise. Walter then turned to me and said, 'Mr. Michaels, could I get a picture of you and me?' I agreed, on one condition: that he called me John and that we also took a group picture with Alex in it, too. He readily agreed and Walter had an employee fetch the store's digital camera. The three of us talked for a few more minutes, and then Alex and I left for the coffee shop. We were there for about 35, maybe 40 minutes; I did most of the talking. I told him about my exploits trying to find him, about the reunion, and about what I had planned for the show's finale."

"What did he say?" Stella inquired.

"He readily agreed to help. I could tell that he was excited about seeing you again, Stella."

Tears started to well up in Stella's eyes. Not wishing to start crying, she removed her handkerchief from her purse and dabbed her eyes.

"I told Alex that he would need to come to the college's auditorium after he got off from work the following evening so I could introduce him to my crew and then run through the mechanics of the illusion. He surprised me by saying he would call in sick. Alex then asked if I had any plans for that night and I told him that I had dinner plans with you. He asked how you were doing and if you were still living on 93rd Street. I told him you were fine, that you still lived there and that there wasn't a day that went by that you weren't thinking about him. I could tell he wanted to say something, but he didn't know how to go about it and I didn't pursue it."

John paused.

"Since he was taking Thursday off, I asked him if he would come down to the hotel about 9:00 a.m. so we could talk some more and catch up on things. He agreed, and then we shook hands and said goodbye. He went home and I returned to the hotel. I hope you're not mad at me for not telling you that I found Alex."

"I can never be mad at you, John. I'm just elated that you were able to find him at all. Finish the story."

"Around 8:45 the following morning, I headed down to the hotel lobby to wait. He arrived promptly at 9:00 and we went directly to the dining room to grab some coffee. An hour later we moved to one of the hotel's lounge areas to talk. We stayed there till the dining room opened at 11:00. After a quick lunch, we walked to the college. When we got there, Dave and the stage crew were almost finished unloading the truck. Once everything had been moved inside, I introduced Alex to Dave. I told Dave that since we had about 90 minutes before I had to leave for the hotel to meet Patty, Sally and Maria, that perhaps we should get a head start and show Alex the illusion, how it worked and our plan for presenting it. Dave agreed.

"At 1:30, I walked back to the hotel. The airport limo taxi arrived a few minutes after I did. As they were being checked in, I told Patty, Sally and Maria that I had found Alex and that he was at the college with Dave. I also told them that we had already given Alex a quick lesson on the illusion. Alex was a quick learner and by the time we wrapped up the fourth run-through, we felt he was ready for the show. Since we still had a few hours to kill, we had Alex uncrate the other illusions and move them to their different holding areas in the wings on both sides of the stage. While he did this, Dave, the ladies and I set the various floor markings. The six of us had dinner at the hotel on Thursday night. Of all the topics in the world that one could talk about, all we did was share stories about our early high school days. It was reminiscent of a cramming session, except it wasn't for a test; rather it was for a class reunion."

Sensing Stella had a question, John paused.

"Was he living in that boarding house?"

"Yes; for almost two years, he told me."

"Did he mention why he disappeared?"

"No, and I didn't ask. I think he'll eventually tell you everything, Stella. You'll just have to give him some time."

"When he came down from the stage he hugged me and told me that he was sorry for what he did. I asked him to come over to my apartment; I told him that we needed to bring closure to this," Stella said.

"It's the right first step," John answered.

"I know it was."

John smiled as he nodded his head up and down.

* * * * * * * * * * * * * * * *

The limo driver double-parked in front of the apartment building. Since there were no cars on 93rd Street at this time of night, they exited on the driver's side. John told the driver that he would be back down in five minutes. The driver acknowledged

John with a simple, "Yes sir." John escorted Stella up to her apartment and waited for her to unlock the door.

Turning back around she said, "I know it's been a long day and you want to get back to the hotel to get some sleep. I just wanted to tell you that I had a wonderful time today."

"Me, too," John replied.

Stella paused a moment.

"Don't worry about coming to pick me up in the morning, I'll take the subway."

"Are you sure? It's no problem for me to pick you up," John answered.

"I'm positive; besides, it'll give you a chance to catch a little more sleep. Where shall I meet you?"

"In the hotel lobby. The group isn't gathering till 8:30, so let's plan for 8:15, is that okay?"

"That's perfect," Stella answered.

John leaned forward and gently pulled Stella close, and then gave her a lingering kiss goodnight.

"I'll see you in the morning, Stella," he said. "Wait a minute, it's already morning," he then added; "I'll see you in a few hours."

John winked at her as she closed the door. He waited till he heard the lock being turned before heading back downstairs.

CHAPTER TWENTY SIX

July 1, 2000

It was almost 1:00 a.m. when the limo driver pulled up in front of the hotel. He didn't want to be late meeting Stella for breakfast in the morning, so he stopped at the check-in desk and asked the night clerk for a 7:15 a.m. wake-up call.

* * * * * * * * * * * * * * *

The ringing phone startled John. Still sleepy, he rolled over on the bed and picked up the phone handset on the night table.

"Good morning, Mr. Michaels," the voice on the other end said. "This is the front desk; you asked for a 7:15 a.m. wake-up call.

"Good morning," John replied. Then after a short pause, he said, "No, I won't need room service this morning. Thank you."

When John reached the lobby at five minutes to eight he sat down in one of the overstuffed chairs with a view out the hotel's front doors, to wait. He was wearing a black button down shirt, tan-colored khakis and loafers. Stella was always a few minutes early whenever she had an appointment, so unless the subway trains were running slow this morning, she would be coming around the corner in about 10 minutes. The only people in the lobby at this early hour were hotel employees and some guests who were on their way to the dining room for an early breakfast. Dave saw John as soon as he exited the elevator.

"Morning, John," he said, as he approached him.

"Morning, Dave," John replied, as he stood up.

"How long have you been down here?"

"Just a few minutes; where are the ladies?" John asked, as he looked around the lobby.

"If you haven't already seen them, they're probably still in their rooms," Dave answered. "It's still early; we said we'd meet at 8:30 a.m. What time is Stella arriving?"

"About 8:15."

"I guess the best thing to do is to go into the dining room and get a table for six, before the rest of the morning crowd gets in."

"That's a good idea because we're probably not the only ones who thought about having an early breakfast."

"All the more reason for me to reserve a table; besides, I could really do with a cup of coffee right about now."

"I'll be in as soon as Stella gets here. And if the ladies come down beforehand, I'll send them to the dining room."

"All right; see you shortly."

As Dave was about to leave, John said to him, "Dave, do me a favor please."

"Sure, what's up?"

"Hold these envelopes for me until Stella and I get to the table."

John had written Dave, Sally, Patty and Maria's name, respectively, on the front of each envelope. He then turned the top envelope over so the name wouldn't be visible and then wrapped a rubber band around the entire packet.

"Okay."

Dave took the envelope packet and then headed for the dining room; John sat back down in the chair. He was looking out the hotel's front doors when he saw Stella round the corner, shortly after 8 o'clock. She was wearing a powder blue blouse, gray slacks and black penny loafers. He stood up and then walked outside to meet her. They embraced and kissed each other on the cheek.

"You get enough sleep, John?" Stella asked. "You look tired."

"I think I did," he replied. "Had it not been for the wake-up call from the front desk, I'd probably be sleeping right now. How are you feeling?"

They held hands as they slowly walked back towards the hotel entrance.

"Same as you," she replied as she gently squeezed John's hand, "except I had to rely on my alarm clock to wake me. So what's on the agenda for today," she asked.

"Right after breakfast, Dave will be driving the truck back to the warehouse in Virginia Beach. Patty, Sally and Maria are due to fly back this afternoon, but I've a sneaky suspicion that they've decided to stay a few extra days."

"What makes you say that?"

"When we were on tour, we rarely had a chance to sight-see. The majority of our shows were one-niters, which meant that early the following day we'd head out to the next city or town. However, if we were in town for two or three days, we usually scheduled television appearances and did some publicity promotions to advertise the shows. Now that we're no longer touring, I think Patty, Maria and Sally may have called their respective husbands to say that they were going to stay a couple of extra days in the city and play tourist. I'll know shortly, I'm sure."

"So how come Dave is not staying?"

"Dave is a native New Yorker; Queens to be exact. Since he is an only child and has no family here, his parents passed away many years ago, I think he'd rather be home with his wife."

"And what about you," Stella asked, as she looked him in the eyes.

"Other than tonight's dinner get-together with Alex, I'm not sure, yet," replied John.

"What does that mean?"

"Nothing in particular," he answered, as they entered the hotel lobby. Intent on quickly changing the subject, he added, "Dave's already in the dining room."

The dining room was half-full by the time John and Stella walked in. As soon as Dave saw them, he stood up and raised his right hand to signal his location. John raised his hand in return.

"There's Dave," John said, "but I don't see Patty, Sally or Maria. They must still be in their rooms."

Dave was wearing his standard fare: blue jeans, sneakers and a short sleeve, pullover shirt.

"Dave dressed comfortably for the drive back to Virginia," John said.

"I don't blame him," Stella said. "I'd prefer to dress comfortably if I knew I had a long drive ahead of me, too."

"You're right. I just think that one day Dave's going to surprise everyone by wearing a pin-striped suit and tie."

"You think so?"

"Well, maybe not; Dave will always be Dave."

* * * * * * * * * * * * * * *

"Good morning, Stella," Dave said, as he stood up.

"Hi, Dave; good morning," Stella replied.

John pulled out a chair for Stella to sit, and as he did he saw Patty, Sally and Maria walking through the lobby, and heading towards the dining room. John waved to them and they waved back.

"Good morning, everyone," they said in unison after arriving at the table.

"Good morning," Dave, John and Stella replied.

After John sat down, Dave slid the envelopes across the table to John. A waitress approached the table and greeted everyone as she handed out breakfast menus. When she had finished, she took their drink orders and then said she'd take breakfast orders when she returned. Everyone asked for coffee.

"Before I forget, these are for you," John said; he gave an envelope to Dave, Patty, Sally and Maria.

John and Stella watched as each one opened their envelope to find a check with their namc on it.

"Thanks for coming out of retirement to do last night's show," John said.

Dave, Patty, Sally and Maria exchanged looks of surprise with each other and then they all turned to look at John.

"You don't owe us anything, John. It was our pleasure to do the show," Patty said, as she put the check back into the envelope and placed it on the table directly in front of John.

"I agree with Patty," said Maria, who did likewise.

"Me, too," Sally added.

Dave placed his check back into the envelope, but said nothing. He knew that once John made up his mind to do something, there was nothing anyone could say to change it and that John would not take back these checks.

The waitress arrived with six cups of coffee, took everyone's breakfast order and then left.

John looked directly at Patty, Sally and Maria.

"I appreciate your thoughtfulness, but it wasn't just yesterday's show; it was all the preparatory work last week. I look at it this way: you've all worked, so you should be paid."

Stella sat quietly and listened.

"But wasn't this a pro bono show?" Patty asked.

"It was," John answered.

"If you were working for free, so were we," Maria responded.

"Thanks, but I insist on paying each of you," John replied.

Patty, Maria and Sally then surprised everyone by having a "girls' only huddle" right at the table. They moved their chairs together, leaned in close and whispered amongst themselves.

"Isn't it kind of early for a huddle?" John asked.

They ignored him. A smile crept across Stella's face and then she began to giggle. So did Dave.

"My ears aren't ringing so maybe they aren't talking about me, after all," John said, trying to elicit a response from the three women.

They continued to ignore John and kept on talking amongst themselves. A few moments later, the huddle ended and the chairs were moved back to the table. Dave and Stella shifted their eyes back and forth between John and the ladies.

Patty, Maria and Sally looked at each other and then simultaneously the three of them got up from their chairs, walked over to John and surrounded him while he sat in his chair. One by one, they each gave him a hug and a kiss on the cheek. John smiled.

After the ladies returned to their seats, Dave turned to John and said, "I'll just shake your hand, if that's okay with you."

Patty, Sally, Maria and Stella, started laughing.

* * * * * * * * * * * * * * *

"When's the next reunion, John?" Sally asked.

"It's funny that you ask because last night I overheard someone saying we should do this again in five years. I'll just have to wait and see."

In between bites of food, Patty, Sally, Maria and Dave told John and Stella some of the stories they heard about the Class of 1970.

"You guys really turned things upside down during your senior year. It's a wonder they let you all graduate," Dave said.

"I think they were glad to see us go," John said. "I don't think they've ever had a class like us before. And I think I can safely say that there has never been another like us, since."

When the waitress returned, she refilled everyone's coffee cup and then began to clear the table. Before she left she asked if anyone wanted anything else. They didn't.

"Dave, are you sure you want to drive straight to Virginia and not make an overnight stop along the way?" John asked.

"It wasn't a problem coming up so I don't envision one going back," he replied.

"All right."

John turned towards Patty, Maria and Sally.

"Ladies, what are your plans for the rest of the morning?"

"We've decided to stay in the city until Wednesday afternoon," Maria said.

"And we've already called the airlines and made the arrangements to change the return trip date," Patty added.

"Okay, then I'll call the limo service and change the pickup date," John said.

"No need to do that," Sally said. "I've already done that for you."

John looked at Stella and then turned towards the ladies.

"I told Stella earlier that I had this hunch you all were going to stay a few extra days in town. I don't mind, but I hope you've also called home and told your husbands about your sudden change in plans," John said.

"Yes, we have," replied Patty. "That's why it took us a little longer getting down here."

"All right, then I'll take care of the hotel bill," John said.

"But…" Maria began; however, John stopped her in mid-sentence.

"It's the least I can do; enjoy playing tourist, but please be careful," he added.

Once again, the three of them got up from their chairs, walked over to John and gave him a hug and a kiss.

"What, no huddle?" John asked.

"Not this time. Just our thanks for being such a great guy," Patty said, as the three of them sat back down.

Dave looked at his wristwatch and said, "Well, if I'm going to get back at a decent hour, it's time I hit the road."

Dave got up from the table, said goodbye to the ladies and he also reminded them to be careful as they strolled around the city.

"Say hello to Melissa for me," John said.

"I will."

"Stella, it has indeed been a pleasure to have met you. I hope we'll see each other again real soon."

"I hope so, too, Dave," Stella replied, smiling as they shook hands.

Dave and John shook hands, and then Dave left the dining room.

"Stella," Maria began, "could you give us some directions to Central Park?"

"Of course!"

As Stella explained where the park was located in relation to the hotel, Sally wrote down the directions on a napkin.

"If you think you are lost, you can always flag down a cab and ask for directions, or simply stop in any store and ask an employee; they'll gladly help you," Stella said.

All three ladies gave John a goodbye hug and kiss, and they then exchanged goodbyes with Stella.

"I know I speak for Sally and Maria when I say that we hope we'll get to see you more often, Stella," Patty said.

"I hope so, too," Stella replied. "Oh, before you leave, let me give you my home and work phone numbers. If you need something while you're here in the city, please call me. I'd be happy to help."

"Thanks, Stella," Maria said.

Shortly after the ladies left, the waitress came by and handed the bill to John.

"When you're ready to pay, sir, just raise your hand and I'll come over and pick up the bill," the waitress said, and then walked away.

Stella burst out laughing while John shook his head back and forth.

"My crew did a vanishing act on me," John said.

"Indeed, they did, John," Stella answered. "And it was a good one, too."

"Some things never change," John replied, and then he started laughing, too.

John drank the last of his coffee and then looked at Stella.

"Are you ready to go?" he asked.

"Just about," she answered.

Stella paused a moment.

"John, you never did answer my question," Stella said.

"Which question was that?" he innocently replied.

"What your plans were for today?"

"I did make some feeble excuse for an answer, didn't I?"

"As a matter of fact, you didn't answer me at all; you changed the subject rather quickly."

"Well, can I have a second chance to answer?"

"You most certainly can."

John turned in his seat, reached over and took hold of Stella's hands. She suddenly had a chill run up and down her back, and neck.

"When do you plan on retiring?" John asked, as he looked directly into her eyes.

"I'm too young to retire," Stella replied. "Why are you asking?"

"No particular reason," John replied.

"John Michaels, I know a trumped-up line when I hear it," she lightheartedly said.

John paused a moment.

"Stella, over the past 18 days I've been an extremely lucky man. I reconnected with two very special people. One of them was Alex. And, I must admit that I almost gave up on finding him."

John continued to hold Stella's hands, as he spoke.

"While some might say it was pure luck, I believe it was persistence on my part. I simply followed the same techniques that I had successfully used over the years when I wanted to create a new magic illusion. However, unlike a magic illusion, which is based on general principles of math and science, this task was much more complicated."

Stella was looking directly into John's eyes and he felt her stare was reaching deep into his soul. He had never been this nervous in all his life.

"That other person," John began, "is you, Stella. Though we've been physically apart all these years, you were never missing from my heart. I knew, from the very first day that I met you, that you and I were destined to be lifelong soul mates."

"What are you saying?" Stella inquired, as her eyes started to slowly well up with tears.

"Stella, if you have nothing planned for the rest of your life, would you spend it with me?" he asked.

"Are you proposing to me?" Stella asked, her tears now beginning to roll down her cheeks.

John stood up and then knelt on one knee in front of her; tears began to roll down his face.

"Yes, I am," replied John.

"Then my answer is … Yes!"

John was talking loudly because everyone in the dining room suddenly stood up and began applauding. Both Stella and John's faces began to turn red. Suddenly, from the back of the room, an unmistakable voice bellowed out.

"She said yes, so kiss her for gosh sakes. You're holding me up from getting back to Virginia at a reasonable hour this afternoon and the ladies want to go to Central Park while it's still day time."

The dining room had quieted down when Dave began speaking. John and Stella quickly turned around. Much to Stella's surprise, standing alongside Dave, Sally, Patty and Maria, was Alex.

"We're waiting," Alex said.

For a change, John did as he was told, much to the delight of the dining room patrons who then began to applaud once again, amidst the many audible congratulatory well-wishes. Dave, Patty, Sally, Maria and Alex quickly walked to the table.

"It took you long enough," Patty said.

"I'll say," added Maria.

"You know we love you, John," Sally said. "That's why we give you such a hard time."

There were a lot of hugs, tears of joy and handshakes as Alex, Patty, Maria, Sally and Dave took turns to congratulate John and Stella, and celebrate in the excitement for a few minutes.

* * * * * * * * * * * * * * *

"I'm really leaving now," Dave said with a laugh. "I'm sure I'll hear from you sooner or later."

"If you don't mind, Dave, please check on my house for a few more days," John asked.

"I certainly will."

"And we're off to Central Park," Patty chimed in. "You know where we'll be for the next few days, if you need to contact us."

"I know," John answered.

"Stella, John; don't forget our dinner plans for tonight," Alex said. "I'll meet you at Stella's; 6:30 p.m. ... don't be late," Alex mischievously added.

"We haven't forgotten. We'll be waiting for you," John replied.

John and Stella watched everyone as they left and then they sat back down at the table.

* * * * * * * * * * * * * * * *

The dining room had since returned to its normal clatter of people talking in semi-hushed tones, tables being cleared, knives and forks striking the breakfast plates and spoons being tapped on the edge of coffee cups.

"I guess we should go, too," John said.

"Don't forget, you need to pay the bill first," Stella reminded him.

"That's twice – in one day. I can't believe I let them get away a second time," John said.

"John Michaels, you're a nut … but I love you anyway," Stella said, with a twinkle in her eyes.

"And I love you, Stella."

John paused a moment.

"Stella, have I showed you this new trick I've been working on … it's called 'the disappearing restaurant bill.' First thing you need to have is…."

CHAPTER TWENTY SEVEN

It was 6:15 p.m. when the doorbell rang.

"John, would you see who is at the door," Stella asked, from inside her bedroom.

John was in the kitchen watching the early evening news broadcast.

"Certainly," he answered; he turned off the television.

"Hey Alex," John said, after opening the door. "Come on in; Stella should be ready any minute now."

They sat in the living room.

"Did you just get here?" Alex asked.

"I've been here about 10 minutes," John responded. "I dropped Stella off about an hour and a half ago and then went back to the hotel for a change of clothes."

"I'm ready to go if you guys are," Stella said, as she walked into the living room.

"We're ready," John replied.

"Are we driving or taking the train?" Stella asked.

"I suggest we take a taxi," Alex replied.

"Okay by me," Stella answered.

* * * * * * * * * * * * * * *

There was a long line of patrons waiting to get into the Hacienda del Sol when the taxi pulled up in front of the restaurant on 49th Street.

"Don't worry about the line," Alex said, as he paid the taxi fare. "I know the owner, Burton Quintana; I called him yesterday afternoon and he reserved a table for us."

"I feel bad for the people who are waiting to get in," Stella replied.

"Ah, they're tourists," Alex answered. "Locals know that they need to make reservations."

"How long have you known the owner?" John asked, as they walked towards the door.

"A little over 20 years; he's a friend of Walter Reddman, the owner of Walter's Music. Mr. Quintana's son, Bobby, was one of my first guitar students."

"Did the son continue taking lessons?" John asked.

"Yes, he did. He and his Dad would always come in a few minutes before class started to say hello to me," Alex replied. "I'd ask him how his lessons were coming and he'd show me what he had just learned."

"Do you know if he still plays guitar?" Stella asked.

"He took lessons for about four years, so I would imagine he does," Alex replied.

As soon as they stepped into the restaurant waiting area, Alex spoke with the hostess and a moment later they were escorted to a private booth in the back of the room where they could talk. Stella sat between Alex and John.

"Aside from the great food and the service, the reason this restaurant is so popular is because they have a live jazz ensemble on weekends and they alternate between classical and Flamenco guitarists on Wednesday nights."

Moments after sitting down, Burton Quintana approached the booth.

"Hi, Alex," he said. Then he turned towards John and Stella. "You must be Stella," he said as he extended his hand to her.

"Yes, I am," she replied.

"Burton," he offered as he gently shook Stella's hand. "Alex has talked about you on a few occasions," he said. "You're every bit as attractive as he said," Burton added.

Stella blushed.

"Mr. Michaels, it's an honor to have you as a guest in my restaurant."

"John," he answered, shaking hands; "I'm glad Alex brought us here."

"A waiter will be here momentarily with a complimentary bottle of champagne," Burton said, as he made eye contact with both John and Stella. "I understand you two are planning to tie the knot; congratulations."

"Thank you, Burton," they said.

Stella then turned towards Alex and said, "News travels fast."

Alex shrugged his shoulders as if to imply he knew nothing about it.

"I hope you'll stay for a while and enjoy the music."

"We will," John answered.

"May I make a couple of menu suggestions?" Burton then asked.

"Please," Stella replied.

"Try the mint/zinfandel glazed pork loin; it's the best in the city. However, if you're in the mood for seafood, then I'd heartily recommend the shrimp mojo de ajo with chiltepin salsa."

"Sounds wonderful; thanks," Stella said.

"My pleasure; enjoy your meal," Burton said.

After shaking hands with Alex, Burton walked over to another table to chat with a group of people whom he recognized. A few moments later, a waiter stopped at the table and filled the water glasses.

"I'll be back in a few minutes to take your orders," he said.

Right after the waiter left, another one approached the table. He was holding three crystal glass flutes in his left hand and was pushing a chrome-plated circular serving cart, with a silver bucket cooler. Resting sideways against the bucket's inner lip was a partially immersed bottle surrounded by a blanket of ice cubes. After gently placing the flutes on the table, the waiter removed the champagne bottle from inside the bucket and peeled away the foil around the outer wire cage. He then removed the towel that was neatly folded over one of the bucket's handles, draped it over his wrist and with his left thumb pushing against the cork he slowly turned the base of the bottle. The cork eased out with a soft *whoof.*

The waiter slid the towel and cork down around the bottle's neck, and then slowly poured champagne down the side of each crystal flute. Before leaving, he placed the bottle back into the bucket, folded the towel and then placed it on the cart's lower shelf. Alex picked up his glass of champagne and then made a half-turn to his left.

"I'd like to make a toast," he said, and waited for Stella and John to pick up their glasses.

"There are good ships, and there are wood ships; the ships that sail the sea; but the best ships are friendships, and may they always be," Alex recited.

"Cheers," John and Stella said in unison as they touched glasses with Alex.

"Cheers," Alex replied.

After placing his glass down on the table, Alex picked up his menu and said, "I think you'll be quite pleased regardless of what you pick."

John and Stella looked over the numerous menu offerings, but they ultimately decided to try Burton's recommendations. John and Stella chose the shrimp; Alex opted for the pork.

* * * * * * * * * * * * * * *

Alex was staring at the champagne in his glass, deep in thought, when Stella broke the silence at the table.

"Is something wrong, Alex?" she asked.

"I just don't know if this is the right place for us to talk, or simply the wrong time."

"Is there such a thing as a right place or wrong time, Alex?" Stella gently asked.

"Perhaps not," he answered, looking directly at her. "It's just that it's been a long 24 hours for me."

"That makes two of us," Stella said, "for more than one reason."

"Since leaving the hotel restaurant this morning, my mind has been racing a mile a minute. I've been asking myself over and over whether now was the time to dredge up the past, and I don't have an answer to my own question."

Alex took a deep breath of air and slowly exhaled.

"What is your conscience telling you to do Alex?" Stella asked, as she looked him in the eyes.

"To talk," Alex replied. "Because I'm hoping that when the three of us leave here later this evening, we'll leave the same way we arrived – together."

Stella took another sip of champagne.

"Alex, we can't undo the past; we can only go forward," Stella said.

"I know," was his reply. He paused a second and then added, "I'm just not sure where to begin."

"New Years Day, 1974," Stella said.

"In order for this to make sense, I have to go back further than that."

"All right," Stella replied.

Alex nodded his head up and down, and then took a sip of water.

"It wasn't until I was actually back home that I began to feel more at ease knowing that I had completed my military obligation and that, in all likelihood, I would not be recalled to active duty. Like many others, it took a while for me to become accustomed to being a civilian and not a combat soldier in Vietnam," Alex began. "While I had a smile on my face all the time, my emotional state was slowly trying to regain its sanity. I was grateful that I made it home alive; a lot of my friends weren't as lucky. I'm sure John had friends who were killed or badly wounded."

Stella turned her head to see John nodding his head up and down. Alex took this moment to take another sip of champagne before continuing.

"By the end of the summer of '73, everything was about as perfect as it could be; I had gotten a stress-free job and the time I spent with Julie was uplifting. But everything abruptly changed when the police chaplain knocked on my door."

Alex saw the waiter coming towards the table so he stopped talking. After the waiter had finished taking their dinner orders and left, Alex continued.

"I remember staring at the chaplain, as he stood outside the apartment door, and me not saying a word to him. He finally asked if he could come inside. I apologized; I didn't know what else to say at that moment, though I knew his presence meant bad news was coming. And it did. After learning of my parents' death, my state of mind rapidly spiraled downward in an out-of-control tailspin. When I finally snapped back into reality, I heard the chaplain asking me if I had any other family members who would need to be notified. That's when I realized that I needed to call you."

"In the weeks following the funeral, I got the impression that you were still bummed out."

"I was."

"Why didn't you see a doctor or attempt to get some counseling?" Stella asked.

"I thought it was just a temporary bout of desolation; something that everyone goes through when there is a death in their family. I was sure it wouldn't last long."

"But it didn't go away," Stella said.

"No, it didn't," Alex replied.

"Did it ever occur to you that perhaps you were suffering from something much worse?"

"I thought I just needed more time to grieve. I had been away for two years and had only been home for a few months before this happened. Knowing what I know now, I can honestly say that I was afraid to admit that I needed help."

Stella stared at Alex. He sensed that she had something more to say, so he waited.

"How often did I come over to see you, to talk with you and to get you out of the apartment?" she asked.

"Many times," Alex solemnly responded.

"I did everything I could possibly think of, and I'm sure Julie did the same. I even asked my Mom and Dad to call and check in on you. We rallied behind you knowing, full-well, that it was going to be an uphill struggle, but we were committed to helping you get through that difficult period."

Alex listened intently as Stella verbalized the grief that she had held onto for all these years.

"I thought I saw a glimmer of hope shortly before Thanksgiving Day. You looked happy and I thought that you were finally coming around. And then, a little over a month later, on New Year's Day, the other shoe dropped … you simply disappeared into the night, without saying a word to anyone. You can't imagine the anguish all of us felt once we realized you were gone. We checked hospitals; we called the police; at one point we even called the morgue. Not knowing what had happened to you was devastating."

Alex looked away from Stella and lowered his head down. Stella waited for him to turn back in her direction.

"Why didn't you confide in me, Alex?

"I don't know, Stella."

"You know I would have done anything in the world to help you."

"I know. If I could turn back the clock I would certainly do things differently."

There were no tears in Stella's eyes as she talked. The heartache in her voice was enough for Alex to understand her sadness. Stella picked up her water glass and took a small sip. John placed his right hand on Stella's lap and she gently squeezed it with her free hand.

"In early February 1974, I finally took a day off from work to see a doctor," Alex began. "He told me that I was suffering from *dysthymia*, a depressive disorder with similar, but longer-lasting and milder symptoms than clinical depression."

"I think we're about to be served," John interjected, as he watched a waiter head towards their table.

Both Alex and Stella stopped talking and turned their heads forward.

"Can I get you all anything else?" the waiter asked, after he placed the last dish on the table.

"No, thanks," they each replied.

"Enjoy your meal," the waiter said.

Alex and Stella continued to talk as they ate dinner.

"I'm lucky that my doctor immediately recognized my symptoms and quickly referred me to a mental health professional for treatment. Unfortunately, many patients are often initially misdiagnosed and don't see a specialist right away. Consequently, when they do, they're already suffering the effects of clinical depression. The day after I was diagnosed I stepped into a phone booth and began to dial your work phone number. I got as far as the prefix when I stopped and hung up the receiver."

"Why?" Stella asked.

"In my mind I was sure that you would hang up on me before I had a chance to explain my actions and apologize," Alex said.

"Did it ever occur to you that that was irrational thinking on your part?" Stella asked.

"At the time, no," Alex replied. "In hindsight, of course it was irrational, but that's one symptom of dysthymia."

Stella looked away from Alex and turned towards John.

"I'm sorry, John," she said. "This is probably not the dinner conversation you expected."

"You don't need to apologize, Stella; and neither does Alex. I think it's a therapeutic first step to mutual reconciliation."

Stella leaned in close to John and kissed him. Then she turned back towards Alex.

"Obviously, your therapy sessions were beneficial; otherwise we wouldn't be here," Stella said.

"I was very proactive," Alex replied. "It was a two-part treatment plan involving cognitive and behavioral therapy," Alex added.

"Can I ask what you learned?" Stella asked.

"Sure. Without getting into the minutia nitty-gritty, my cognitive therapy sessions taught me how to recognize negative thought patterns and then how to replace them with more realistic ones. The goal of my behavioral therapy sessions was to emphasize the important role thinking plays in how we feel and what we do. Once I was able to recognize these symptoms, I would attempt to change the way I felt, or acted, even if the situation did not change. In addition to therapy, I also made it a point of taking early morning walks in Central Park. The solitude of the park offered me the opportunity to express my feelings aloud and without the fear of being branded a nut case. To this day, I still find it revitalizing to walk in the park in the early morning hours.

"I also made short-term and long-term goals for myself, and at each session the therapist and I would discuss the goals that

I accomplished. There were times, in the very beginning stages, when I thought I'd never break free. While improvements didn't happen overnight, I soon realized the positive changes that were taking place. As I learned how to take back control of my thoughts and feelings, I was slowly weaned from multiple visits each week. As the months rolled by, my appointments were gradually reduced and after seven months, stopped altogether."

"It's now early October 1974," Stella said. "Three-quarters of a year passed."

"That's correct," Alex responded. "And while I had overcome my bout of dysthymia, I still couldn't bring myself to contact those whom I truly cared about. It's the one issue I didn't know how to overcome in spite of everything I had learned."

"So you opted to do nothing," Stella said.

"Regrettably, yes," Alex replied.

Stella looked at Alex, but said nothing.

"Every day is a new day for me, Stella. I'd be lying if I said that the past 25 years have been totally stress-free. They weren't. But, I can truthfully say that the object lessons I learned in therapy have been the cornerstone of my survival and have effectively kept me from suffering a relapse."

* * * * * * * * * * * * * * *

They had finished eating dinner and passed on the offer for dessert, but they did ask for coffee. Stella was more at ease now that she had heard a part of Alex's story. She wanted Alex to continue, but knew it would be better for him to take as much time as he needed to open up some more. She was willing to wait. While they sipped their coffee, the conversation reverted back to the previous night's reunion. In the background, they could hear the jazz ensemble as they performed various selections from their repertoire of jazz, classical music, film music, and contemporary pop. It was easy to see why there was a long waiting line to enter the Hacienda del Sol. The food was superb, the service outstanding, a friendly atmosphere, and some really great music. The restaurant had it all.

* * * * * * * * * * * * * * *

It was 10:45 p.m. when John, Stella and Alex said good-bye to Burton Quintana and left the restaurant.

"John, when are you going back to Virginia Beach?" Alex asked, as they slowly walked down 49th Street, towards the corner of Sixth Avenue.

"Early Tuesday morning," he answered. "I need to catch up on my mail, since I have not been home for two weeks. The bills still have to get paid, you know. I'm also scheduled to perform at two different fund-raisers on Wednesday and Thursday evening. I've had these engagements on my calendar since January."

"Stage shows?" Alex asked.

"No, I'll be performing walk-around magic."

"Is that where you mingle with the guests and perform while you're standing in front of or alongside them?" Alex asked.

"Yes, but I also entertain guests who choose to sit at a table."

"When are you coming back to the city?"

"Friday afternoon."

Alex nodded his head up and down.

"Stella, are you going with John?"

"No, I'm not," she replied. "I have to go back to work on Wednesday."

He turned towards John, again.

"I'm sure I'll catch up with you at Stella's place," Alex said, as he extended his hand to John.

"There or at the hotel," John replied, as he shook Alex's hand.

"Same one you're at now?"

"Yes."

Alex then turned towards Stella and gave her a hug and a kiss on the cheek.

"I'll call you on Tuesday evening, about 7:30; is that all right, Stella?" he asked.

"Of course," she replied with a smile.

"Great."

Alex turned and walked up Sixth Avenue; Stella and John stood quietly on the corner, watching him. A few seconds later, John stepped into the street and flagged down a taxi.

CHAPTER TWENTY EIGHT

July 5, 2000

"How was your Tuesday shopping trip with Patty, Sally and Maria?" John asked.

"Really nice; it had been a long time since I went on a shopping spree with friends."

"Did you all leave anything for other customers to buy?" John asked.

"You make it sound like we bought the entire store."

"I know how much the ladies like to shop."

"Wait till I tell them that you referred to them as 'the ladies,'" Stella said.

"Terrific. That's all I need; to have them converge at my house right after they get back to Virginia Beach. They won't stop and see their husbands, first. They'll come directly to my house, ring the bell and then as soon as I open the door I'll be read the riot act."

Stella began laughing.

"You know that they'll do that to me, don't you?" John said.

Stella continued laughing.

"In the past, it was always Dave who received the 'if looks could kill stare' and then had the riot act read to him like there was no tomorrow," John said.

He paused.

"I always felt sorry for Dave, even though it was all in good fun; but knowing what I know, I'm not so sure I'd like to be on the receiving end," John said.

Stella was laughing so hard she had to stop and catch her breath.

"I'm glad you see the humor in this," he then added, with as serious a voice as he could muster.

Stella started laughing again.

"Take your time; I'll wait till you finish laughing at me," John said.

It's a good thing the phone didn't have a monitor otherwise Stella would have seen John softly laughing, as well.

"You know I love you, John," Stella said.

"I would hope so," he replied.

He paused again, as he waited for Stella to stop and catch her breath, a second time.

"So what did you do after the shopping spree was over?" John then asked.

"We went to The Artisan, a French bistro on 60th Street and Fifth Avenue."

"You all had quite an outing."

"We had a lot of fun," Stella said. "I'm sure you know that Patty, Sally and Maria think the world of you."

"We hit it off from the very first day I met them. I'm very lucky to have such wonderful assistants, but I'm richer for having you, Stella."

There was a moment of silence as Stella thought about what to say.

"I'm glad they had a chance to enjoy their mini-vacation in the city," John said, breaking the tension. "Now that I'm thinking about it, I wonder how many rounds of golf their husbands managed to get in?" John added.

"It's profound that you mentioned that because they said the same thing to me. On a similar note, I can tell you that they're looking forward to coming back here with their husbands," Stella replied.

"So, did Alex call?" John then asked, changing the subject.

"Yes, he did. That's why I'm calling you so late."

"Was he upbeat?"

"He was very cheerful and said he had a great time on Saturday. During the course of our conversation he said that he would be in the vicinity of the bank on Thursday and asked if we could meet for lunch. I told him that I'd love too."

"I'm happy to hear that, Stella. I think everything is starting to fall back into place and he's anxious to make up for lost time."

"I agree. I know, deep in my heart, that we'll eventually have the same close relationship we once enjoyed."

Stella paused a moment.

"Are you ready for your two engagements?" she then asked.

"I'm as ready as I'll ever be," John replied.

"How long will you be staying at each function?"

"My contract is for two hours, but I may stay an extra 30 minutes if the crowds are larger than expected. I want to ensure that I get to meet and entertain as many guests as possible."

John paused a moment.

"How long do you think it will take for corporate headquarters to process your request?"

"No more than two weeks," Stella replied.

"Okay, next question; do you want me to come directly to the bank or meet you at your place, on Friday?" John asked.

"If you don't mind, please come to the bank," Stella answered. "I'd like you to meet my co-workers."

"I'd be delighted."

They talked for another 30 minutes.

* * * * * * * * * * * * * * * *

"I think we should go to Silverman's for dinner, on Friday, so we can tell Regina that we're running off to elope. What do you think?" John asked.

"Oh gosh, no," Stella said, laughing. "I'd never hear the end of it."

"I'll take that as a 'yes' for dinner, but a 'no' for eloping," John said. "I'll have to remember to bring my Irish, 50-pence coin with me when we do go there to give her the good news. You were planning on telling her, right?"

"Of course," Stella answered.

"Excellent. I don't want to leave home without my good luck coin. It was a gift; given to me by a leprechaun. Besides, I may need it."

"The coin or good luck?" Stella asked.

"Both," John replied.

"What am I going to do with you, John Michaels?" Stella asked.

"Believe," he replied. "Believe."